ILMAR TASKA is best known in his native Estonia as a film director and producer, and for founding a national television network in Estonia, Kanal 2. *Pobeda 1946: A Car Called Victory* is his first full novel, and is based on a prize-winning short story from 2014. This novel, set in the immediate aftermath of the Second World War and the first years of the Soviet occupation of Estonia and the Baltic countries, quickly became a best-seller, dealing with issues that are still sensitive for generations of Estonians seventy years later. It is a thrilling, fast-paced novel of suspicion, intrigue and the betrayal of trust in a burgeoning totalitarian society, and much of it is based on events in the life of the author and his family.

CHRISTOPHER MOSELEY, the translator, is Teaching Fellow in Estonian language at the School of Slavonic and East European Studies, University College London. His translations include *From Baltic Shores* (Norvik Press, 1994), Indrek Hargla's *Apothecary Melchior and the Ghost of Rataskaevu Street* (Peter Owen, 2016), and Andrus Kivirähk's *The Man Who Spoke Snakish* (Grove Atlantic, 2017).

Some other books by Norvik Press:

Johan Borgen: *Little Lord* (Translated by Janet Garton)

Jens Bjørneboe: *Moment of Freedom* (Translated by Esther Greenleaf Mürer)

Jens Bjørneboe: *Powderhouse* (Translated by Esther Greenleaf Mürer)

Jens Bjørneboe: *The Silence* (Translated by Esther Greenleaf Mürer)

Vigdis Hjorth: *A House in Norway* (Translated by Charlotte Barslund)

Anton Tammisaare: *The Misadventures of the New Satan* (Translated by Olga Shartze and Christopher Moseley)

Kirsten Thorup: *The God of Chance* (Translated by Janet Garton)

Selma Lagerlöf: *Mårbacka* (Translated by Sarah Death)

Viivi Luik: *The Beauty of History* (Translated by Hildi Hawkins)

Dorrit Willumsen: *Bang: A Novel about the Danish Writer* (Translated by Marina Allemano)

For our complete back catalogue, please visit
www.norvikpress.com

POBEDA 1946
A CAR CALLED VICTORY

by

Ilmar Taska

Translated from the Estonian by
Christopher Moseley

Norvik Press
2018

Originally published in Estonian by Varrak as *Pobeda 1946* ©
Ilmar Taska 2016.

This translation © Christopher Moseley 2018.

The translator's moral right to be identified as the translator of
the work has been asserted.

*A catalogue record for this book is available from the British
Library.*
ISBN: 978-1-909408-42-5

Norvik Press
Department of Scandinavian Studies
University College London
Gower Street
London WC1E 6BT
United Kingdom

Website: www.norvikpress.com
E-mail address: norvik.press@ucl.ac.uk

Managing editors: Elettra Carbone, Sarah Death, Janet Garton,
C. Claire Thomson.

Cover design: Essi Viitanen

Printed in the UK by Lightning Source UK Ltd.

Produced with the generous support of Eesti Kultuurkapital

EESTI KULTUURKAPITAL

CONTENTS

What kind of gibberish is this? thought the man, looking at the date on the letter. It was already a few months old. He took a Sport cigarette from its pack, crushed its long hollow cardboard filter, and put it between his lips. He lit it, settled back into his chair, and read the letter once more.

Dear Alan,

Before the end of the war the opera house was bombed. I wasn't on the stage at the time. A spectacular ballet called Kratt *was being performed. The horned beast, who escaped from the stage with his life, ran in his red costume across the square in front of the theatre into town. Bystanders watched the National Opera House in flames and the Devil running out of it, apprehending that Dostoyevsky's demons had penetrated the town. Those demons are still here. In the meantime they have multiplied and there are more and more of them every day. They have taken over the town, although they don't dance on the opera stage. I don't sing there any more either, because there is no stage. I do not intend to start singing Aida and Carmen at the culture houses and cinemas. Let the demons sing Dunayevsky's marches there. I am still thinking of my Rinaldo in London.*

Your Aida

The man put the letter down with a frown. Even the translation seemed wooden. *We should hire more girls with language skills,* he thought. He picked up a shiny black trophy fountain pen, twisted it open and noted with satisfaction that the ink in it hadn't dried yet. The Third Reich had lost, but their fountain pens worked.

His secretary appeared in the doorway, twiddling a key between her manicured fingers.

"They delivered it!" Anna exclaimed cheerfully. The man pushed himself away from the desk and jumped up. He snatched the key from Anna's hand and rushed downstairs. Parked there in the courtyard it stood in honour and glory. A brand new car called Victory. The man opened the door of the Pobeda and sat inside. The leather seat squeaked and bounced nicely under him, like a bourgeois sofa. He straightened his back and his head didn't hit the ceiling. Hurrah! There was even room for his knees and he could almost stretch out his legs. He sized up the width of the passenger seat and lay on his side. Now he saw the car from a different angle – underneath the dashboard. A few cable-ends and an unfinished paint-job showed. *Still can't shake off the Potemkin village of the Tsarist times,* he thought, and smirked. Then he turned on his back. *Here you could even sleep or fool around with someone.* He wrinkled his brow and chuckled. *You don't even need to climb into the back seat.* He sat up again and gripped the elegant steering wheel with both hands. He gazed at his well-maintained hands and felt that this vehicle would submit to his every hand movement. Yes, he was at the helm. He settled down and looked in the rear-view mirror. With a face like that he could have been an actor. But now he had to act in the national theatre of everyday life.

The man pressed the pedals and turned the ignition key on. The engine growled like a bear. "Mmm," he murmured with satisfaction. The sound was powerful and promising. He toyed with the accelerator and the engine growled more savagely, then more tamely. It obeyed the tamer's words. There was no need for provocation.

Where will I go now? wondered the man, releasing the clutch, and then turning slowly out of the gate. To get past the crowd of immigrants blocking the way with their bundles, he had to drive on the kerb. A big pothole in the road shook the car. It didn't throw the man's head against the ceiling or shake his innards like other old cars. *It really does have good shock-absorbers,* he thought. He turned right towards the residential district. The houses on the fringes of the town were still in ruins and covered in winter dust, having just awoken from the cold mud in spite of the warm weather. There was rubbish from the war everywhere, as if the war had never ended. The town looked like a rape victim. The shiny brand-new vehicle slid through it like an alien body from another planet.

The man adjusted the rear-view mirror, hitched his pants at the groin to allow himself more room, and accelerated.

*

The boy had to be silent again. Daddy said, with a frown as always: "Don't talk so loudly."

"He can talk," interjected his mother, "but you have to be quiet and don't boom in your deep bass."

But what's the use of talking alone, thought the boy, *if Daddy isn't allowed to answer and Mummy doesn't want to?*

The room was dark and gloomy. The boy climbed onto the window-sill and looked out between the curtains. The street was getting dim and damp as well. Yet muted lights shone from the windows of the house next door and the boy saw shadows moving. They were running, playing, maybe even laughing there.

His mother said in a quiet, scolding tone: "Close the curtains."

The boy was sad that his father was sullen, while his mother was always angry about something. Mummy was always busy,

11

making meals, washing dishes, ironing clothes, mopping the floors, darning socks. Always in silence. She didn't like the boy laughing, shouting, or asking her anything. She liked it even less when Daddy did it. He wasn't allowed to talk at all. Not to go to the door or the window. He always had to hide from everyone, but he never wanted to play hide-and-seek with the boy. He sat or lay in the back room, reading old, bad-smelling books. Once the boy had found an old photograph album with pictures of Mummy and Daddy in which they were laughing and beautiful.

"Now you look quite different. Horrible," the boy had said, at which his mother took the album from his hands and put it on a high shelf, so that the boy could no longer get at it.

"I'm bored," he told his father. Daddy was smoking, and didn't raise his eyes from some old magazine with yellowed pages.

"You want to look at pictures of tanks and armoured cars?" asked his father. Those pictures the boy had seen countless times, however, and knew the make of every armoured car by heart.

"May I go outside and play?"

"Off you go," said Daddy, without looking up.

"But not far from the house," warned his mother, nervously brandishing the iron.

The boy was already grabbing his cap and sprinting out into the brisk air. He climbed onto a woodpile on the other side of the street and sat down on a thick log that extended from the stack, as it rocked under his weight. Finally he was back in the driver's seat. He switched on the engine, put it into gear and felt the bus starting to move under him. He rocked himself on the wooden seat as he drove along the potholed road, and the noise of his bus got louder when he changed gear. As he drove and battled with the bumps in the road, he noticed two lights approaching from the end of the street. A splendid shiny car was slowly approaching. It was brand new, and beige in colour.

"Psssh" – the boy was pressing the button to open the bus doors. "Last stop! All passengers please get off."

The approaching Pobeda had stopped on the other side of the road. The boy climbed down from the woodpile and stepped closer to the Pobeda, curiously, his heart pounding. He had seen beautiful cars before, but none so brilliant and new. Sitting in it was a tallish man in a grey coat, who had noticed the boy and was looking at him, smiling broadly. He didn't get out of the car or turn off the engine. The boy approached the car with a self-conscious gaze. He made a circuit around the car, bent down behind it and sniffed the exhaust-pipe gases. Even that smelled wonderful. The man wound down the car window and leaned his head out toward the boy: "Do you want to be a car mechanic?"

"No, a bus driver," replied the boy.

"So cars don't interest you much?"

The boy moved alongside the car closer to the man, rose on tiptoe and looked in the window. Coloured lights shone on the dashboard and the seats were covered in leather.

"Do you want to get in?" the man asked the boy with a friendly glance. The boy knew that he mustn't talk to strangers, but sitting in a car like this was worth breaking the rules for. He could simply sit in it quietly. The man opened the door, stretched out his warm hand and pulled the boy up onto the seat. He looked slyly at the boy and flashed the dashboard lights to please him. The man laughed. His hair was nicely styled and he was clean-shaven, not like Daddy. It was hard to sit silently when such an amusing man was wanting to chat. And they did chat for a bit, about cars.

Then the man inquired: "What's your name? Where do you live?" The boy didn't answer those questions. Mummy had forbidden him to answer such questions. He didn't understand why, but Mummy and Daddy didn't let him talk to strangers. He stretched out his arms and tried the steering-wheel. It was cold, smooth and curved. How nice it would be to hold onto, not like the stick with which he drove his bus. The man seemed to read his thoughts, shifted aside and said: "Come, sit closer and hold onto the wheel like proper bus drivers do." The boy placed both hands on the wheel and looked straight ahead through the windscreen. The man pressed some button and the wipers suddenly sprang into action. The boy squealed in surprise and they both laughed. The man took the boy's hand, pressed the button again and the wipers stopped.

"Now you try. Does your father have a car too, or does he go by bus?" asked the man.

"My Daddy doesn't go out at all," the boy blurted out. He looked at the man, startled. But the man only smiled. He stared deep into the boy's eyes and replied, almost consolingly, "Not all guys are car enthusiasts like we are." *This man can be trusted,* the boy thought.

"My Daddy is only interested in tanks and armoured cars." But now his mother's perpetual warning rang in his ears again: "Never talk about Daddy to anyone."

"Has your Daddy driven a tank?" asked the man curiously. "What has he told you about them?"

The boy pressed his lips together firmly. He wouldn't say anything more about it.

"Do you want to go for a drive?" asked the man.

"I'd like to, but I'm not allowed," the boy answered glumly. "Now I have to go home."

The man was silent for a moment. "All right then, bus driver. Maybe we'll meet again."

He gave the boy an encouraging look.

"You could sit at the wheel yourself tomorrow evening. I'll teach you how to drive. Since your Mummy and Daddy don't especially care for cars, let it be our little secret!" He looked deeply into the boy's eyes and asked: "Can you keep a secret?" The boy nodded solemnly.

The man reached out his big hand, took the boy's hand in his own palm, and squeezed it firmly.

"These are things to be kept between drivers," he said. "Let's meet here again tomorrow, if you're able to come."

He leaned over the boy and pushed the car door open, so he could leap down from the seat.

The boy was sorry to leave the warm car. He could still feel the upholstered leather seat under his bottom and the pleasant aroma of the car in his nose. It was an unfamiliar smell that was a mixture of petrol, cologne, leather seats and the scent of the dashboard. He plodded slowly towards his home, stopped at the door and glanced backwards. He saw the Pobeda slowly and almost noiselessly slipping away behind him.

The boy knocked on the door. He heard the shuffling of his mother's slippers, the grating of the key, and then saw the door crack open and his mother's glaring eye appear. "You must be chilled through! Come and eat some soup."

The boy didn't reply. He wasn't cold, and he'd been having drivers' talk with the man. Their own secret.

He entered the smoke-fusty room, where apart from the smell of broth there were the smell of damp wood and the crackle of the stove being heated. His father opened the door of the back room a little.

"I'd like some soup too," he said in a whisper.

The boy didn't know why his Daddy wasn't as bold as the friendly man in the splendid car and why he always hid away in the back room if anyone came. Why couldn't they ever laugh together?

They ate the soup in silence.

"Time for you to go to bed," said Mummy. And so the boy did. He was sorry that he couldn't talk to his father about the man's car.

*

Johanna was heading down the street in the direction of the tram stop. Life had become totally unrecognizable since the Soviet troops' triumphal entry. She stepped cautiously in her suede shoes, since the cracks in the pavement seemed bigger than the paving stones. They were filled with discarded cigarette butts, rubbish and manure. *I haven't seen any street-sweepers for a whole year,* thought Johanna. *The rubbish bins have been stolen and all the sweepers have been sent to the Higher Party School. The war and the new era have brought the freedom to spit, urinate and throw rubbish anywhere you please.*

Johanna had sung Verdi's *Aida* and was able to identify with the enslaved Nubian princess, whose country had been devastated by the soldiers of the Egyptian army. Over the past few years, foreign forces and immigrants had repeatedly taken over Johanna's home town, ultimately covering it in a layer of ash and the dust of ruin. Since the Red Army regiment of female aviators had dropped bombs on the opera house, Johanna had kept away from the theatre. She had become an independent soloist before the war so that she could sing on other opera stages as well. Now she had lost even those opportunities, because the borders were closed. A singer in her forties could devote herself to playing bridge as well. Yet Madame Butterfly and Tosca still haunted her in both daytime and dreams.

The street ran past the ruins of houses, and Johanna sharpened her gaze. *There isn't someone hiding behind the wall, waiting to rob and murder me, is there?* Her friend the baritone had told her how even illegal sausage factories were flourishing in the shadow of political repression. Someone had allegedly found a little fingernail in a sausage bought from the market. Johanna had also just paid a visit to the market today, and had purchased flour in exchange for her genuine freshwater pearls. She hadn't much of an appetite for sausage, though it was on sale at the market too. People were really disappearing from the streets daily. Johanna thought that most of them were vanishing to Patarei Prison. Everywhere were the big ears and suspicious eyes of Stalin, seeking out enemies of the people. Stalin and Beria had wanted to relocate the entire nation to Siberia, but the war had spoiled their plans.

Johanna glanced instinctively backwards. Slowly approaching her was a handsome, brand-new, light beige car. She had not seen that make before. *Is someone following me again?* At the wheel was a nice-looking youngish man who didn't seem dangerous to her. The man was watching Johanna through the car window and smiling. Johanna calmed down and looked at the road again. There was no need to fear a car like that. People were rounded up in dark lorries, the Black Ravens.

A noisy bunch of drunken sailors emerged from the building next door and cast their bleary looks at the well-dressed Johanna, and then at the new car that was passing. "*Смотри, Победа, какая красавица!* Look, a Pobeda, what a beauty!" cried one of them as he noticed the car, and whistled. Thinking the whistle was directed at her, Johanna quickened her pace, and the man driving the car also accelerated, whizzing past her.

Parked at the intersection was an old taxi with an eternally waiting driver yawning in it. *I'd take a cab, but God knows where it would take me,* thought Johanna. *My coat and hat would guarantee him a month's easy living,* she reckoned bitterly, continuing toward the tram stop. A horde of absolute newcomers was already standing there, people she hadn't seen in the town before, ready to attack the tram door. Since the tram was still not in view they turned and scowled at Johanna as if she were an approaching apparition. Somebody seemed to even recognize her and merely stared with a glazed expression. The blinkers on the heads of the elegant, forward-looking horses of Johanna's youth sprang to mind. She would have liked those defences for herself now, but she didn't lower her gaze.

Two men in soldiers' uniforms strolled closer, observing her suspiciously with narrowed eyes. *What on earth have the war and this new regime done to us,* she thought. *Look at these comrades' posture; their bad-tempered furrowed brows. Gone are the easy-going attitudes, the relaxed smiles. Equality, fraternity, but not a speck of love for your fellow man. Even getting on a tram you have to fight for your spot under the sun. But the Soviet sun doesn't warm or shine.* Instead of cologne, a bouquet of garlic, two-day-old sweat and sperm wafted toward her from the men. Johanna turned her back to the men, adjusted the silk scarf around her neck, and inhaled the traces of old perfume deep in its folds. She recalled the cologne that her London gentleman, Alan, wore – Mischief. His subdued English smile and impeccable manners. She turned up her crimped coat collar and looked at her watch. The hands were moving too quickly on their accustomed course. She stared at the rails and felt herself frowning. *Have I already become like them?* The tram still hadn't come. To calm her mind she hummed the leitmotif of *The Ring of the Nibelungen*. She was exiled from the company of the gods to the mortal currents of the underworld. She eyed the crumbling plaster and cracked paint on the walls of the building opposite and was sure that as long as the English fleet had not docked in Tallinn harbour, it would continue to crumble for all eternity.

*

The boy couldn't wait for the Pobeda man to come again. He perched on the woodpile, his gaze fixed steadily on the end of the street. Then he saw the familiar Pobeda slowly turning the corner.

"Citizen passengers! The bus is broken. You all have to get off now," he said briskly, and pressed the button for the door. Pssssh! The doors opened.

The boy leapt off the woodpile and ran towards the Pobeda. He could see the familiar man's broad smile through the windscreen. The Pobeda stopped, the door opened and the man extended his arm so the boy could do a panther-leap onto the leather seat. The car emitted its familiar smell.

It was nice and warm inside.

"Great to see you again, bus driver!" said the man cheerfully. "Turn this knob here."

He pointed to a round button on the dashboard.

The boy reached out his hand and turned the knob. The radio started to play. It sounded so good and filled the entire interior, not like the scratchy radio at home.

"Now we'll hear a popular melody from Veera Nelus, soloist of the Working People's Culture Centre," the announcer's cheery voice proclaimed. A lady began singing "Whistle while you work" in a pretty, high voice.

The boy looked over at the man, who was grinning proudly. They swayed along to the rhythm of the music.

A dark-coloured lorry drove past the window. The man's gaze turned towards it. The boy's eyes were now also following the large vehicle, which stopped in front of his house. Men in leather jackets jumped out and headed at a run towards the door of the boy's house.

The man leaned closer to the boy, pulled him over and said "Now we'll do a little test-drive. Put your hands on the wheel. You're driving." He took the boy on his lap and pressed his hands on the wheel. The boy grasped it firmly. He felt the man's legs moving. The man pushed the clutch with one and gave it some gas with the other. The car started slowly moving. The boy turned the wheel, and indeed the car responded. They drove past the lorry and his home. The boy glanced at the house, but the man commanded: "Bus driver, keep your eyes on the road, look straight ahead!" The boy turned his gaze back to the road. What fun it was to drive such a big and responsive car.

They drove past the neighbours' houses, turned onto side streets, and found a parking lot encircled by a plank fence.

"This is the cars' home, where they sleep at night," explained the man. The boy squealed with excitement when the car started to climb onto the pavement. The man's foot pressed the brake and they adjusted the wheel again, and kept driving. Music played and the car drove on. They completed their circuit and arrived back at the boy's house. The street was empty. The lorry had disappeared. The man parked close to the house.

"You're a good driver," he said. "Our work's done for today."

He reached out and gave the boy a manly handshake. The boy was happy. He had become a real driver.

The man opened the door. The boy climbed down from the seat and shut the door behind him. The man waved merrily to him and drove off. The boy followed the receding Pobeda's tail lights with his eyes and strolled toward the house.

The front door was ajar. He pushed it open and stepped inside. His mother was sitting on the floor. She looked frightful: her eyes were puffy from crying and her hair was tousled. His mother stretched out her arms and grasped him in her embrace. The boy felt uncomfortable in his mother's cramped grip. He stared at the door to the back room, which was wide open. His father was nowhere to be seen.

"Daddy went out," said his mother.

*

How long will I have to cry, wondered the woman, drying tears from her eyes with her sleeve. She stepped over to the window and drew back the curtain. Usually, when someone had been lost, the curtains were drawn, as if mourning couldn't stand the light. She had lived behind closed curtains for nearly two years already, and could now pull them open in her sorrow.

An almost blinding sunlight shone in through the window, painful to the eyes. Especially since her eyes were red and bleary from weeping. She had to shut her eyelids for a moment, then cautiously parted them again, squinting.

Maybe it's premature to mourn? My husband was taken away, but perhaps he's still alive? As a member of the National

Committee[*] he had fought for national sovereignty and supported the short-lived independence between the two occupations. Most of his companions had been killed or escaped to the forest; he, however, had hidden away in the back room. *Is there still any hope for him?*

They had heard about the executions, the deportations, the arrests and the vanished war veterans every day. Therefore they hadn't been able to decide anything about their own lives. Even the hope of living in the forests, of the white ships or the friendly English troops arriving in Tallinn Bay had gradually faded. So their family happiness had started to deteriorate in the atmosphere of hopelessness, indecision and passivity, and doubts began to sprout in the woman's soul like potatoes in a spring cellar.

She brushed strands of hair away from her face and stared out the window, as if accustoming her eyes to the new light. She alone was the one who went out, earned a living, bought food, communicated with the surrounding world, raised their child, and took care of the household. At the same time her husband had buried himself ever deeper in the back room, in an ever thicker haze of smoke, like a fuming chimney that doesn't know what it is heating or why it still produces smoke. They had only cast wordless reproaches at each other through the door, blaming each other for the world's injustice and the surrounding social system. For there was no hope.

Neither of them had a choice any more.

Her husband was a man of principle and wouldn't have sold himself to the new regime. Not himself, not his companions, not his principles. They had let the last boats to Sweden, the last ships to western Europe, go without them, because every other vessel was sunk, and the woman didn't want to lose their son in the waves.

Better to live in a bad society than to die on the way to a better one. *And was there a better one any more anyway?* She had guiltily caught herself thinking how much simpler life would be if she didn't have to hide her husband in the back

21

room. But now that he was gone, she missed him.

She watched her son playing on the woodpile outside the window, and reckoned that her sacrifices hadn't been in vain. *There sits my six-year-old, swinging on the end of that board. Alive and well and blissful in his six-year-old ignorance.*

She walked across the room to the other window and drew back the curtain from it as well. *Let there be light,* she thought gloomily, mourning her smoky husband and their irretrievable love, which had faded like daylight in a dark back room.

*

Another rainy night, mused Alan. He was swaying in the slow London Underground, which was nevertheless quicker than taking a cab at that hour. He was reading *The Times,* peppered with more advertisements once again. Life seemed to be improving. Alan turned the page: bold headlines in the international news section told of the Philippines and the liquidation of the League of Nations. The League's last feat had been to expel the Soviet Union when it attacked Finland in 1939. But times had changed in the meantime, and the ally had been found a place in a new Union – the United Nations Organization. Europe had figured at the top of the news during the war. Not any more.

Alan's attention was caught by an article titled 'Are Relations Cooling?' It dealt with the Soviet Union, which was distancing itself from former allies.

There had been no word from Johanna in a long time. The last letter had arrived about three months ago. And after that there had been no more replies to Alan's letters. *I wonder if I should try to send a message through our Moscow correspondent?* he pondered. Asking for a personal favour would be unpleasant.

The train doors had opened and didn't seem to want to

shut again. A draft from the chilly evening outside gusted in and across his knees. Alan shifted and covered his knees with the newspaper. The train didn't move.

"We've a red light ahead," the conductor announced through the scratchy intercom. *Wonder if somebody's jumped in front of a train again?* Alan thought. Constructing a new era of peace should have injected some optimism. The horizon had brightened, although not for everyone. There were still jumpers to be found. *Was the reason a psyche crushed by the war, lost loved ones or limbs, adrenaline deficiency?* The train doors finally closed, and it jolted forward.

Alan entered the soundproofed radio booth of the BBC news studio. He sat at the control desk and switched on the metal-shaded desk lamp. The editor had handed him the evening news. He needed to read through them quickly, and clear his throat of the traces of tiredness, smoke and fog. He knew how to turn the pages so that they didn't rustle.

Again Russia, the Philippines – and not a single item about Estonia.

The light in the studio went on and Alan put on his headphones. The sound engineer's voice came through: "Good evening! Let's do a mike check."

Alan coughed, straightened up, and turned towards the microphone.

"One, two, three, one, two, three," he now said in his liveliest radio voice, articulating each word clearly.

He had a beautiful timbre, a resonant baritone, and yet he didn't have the nerve to sing. His range was narrow; as a boy he had sung too much when his voice was breaking, and almost lost his singing voice. Now he had to listen to others. The loveliest singer of all was Johanna, his darling soprano from Estonia, behind the Iron Curtain. His late love and heartache. *Is it already too late?* wondered Alan. The echo of her song no longer reached him. *Something must be done.*

"One minute to go," announced the sound engineer.

Alan stared at the second-hand's determined but stiff

progress along the wheel of the clock, and waited for the red light to go on. His body tensed in the usual anticipation, as if he were standing at the starting blocks of a sporting event. *Now!* announced the red light on the fabric studio wall.

"Good evening! This is the BBC News from London. This is Alan Hanley, broadcasting live from the BBC studio. The evening news from Britain and the world," he read in a fluid, formal tone.

*

Peep-peep. "We begin our bulletin with an excerpt from Mr. Churchill's speech which he gave in America..." said Alan's voice on the radio box.

Johanna pressed her ear against the pulsating speaker fabric and listened intensely. In the static-filled broadcast it was hard to follow the sense of the words, but what mattered most was to hear her beloved Alan's voice. The radio frequency wavered and the sound seemed to be coming from the depths of the ocean. The wavelength was never clear. Johanna carefully adjusted the pale wooden knob, trying to swim after the oscillating radio wave.

"From Stettin in the Baltic to Trieste in the Adriatic, an iron curtain has descended across the Continent. Behind that line all the capitals of the ancient states of Central and Eastern Europe, Warsaw, Berlin, Prague, Vienna, Budapest, Belgrade, Bucharest and Sofia, all these famous cities and the populations around them lie in what I must call the Soviet sphere, and all are subject to one form or another of not just Soviet influence, but to a very high and, in many cases, increasing measure of control from Moscow..."

The resonance of Alan's voice penetrated Johanna's eardrum and passed directly into her brain, chest and heart, mingling with the blood pumping through it and beginning its circuit through her entire body. It was so good to let it pulsate and warm her rather tired heart. *There haven't been any letters from Alan for a long time,* thought Johanna. *Or have they gone missing… or are waiting their turn on the censor's desk, in line for the glue pot?* She was able to read the signs of resealing on the envelopes, could discern the wrinkles along the flap and the thicker layer of glue.

Johanna's shoulders shivered, and she glanced at the window. It was shut, but she could feel a draught.

How nice it would be, she thought, *if Alan's embrace could protect me from the invisible wind now too.* She felt the easterly wind blowing more strongly now than she ever could have believed. It even blew through the walls and the closed windows of the house, and there was nowhere to hide from it any more.

*

The man stared, bored, at the thick file of foreign-language letters in front of him on his desk, forwarded to him from the secret mail inspection department. Then he turned his gaze to the arrest warrant awaiting his signature on the other corner of the desk. *The war is over, but there are still plenty of enemies,* he thought. *The wrong people always got killed. The enemies could have been executed and the refugees on their boats could have been sent to the bottom…* But then he would have to choose a new career. A growing stack of imaginary dossiers appeared before him on the desk. It grew to the ceiling at the edge of his vision and started to bore a hole in it.

The man glanced at the clock and whistled. Although he was head of department, he could do operational work too. He was permitted to do anything as long as it fitted even vaguely with the duties of his office. One of the first of the new Pobedas had been entrusted to him, as a reward for exemplary service. He was sharper and more skilled than the others. Cleverer and more handsome too. Both his allies and his enemies liked him. Nor was he any longer the tallest man, or the one who was a head above others in society and should be cut down to fit. Now he could remove other people's heads. But the ease of his success was deceptive. Brute labour lay behind it all. You had to be harsh, astute and logical. The job also required imagination and playfulness. With the new car it was fun searching for targets. First you had to wade through the mud, get your hands dirty. Then you could wash them with soap and pick up your favourite pen with clean fingers in order to sign freshly-printed warrants for search and arrest. He was the one who decided who died and who lived. Who was a weed to be eliminated from the flower-bed, and who would be planted in their place. Those kinds of flowers that could be smelled or eaten.

The man felt for the car key in his pocket and stood up resolutely from his chair. It was time to test the shock absorbers on the potholed roads again. *No matter; soon we'll erect buildings with towers and tall pillars in the bomb craters; we'll put new people in them. We'll attach loudspeakers on the tops of new telephone poles to play rousing songs, and we'll speed into a future smelling of new, dark grey asphalt,* he mused, conjuring up images of freshly painted facades, carpets of green lawns, fountains, colourful flower-beds, and a large bronze statue of Stalin.

*

The boy was perched once more on the woodpile, driving his passengers around.

"Caution, the doors are closing. Next stop: Tondi."

He raised his glance to the rear-view mirror and had to push the button again to open the door. Some man who looked like his father had got the front of his coat stuck in the door. *Psssh*, the door opened with a hiss. The boy frowned. *Please don't jump onto the bus at the last moment!*

He didn't understand why his father had rushed off somewhere like that, without even saying goodbye. Otherwise he had only sat in the back room and never rushed anywhere.

Now the boy noticed the Pobeda turning the corner into the street. *Pssssh:* he quickly pressed the door button and jumped down from the woodpile. There was no time left to give instructions to the passengers or say goodbye to them.

He hurried towards the car. The man waved to him through the windscreen and parked the car in the shade of the trees far along the edge of the street.

"Hello, bus driver," called the man's familiar cheerful voice. The man threw open the passenger door with a flourish and reached out his hand. It was nice to grab that hand and jump onto the warm seat of the car. The man turned on the radio, and mellow music rolled out, filling the whole interior.

"What's new, friend?" asked the man, looking happily at the boy.

The boy didn't want to spoil the man's mood, but his heart was heavy. It would be so good to get it off his chest now.

"Everything's fine, it's just that Daddy left and Mummy's crying," he said in a brave voice.

The man shook his head, concerned. "Then you should certainly comfort your mummy," he said, trailing off into thought.

"I don't know how..." The boy looked pleadingly at the man.

The man turned the radio knob. Some man was singing in a dreamy voice: "*Do you still remember, when you gave your hand with tearful eyes...*"

"You know – I do know how to comfort mothers," he said decisively, and looked brightly at the boy.

A ray of hope appeared on the boy's face.

"But to do that we have to think up a new game and keep

a secret again." The man's stare bored into the boy's eyes, waiting for a response.

The boy nodded.

"We'll tell her that you ran in front of my car and I brought you home. That will set her mind on something else… and so we'll get to know each other."

The boy was a little confused. It wasn't good to run in front of a car. He didn't understand the man's idea properly, but well, the man knew best how to talk to Mummy.

"It'd be a bit odd if a complete stranger knocked on the door and started to comfort someone right away, now wouldn't it?" explained the man.

The boy nodded again. The man was right.

"Don't say you know me. It's better that way."

The man stretched out his hand to the boy. "If you agree, let's shake on it!"

It was good to grasp the man's warm hand and shake it firmly. It wasn't moist like his mother's.

They jumped out of the car and the boy shut the door with a slam.

"You're strong," laughed the man, "but hey - not so hard!" He looked across the bonnet at the boy.

"Doors don't like being slammed. They have delicate locks inside them." His voice didn't have the scolding sound of Mummy or Daddy. The man was keen to know whether the boy was following his thoughts. The boy followed him attentively. The man asked: "Do you know how to lock the door?" The boy shrugged awkwardly.

"Come and try it," he said, brandishing the car-key.

The boy ran quickly around the car and stopped to watch the man obediently. The man handed him the key.

"You put the key in carefully and then you turn it gently to the right. You'll feel the key in the lock, moving into the right place…"

The boy pushed the key into the hole. It didn't want to go in.

"Not so fast - move it a little bit. Find the right position!" The man put his hand on the boy's fingers and together they slid the lock smoothly shut with a click.

The boy's face spread into a chuckle.

"Great, bus driver! Now give me your hand." The man took the boy by the hand and led him toward the door of the house. It was nice walking hand in hand with the man. Just like two friends.

They reached the street-door and knocked. Mother's face appeared in a crack in the door. She looked at them apprehensively.

"Hello there!" announced the man with a smile. "I've brought your young man home."

"What happened?" asked the mother, looking at the boy quizzically. "What's wrong?"

"Nothing bad," said the man easily. "May we step inside?"

The boy wanted to bend down and take his shoes off, but the man was still holding his hand firmly in his palm.

"He's quick on his feet. Ran in front of my car... but I managed to brake."

Shock appeared on the mother's face and she bent down toward the boy. "Were you hurt?"

"No, no. The car didn't even touch him. Maybe just a little fright," said the man calmly.

The boy looked in bewilderment at his mother, then at the man. His mother gave him a penetrating look.

"Do you feel all right?"

The man squeezed the boy's hand again and gave him a friendly look.

"Yes, all right," repeated the boy.

"I've told you a thousand times to look out when you cross the road!" She was raising her voice. The boy didn't like his mother's words, but he put up with them, to please the man.

"Well, what do you say?" – his mother's voice was becoming demanding.

The boy cast his eyes down. He wasn't guilty!

29

He felt increasing pressure from the man's hand. The man defended him gaily: "He's a good boy. Sometimes we're all in a bit of a hurry."

The man took a step closer to the mother and cautiously touched her hand with his other hand. The mother withdrew her hand.

"Let's not scold him," he said amiably. "He's had a fright."

The mother looked at the man in confusion, and it seemed to the boy that his mother had noticed the man's laughing blue eyes. It would be all right. Nobody had got hurt, their glances seemed to say. Tears appeared in his mother's eyes. The man let go of the boy's hand and now supported his mother's elbow. "We're alive and well!"

Through her tears the mother looked at the man again: "Thank you so much." Then she hunched herself up and turned away again. Her shoulders began to shake.

The boy looked on with interest as the man comforted his mother, and wasn't quite sure that he was succeeding. The man stroked his mother's arm. "Shh, calm down, it's all right…" The man made the sort of noise the boy would make when he opened the door of the woodpile bus. This only unleashed a new wave of tears.

"I'm sorry, I just couldn't bear another loss," the mother whispered, clutching the boy to her bosom. The boy looked between his hands with curiosity at the man, who was holding both his and his mother's elbows, and was no longer worried about anyone. *All three of us are bound together now,* thought the boy. Although his mother was crying, it was a more beautiful weeping than before. As if she felt more secure beside the man.

"We've had some hard times," came the mother's broken voice through her sobs.

"We all have hard times now," said the man in a gentle voice, delicately supporting the mother's arm from below.

The man looked conspiratorially at the boy. "Do you have any sugar? Your mother could do with a little glass of sugary water."

"There's no sugar, and the potato syrup has run out," said the boy, licking his lips.

The man took a long look at the boy and then his mother, and grinned to himself.

"Tomorrow evening I'll bring you something sweet that will put you in a better mood," he said, giving them another long look, bowing and stepping out of the door.

*

Alan was sitting alone in the kitchen eating oven-hot roast beef and Yorkshire pudding. He looked out of the window, wondering why the London fog was regarded as romantic. Again the fog had cut him off from the outside world, made his house a solitary island in the capital city of an island nation.

The world was foggy in every sense. The war had ended and now seemed to have started again, at least for him and Johanna. He had waited for the end of the German occupation in Estonia, then the end of the war in Europe, so that he could travel by air again, and by train on the continent. But the former friendly allies had again closed the borders in the Baltic. He had applied for a visa, and hadn't yet had a reply. The visa application was composed of endless questionnaires. Maybe the Soviet side was afraid of him as a journalist who might make a note of something in the Communist paradise that it was better to be silent about. He was a newsreader on the air, not a news writer. He was just a voice. *Were they afraid that my voice was passing on secret codes, as in wartime, when the news contained secret signals for the French resistance?*

In Central and Eastern Europe the partisan groups, the Forest Brothers[*] and the underground liberation movements were now fighting. *Why didn't we liberate them all? With the Americans we were superior to the Russian armed forces. We were kind to Stalin. A Gentlemen's Agreement. The friendly alliances* *that were like the secret protocols of the Molotov-Ribbentrop Pact. Stalin got as much from us as from Hitler, even though Hitler was now kaput.*

Alan took another piece of Yorkshire pudding on his silver fork, put it in his mouth and let it roll around without any desire to swallow it. Thinking about politics, it always made his blood boil. There was always a need for an enemy. No war could ever be completely ended, there was no truce for weapons. New trouble-spots had to be created, new security threats provoked – divide and rule. The division at the Yalta Conference, though, seemed to have gone wrong. Stalin wasn't interested in trade relations or the Marshall Plan. Half of Europe had been given away and the market there had been cut off. Victory, though, had been by force of arms. Instead of rebuilding London, taxpayers' money was now going once again on armaments. Ideas like that were not popular anywhere. *On our propaganda station we understand the world better. The people are still swooning in the blissful delirium of victory,* thought Alan, putting his fork down. He had no appetite.

He should have let Johanna leave Estonia when the Germans were retreating and the Russians were still only arriving. In the intervening chaos there were still ships moving around, although even they were being torpedoed. He didn't want her to risk her life. Peace would soon come, along with the unshakeable friendship of the allies.

Alan looked at the chocolates in the crystal bowl in front of him. They were supposed to stimulate chemicals in the brain, to improve the mood. It reminded him of the bas-relief at the front of Broadcasting House, in which Ariel, the spirit of the air, was in the grasp of the angels of wisdom and joy.

He took a chocolate from the bowl and slowly put it in his mouth, as if hoping that the slowness of the movement would help his brain to stimulate enjoyment. *Or was it actually an aphrodisiac,* thought Alan, worried. He didn't need that right now, because he didn't want to buy a moment's pleasure for money.

*

The evening had come at last! The boy was looking forward to the man's arrival. His mother, too, had been gentler with him today, talked nicely to him and even played with him.

Finally the long-awaited knock came. Excitedly the boy ran to the door, got up on tiptoe and tried to push open the door-latch.

"Wait, wait!" his mother restrained him. Running her fingers through her hair, she opened the door.

In the doorway stood Mister Pobeda, a joyful smile on his lips. In one hand a bunch of flowers, in the other a box of chocolates. The boy also noticed the neck of a bottle sticking out of his coat pocket.

His mother stepped awkwardly back from the door and the man stepped inside. With him entered a cloud of cologne and that familiar Pobeda smell, and an infectious sense of joy.

A broad smile broke out on the boy's face. A scarcely perceptible curving of the mouth even appeared on his mother's sad visage.

"You can always do with some nice-smelling flowers and some chocolates." The big box with its pattern of mischievous squirrels was pressed into the boy's hand.

"Can you open it?" asked the man. He winked at the mother and set about unwrapping the box in the boy's hands.

The lid opened, and beneath it appeared dark brown chocolates, which the boy had never seen in his life before. He had seen the empty chocolate box in which his mother kept reels of thread. But that was worn, and didn't even smell of chocolates any more. This crisp box exuded a completely new aroma.

The boy rapidly took a dark chocolate and popped it in his mouth. *This is better than a lump of sugar,* he discovered.

"Where do you get hold of things like that?" asked his mother suspiciously.

"The boss gave the box of chocolates to me, his driver. I really don't know where they hand them out to the new big nobs," said the man uneasily. Then he looked the mother straight in the eye: "I think we ordinary folks have a right to eat them too, don't we?"

The mother reached out and quickly popped a chocolate in her mouth too.

The boy grabbed another chocolate and tucked it into his cheek.

"Not all at once!" reprimanded his mother.

"Let him eat. Chocolate stimulates the mind," said the man with a benevolent smile.

"Are we going for a drive in the Pobeda too?" asked the boy.

"Why not? Shall we go for a spin?" The man looked inquiringly at the mother.

"No, now you…it's late!" replied the mother, frowning.

At that, the man took the bottle from his pocket and started unscrewing the top. "May I ask you for some glasses?"

The mother hesitated for a moment, but then stepped over to the cabinet and took out two glasses.

Again the boy was left out of something. He quickly took a third chocolate from the box.

The boy was listening to voices in the next room. His mother's sobs and the soothing melodious voice of the man. Then he seemed to hear a scuffle and his mother's hushed voice: "No, not now!" The boy became worried and sat up in bed. But then his mother's voice subsided and he heard the familiar creaking of the bed. At first it was quiet, but then the creaking grew louder and became rhythmic. He could hear his mother sighing too. Now he was no longer afraid for his mother as he had been at first when he heard noises like that. Then he had run into the next room and watched his parents romping. In those days it was his father. Now it was Mister Pobeda. He didn't like the way the man played with his mother without him.

Once, when his mother and father seemed to be screaming in a muffled way and he ran into the bedroom, his father had said that these games were only for grown-ups. But they must have been good games. And though the boy didn't especially want to grow up, he might do that for the sake of them. For his parents, otherwise so gloomy, were always in a good mood after playing them. For a little while. They would even tell funny stories, until his mother had said: "Quiet now – don't talk so loud," and his father's voice had sunk away again.

The boy was seized with a new worry. *Will the man go on caring about me as much as before and take me riding in the car?* Although he knew they had to comfort his mother, this comforting wasn't so good any more. *Who will comfort me now?* He had been left out of the game. And yet he had found this man and brought him home. *Do I have two daddies now? But everything has its plusses and minuses, as my daddy used to say. One daddy had a Pobeda and the other hadn't. One had come and the other had gone. Interesting,* thought the boy – *if Daddy comes back, will all three of them fit into the same bed?*

Finally the next room had gone quiet, and a smell of smoke came from under the door.

Sleep came over the boy and he turned on his side.

In his dreams his father appeared before him, smoking another cigarette. He was wearing a helmet, and now they had to ride in a tank. The boy took hold of his father's hand. His father's hand was cold. Bombs started raining down from the sky and their tank had vanished somewhere. The two of them were walking around the shell-pocked landscape, looking for their tank. But it was nowhere to be seen.

*

The mother noticed her son's pleasure and it gave her a sense of pleasure as well. The boy was dressed, sitting on a stool by the door. He was listening to every rattle coming from the yard. *Boys and cars,* thought his mother. *Is this man really the cause of the excitement?*

Everything had happened too quickly. While she was crying about her husband she could have lost her son. Now, unexpectedly, she had opened the door to her son's rescuer. What was happening? Was this a debt of gratitude, or something else?

From the sideboard she hunted for her compact and worn-out lipstick from before the war. She opened the compact and looked at her face in its cracked mirror. She inspected the bags under her eyes, from crying and sleeplessness, and dabbed a little powder on them. *Who was this man? Suspiciously handsome and smooth. And too masterful in bed.*

"Don't be sad, Mummy. Soon me and the man will be comforting you," her son interrupted her train of thought, watching her from his stool.

"What do you mean, comforting? Where did you hear such things?" she asked, dismayed.

He bit his lip. "You need comforting, because you cry so much."

She opened her lipstick case. The red stick was worn down very low.

"I don't need comforting. We're going for a drive in the car, because you want to."

She rubbed pomade on her lips and puckered her lips tightly. From the corner of the mirror she saw that the boy was already turning a large imaginary steering-wheel in his hands.

How good that the boy was so pleased. She knew she had so little to offer him. *But the driver?*

Her husband had just been taken away. Every corner, every

object, every speck of dust reminded her of his absence. She glanced again in the broken mirror at her split face and wiped the pomade from her lips with her hand. She sighed deeply and hurried to the kitchen tap to wash her hands.

There's even a little lipstick left, and I'm stupidly wasting it! She washed the red colour from her hand, which spread out the grease of the lipstick even further. It reminded her of blood, which might be running from her husband's nose right now. *Are they interrogating him?*

"Mummy, Mummy, come on!" cried the boy from the doorway.

There was a knock at the door.

She quickly wiped her mouth and hands with a towel and headed for the entrance. The boy had already opened the door, the man, brimming with energy and spring sunshine, stood on the step, a bunch of flowers in one hand and a lollipop in the other.

She summoned a smile to her face and felt shy. He looked at her with the same charming glance, as if he knew nothing of her inner scars. She wasn't sure that she could smile back at him. The boy was already clinging to the man's arm and circling around him like a little puppy.

The boy is enchanted – what is this man's magical power?

She felt that something was wrong.

The boy grabbed the man's hand and started pulling him through the doorway. The man let him do it and looked toward the helpless woman. He shrugged, grinned and let the boy lead him back out of the doorway.

She closed the door carefully.

What is the boy so excited about? His father might already be dead. But where did my own weakness yesterday come from? I'm not that sort of woman. It must be the alcohol that went to my head.

Now her son was leading this lanky man by the hand onto the street as if they were old friends.

How quickly everything changes. How replaceable we all are.

Isn't it terrible?

She tiptoed after the menfolk. *And me still in my ridiculous party shoes!*

But then the Pobeda came into view. With its shiny silver nickel plating and its luminous streamlining. A real beauty.

Now suddenly she understood the boy's enthusiasm.

The man opened the car door chivalrously and the boy jumped nimbly inside. The man remained standing gallantly beside the car, ready to help the woman in.

"Let him sit in front," she said. "I can sit in the back."

"No, no," said the man, "all three of us can fit in the front."

The car seat still smelt of fresh leather. Nickelled buttons and a round speedometer glistened on the dashboard.

Interesting – who does he usually drive in this car, she thought.

The man smiled proudly to her, flashing his eyes. He selected a gear under the steering-wheel and the car gently moved off. The boy smiled even more proudly, turning the radio knob.

A Russian marching song came on loudly, taking her aback. *And how does the boy know all the knobs already?*

The man put his own hand on the radio knob and tuned it to another frequency.

"Täällä soi Radio Helsinki" intoned the crackling radio. A genial announcer introduced the Andrews Sisters' song *Bei Mir Bistu Shein.*

The boy sang along, without understanding the words. The man joined in too. He had a fine tenor voice and even kept in tune. He threw merry glances now and then at the boy and the woman in turn. The car rolled through the vernal suburban streets with a sort of inexplicable lightness.

The woman gazed at her happy son and the joyful driver, and beyond, at a cherry-tree in a garden gliding past, and she again wanted to cry. Happiness was not her strong suit, and her family happiness she had recently lost. *So what's happening to me? Might everything be repeated?* She knew that wasn't possible.

The man threw her another mischievous grin, singing: *"Please let me explain – bei mir bist du shein."*

She smiled awkwardly.

The man beat time with his hand and boldly indicated the back seat: "We're empty at the rear – shall we pick up some of your friends?"

She shook her head. "I don't have any friends left. They've all left… or been taken away. They've been replaced by people whose language I don't understand."

She detected a sharp new gleam in the man's look.

"What times these are," sighed the man, letting his right hand fall from the wheel. He lifted the boy's hand to the wheel. "Now let's drive together!" The boy shrieked with pleasure.

She looked out the window to hide the tears welling in her eyes. The man's bright blue eyes and the boy's ringing laughter were so beautiful, they made her feel sick. *This can't be true – taking with one hand, giving with the other.* The car passed over a hole in the road, but it didn't judder as they usually did. The car just swayed a little and the leather seat vibrated.

The man's hand took hold of her wrist and squeezed it lightly. It was neither dry nor moist, neither cold nor hot. It simply held her arm with a secure assurance.

The man smiled, flashing his white teeth again. She looked at him without wanting to get excited, but she could feel the man's effect on her. *Those teeth of a stranger had touched her lips and skin. This man was able to fill her, from top to toe.*

Straight ahead red lights were flashing. A level crossing. A boom descended onto the road and bells sounded a warning.

*

The boy was running happily across the room, imitating the sound of the Pobeda.

"Brmm-brmm-brmm, we're revving up," he shouted. "Chhh,

now we're braking. There's an enemy tank in front of us."

"We don't talk about tanks any more," interjected his mother. She was splashing the washing-up in the sink.

"But that Pobeda is a nice car, isn't it?"

"It is," said his mother, adjusting her apron. The boy ran to his mother clutching a steering-wheel, shouting "Toot-toot, out of the way!"

"You can turn around," said his mother, without moving aside. She turned on the tap. Water spurted in a wide cascade.

"Oh, it's started to rain – workmen, get to work! Chop-chop!" The boy made a movement with his hand imitating the movements of windscreen-wipers.

"Do you know, Mummy, that when the man put the workmen to work the first time, I got a fright!"

His mother put a plate down and looked straight at the boy.

"But it didn't rain today…"

The boy stopped. He felt uncomfortable. "Toot-toot – but it might still start raining." The boy drove out of the kitchen. He heard his mother turning off the tap and following him out of the room in her carpet-slippers, rustling on the floorboards. *Now I've had it!* thought the boy. He had given the man a promise. *I should have kept my word.*

"When did you go for another drive with the man?" asked his mother behind him.

The boy had promised the man he would keep a secret, but it wasn't good to lie to Mummy either. He simply made a car noise and drove off into the bathroom. His mother came after him.

"Wait," said his mother. "Look me in the eye. When did you go driving with the man in the rain?"

The boy lowered his eyes. "It wasn't raining. I didn't go. He just showed me how it's done."

Tension had appeared on his mother's face. "When?"

"I don't remember."

The mother grasped the boy by both hands, crouched

40

down, her face approaching the boy's eyes. Her face was pale and serious. Her eyes bored into his. "When did he show you?" she asked.

"I'm not allowed to tell you about it."

"Why not?"

"It's a secret," replied the boy. He felt uncomfortable in his mother's hands. He tried to shake free, but she held him firmly.

"You don't need to have secrets from me," she said angrily. "What else did you tell him?"

"I can't think."

The boy felt the corners of his eyes smarting. He wanted to cry.

"Did you run in front of his car?"

Now the boy felt his tears welling forth all over his face and the room. He nodded and then shook his head. He didn't want to stand here any longer looking straight at his mother. He didn't want to lie and he didn't want to break a promise either. He didn't know what to do.

"There are only two of us now, we mustn't have secrets from each other," she said with trembling lips.

The boy was afraid that if he let his mother into the secret he would lose the man and the gleaming Pobeda. He pressed his lips firmly together and decided not to say any more. He suddenly felt very bad. His heart had jumped into his throat and his head felt like splitting.

His mother left the bathroom.

Through the half-open door he saw his mother going to the cupboard and taking a suitcase from the back of it. She opened it in the middle of the room and started feverishly packing things into it.

Is Mummy leaving too, leaving me alone? thought the boy.

A sob was throttled in his nose.

He felt afraid, and his heart was beating even harder. He threw open the bathroom door, shouting: "Are you leaving me too?"

"We're both leaving," said his mother, putting the boy's

41

jacket in the suitcase.

"But the man is coming soon and we're going for a drive in the Pobeda," protested the boy.

She turned around and took a long look at him.

"Today the two of us are going for a ride on a tram."

She turned back and continued packing. The boy saw that her hands were trembling.

*

Alan stopped in the corridor of Broadcasting House and leaned on the window ledge. He had finished reading another news bulletin. In this position he could get his breath back. He suddenly noticed how dusty the ledge was. Yet this window was hardly ever opened and the cleaner was continually dusting. Alan lifted his hands from the ledge, stood up straight and rubbed his dirty hands together. *Did even radio waves create dust? Or was it only the brain that got dusty?*

Alan knew that every year by its gravitation the Earth draws thousands of tonnes of all kinds of material from cosmic space. All kinds of cosmic rubbish falls onto his and his fellow citizens' heads. Even onto this window ledge. Luckily most of it burns up in the upper atmosphere and then falls to earth as invisible dust. Alan imagines himself as a vacuum cleaner which has to absorb the dust of cosmic meteorites, suck into his nose the invisible refuse of the universe.

If Alan had not happened upon Broadcasting House as a young man, he could have become a geologist or a musician. Maybe even a researcher of the cosmos? He had followed the call of the latest discovery in science and technology – radio – and rushed into the competition for announcers. His mother wanted him to be an orchestral musician, but it was so exciting to listen to music without having to play it oneself, not even being played in the same room, but reaching one's ear invisibly through the air. To listen to a little box in a cosy living-room giving live reports of natural disasters in distant lands. Those invisible vibrations were more interesting to him than the structure of crystals, as described to him by his father, a geologist, or the daily squeaking of a violin, as demanded by his mother. His parents had deplored him ruining his future prospects with this radio tomfoolery, and thus taking time away from his studies. He had disappointed both his mother and his father by choosing the profession of announcer. Yet his mother's music and his father's geology were etched into his subconscious, and this manifested itself in a love of opera and the composition of the Earth. For this he was deeply grateful to his forebears. He could appreciate both the vibrations of music and the inevitability of dust.

Journalists were invited everywhere, and he didn't fail to take up invitations even to musical events that the BBC didn't cover. At one such concert he had heard Johanna singing and forgotten about the cosmic dust for a moment. A burning meteorite had landed right at his feet. It had thrown out sparks even at the cocktails after the concert. It was still hissing. But he no longer saw the sparks, nor had he heard Johanna's voice for a long time. He had to send an SOS signal into the depths of space.

Alan turned around decisively and went further along the corridor. He stopped at a door marked *Special Operations Executive*. He knocked, waited for a moment and then turned the doorknob. There in an aureole of light streaming in from the window sat Simon, like a granite statue. The contrasting light turned him into a dark grey silhouette.

"Alan, old chap," said Simon, raising his eyes from the papers on his massive desk. "What's afoot?"

Alan squinted to catch Simon's expression. "Got a moment?"

Of course Simon could find a moment when he saw Alan's worried face. "Take a seat," he said amiably.

"I have a personal question," began Alan, fidgeting with embarrassment. He wasn't sure whether it was sensible to go into detail.

Simon nodded encouragement.

"I have a girlfriend in Estonia, a well-known opera singer. I'd like to visit her… but there doesn't seem to be any response to my visa application."

A silence came over the room, like a burst of cold air. Simon gave him one of his "trust-me" looks and asked thoughtfully: "Did you put your exact profession in the application?"

"Yes, of course; they must surely know everything about us."

"They do, but they doubt most of it," explained Simon. "Our function has changed… They don't regard us as a friendly station any longer." Simon grinned discreetly. "They don't see anyone as friendly. Nowadays entry for all foreigners has got harder."

Simon paused, looking at Alan with a quizzical expression. "Apart from those who want to settle there… But there aren't any of those."

Alan smiled ironically. *Might they suspect me even here?* he thought. *A friend behind the iron curtain might be a security risk.*

"They're trying to lure the emigrants back home. Do you have any friends among them?"

"No, I don't know anyone apart from my little singer," said Alan, shaking his head and looking Simon in the eye.

"Strictly personal. Affairs of the heart." He rolled his eyes and whistled.

Simon grinned, and went on: "The sad truth is that wartime friendships are coming to an end and comfort girls from the eastern front aren't being offered to us any more. If there are any, they're the honey-traps, wearing microphones in their brassieres…"

"That was *pre*-war friendship… From the time when we regarded the Baltic countries as friendly nations." Alan quickly parried the dangerous idea. "You should visit me one day, and listen to her singing on record."

"Casta Diva" – Simon spread out his arms – "singers that aim

straight for the heart." He burst into good-natured laughter, and then added, in a more serious tone, "I'll ring our contact at the Russian Embassy, if you really have such a strong urge to be going there."

"Thanks! Dinner is on me," said Alan, relieved, thinking that he mustn't make such a big issue out of it and show too much pleasure. He slowly got up from the plush chair, straightened himself up and slyly asked: "Who's warming your bones these days, old chap?"

Simon smiled and sighed: "I'm still living on the mercy of strangers."

*

The heavy oak door opened silently and there on the threshold stood Aunt Johanna. Surprise appeared on her face, normally so restrained.

"Well, look who's here!" She smiled at the boy, then looked at his mother, and seeing the suitcase in her hand, asked with concern, "What's happened?"

She stepped inside and put the suitcase down on the floor of the hall.

"I'll tell you."

She turned to the boy: "Look around, there are so many interesting books here. I have to have a talk with Auntie Johanna."

Auntie took his mother in the crook of her arm, led her with a rustle of her taffeta dress into the next room and closed the door.

They have a secret of their own, thought the boy. *What are they talking about now – me, Daddy, the man or the Pobeda?* He still didn't understand why he should not have accepted a ride in the Pobeda before. Nothing had happened, and he hadn't been run over.

He stepped closer to the door and heard his mother's hushed voice: "…isn't it terrible!"

Then Auntie's voice could be heard: "Go back and look as if you don't know anything. Then nothing will happen to you."

"I can't do that."

The boy had no more time to think about what they said, because suddenly a door opened in the wall-clock, a cuckoo came out and repeated several times: "Cuckoo, cuckoo!" *What a nice bird,* thought the boy. He had never seen such a clock before. He quickly took a chair and climbed onto it to look more closely at the bird. But the cuckoo had gone back into its cage and closed the door behind it. *Interesting – when will he come out again?* he thought.

On the wall next to the clock hung a picture in a gilt frame of black boys with turbans, eating fruits whose names he didn't know. Not that he could even guess what those fruits tasted like. Those fruits were only available to dusky boys in turbans. He would have liked to eat apples and gooseberries from Auntie's garden when they ripened.

The boy looked around the large living-room. There was old furniture, and by the wall stood a sculpture of a warrior in armour. In the corner there was a gramophone playing, with a picture of a dog. A scratchy disc was revolving on it, with some lady singing in a coarse voice: *"Einen Mann, einen richtigen Mann."*

He looked out of the window. It was getting dark outside, the trees were murmuring in the wind. He thought of the man who would soon be coming to their door, but they weren't at home.

Outside, it was starting to drizzle.

You see, I was right after all, it did start to rain, thought the boy. He took his shoes off, threw himself onto Auntie's sofa and looked out. He was still regretting that he had mentioned the windscreen wipers. He didn't like the rain. *The rain was to blame for everything.*

*

Johanna was sitting at the head of the sofa in her immutably dignified pose, looking at the sleeping child. She didn't want a child of her own, let alone a visitor, the offspring of her troublesome half-sister. But this negative thought didn't ruffle the polite gentleness of her well-honed features. Now, though, the duty of childcare had fallen on her shoulders, something she had always tried to avoid in life. So far she had had neither the time nor the opportunity for it. She had too much concern with herself to share it with a small creature.

Performances, tours, dress rehearsals, interviews, social life and her English gentleman Alan – they were all demands on her time. *What was left over after that? The wretched remains of a crumbling society and the influx of newcomers.* She idolized Tatyana's aria in *Eugene Onegin,* but she didn't like these new military Tatyanas who were strolling around Kadriorg Park with their officers. She didn't like the new words that had been forced into the language of Pushkin, those new Soviet expressions which sounded false in any language, even Russian. Those demagogic phrases and transparent lies were now even infiltrating the Estonian language. The more shrilly the joyful marches were played through megaphones on the streets, the more grey and miserable became the surrounding reality. *And what had become of Alan?* London, too, had been bombed, just as Tallinn had. Had their love been bombed to smithereens, buried under the ruins? The last letter had arrived in the early spring. Her reply, her 'Tatyana letter', had evidently not reached its addressee. Alan might simply have forgotten her, abandoned her, if no sign of life had come from her. What vanished from sight might also vanish from memory. *Or had the letters reached him and Alan simply hadn't replied?*

While waiting for a letter, Johanna had walked though Kadriorg Park to the Russalka, to see a white ship on the horizon. Like Madame Butterfly. At the tip of the Russalka monument an angel was pointing out a direction with her golden cross. She was looking out to sea, but she had not seen a mist of smoke, a white sail or a sunken wreck. The future was not yet determined. Johanna had stepped down the stone steps of Russalka and turned her head back toward the angel. The angel was swathed in darkness, but her golden cross glowed from every angle.

The boy tossed in his sleep and stuck a bare foot from under the eiderdown. Johanna adjusted the lace-edged blanket. She didn't know if the boy was cold or warm. She knew nothing at all about children. This boy could be her undoing. *If his father was recently arrested and his mother was escaping from a lover in the KGB, what might the charge against herself be? Deliberate shielding of the child of a criminal? People are disappearing every day. Is it my turn now?*

The boy opened his eyes and looked sleepily at his aunt.

"Do you know where you are, darling?" asked Johanna, making a benevolent face.

He rolled his eyes and looked around the room.

"Yes, at Johanna's place. Where is Mummy?"

"You're at Auntie Johanna's place," Johanna corrected him with a polite smile. "Mummy's gone out and left me to look after you."

Now serious concern came over the boy's face. "But I can't stay here."

"Why?" inquired Johanna, taking him by the hand.

The boy pulled his hand away.

"I have to go home. A man is coming to visit me!"

This boy's parents haven't wasted time on bringing up their child, thought Johanna, though still smiling. "No, no-one's coming to visit you today. I'm sure your mummy will fix that up."

The boy started putting on his shoes. He looked out of the window. "Can I go into the garden?"

"No, darling."

Johanna drew the curtains. *I mustn't let him out. What will*

the neighbours say? Whose child has climbed to the top of the
tree? And where would I hide this child?

"It's interesting being indoors here too. You and I can listen
to opera arias and look at picture books."

He looked disappointedly at his aunt and huddled up.

"*Stramm!*" said Johanna. "Young gentlemen should learn to
sit with a straight back from an early age."

Johanna started setting the table. She put a white
tablecloth on the round table and took a dinner service with
gold edges from the cabinet. "One has to preserve form so that
content doesn't disappear forever," she said, throwing the boy
a meaningful look.

The boy's eyes showed interest as he looked at the beautiful
cups and plates. There was a hope of getting something better
than the everyday barley porridge. He sat down at the table
and swung his feet in anticipation.

"We'll have supper now."

Johanna put a couple of dry rusks and a little piece of salted
bacon on the gilt-edged plate.

*

Alan wiped his mouth with his napkin. The many courses of
dinner had been filling and Simon was now looking at the
dessert menu.

"Shall I take the *mousse au chocolat* or the *île flottante* in
honour of our liberated neighbours?" he asked Alan teasingly.
"I suppose you'll be longing for your buckwheat cakes and
jam."

Alan laughed at the inappropriate joke more than he
wanted to. He had invited his benefactor to a French restaurant
for dinner. The visa was worth the gesture. "In Estonia they have
very good pancakes with curds," he said, ceasing to laugh.

"With what?" asked Simon. "By the way, talking of Estonia,

I'm afraid they won't let you in there. You'll have to arrange your rendezvous with your songbird on Red Square, or a picnic in Gorky Park." Seeing Alan's face sinking, he added cheerfully: "Never mind. You put a blanket under the tree and rest. The only problem is that they won't let you anywhere without an interpreter. A *ménage à trois,* you see."

Simon gave another chuckle, but this time Alan couldn't politely respond to him. *Have things really gone so mad,* he wondered, and asked: "Wouldn't it be possible to apply to visit Estonia on some good professional pretext?"

"Estonia no longer exists," replied Simon, growing serious. "We no longer have diplomatic representation there, no-one has diplomatic relations with Estonia any more. It's a Russian borderland. You can only get there through Moscow, and even then it's difficult."

Simon took a sip of wine from his glass and continued without raising his eyes: "We can arrange for you an Embassy employee's visit to Moscow. You have to pay up front for the hotel, transport with a driver, meal, a visit to the Lenin Mausoleum with a guide, an expensive pleasure…" Simon grinned, paused and then lifted his eyes to Alan: "They'll arrange a minder for you there, who won't leave you alone for a minute. As a foreigner they won't let you wander around without an interpreter, for 'security' reasons."

Alan felt the air leaving his lungs, and when he opened his mouth, no voice came out. He coughed, breathed deeply and said: "How do I get a message to her? Letters don't seem to get through."

"We'll send a letter by the diplomatic mail to the Embassy in Moscow and then they post it on under a false name in a pretty Soviet envelope from a street letter-box to the right address."

"And how does she get a reply to me?"

"She writes to the local address on the envelope. Of course, all this is risky. If you request an official meeting with her, she will be processed." Simon's gaze now became extremely clear, despite the bottle of wine. The waiter had come to the table.

"Contacts with foreigners can bring trouble for Soviet citizens nowadays. Eavesdropping, attempts to recruit…" said Simon, raising his eyes to the waiter with his long French apron.

"Would you gentlemen like anything sweet?" asked the waiter.

"*Une profiterole, s'il vous plait,*" said Simon without an accent.

"*Une café - just a black coffee,*" declared Alan in a subterranean-sounding voice, with none of the resonance of a BBC newsreader. Alan's head was swimming and he didn't know if a black coffee would suffice to stop this merry-go-round. The reason was not alcohol. With him it never was.

"Would they dare? She's a well-known singer; she's appeared on various stages in Europe…"

"They dare," nodded Simon. "Every day more and more artists, heroes and even generals are confessing as enemies of the people and traitors."

"I have to go and meet Johanna – before it's too late," said Alan quietly but certainly. "Thanks for your help. I have no other way." Beads of sweat stood out on his forehead.

Simon looked sympathetically at his tousle-headed and worried colleague. *Is this what they call love?* he asked himself, puzzled.

*

The boy woke at dawn. Birds were already singing, but outside it was still dark. He struggled sweatily from under the big fluffy eiderdown and started getting dressed. His movements were quick but quiet. He wasn't sulky, but he was saddened that his mother wanted to imprison him at his aunt's place, in this old house. He wasn't allowed into the garden to play or to run on the street. His aunt's commands and orders were annoying.

Who would want to hide themselves away in a room where the curtains are always drawn? Would that be why Daddy left as well?

He crept along the corridor and passed the half-open door of the room where he could hear his aunt's steady breathing. A floorboard suddenly squeaked under his foot. He stopped for a moment and held his breath. But it hadn't disturbed his aunt's sleep. He was worried that she might find the place where the cars were sleeping. It wasn't far from home. He would get home from here in half an hour. He didn't have the money for a tram ticket, so he could only run to beat the tram.

The street-door key was in the keyhole. He turned it slowly and carefully, just as the man had shown him how to do on the Pobeda's door. Excitement and anticipation of adventure gripped him. He pressed on the latch: the big fat door opened quietly on its well-oiled hinges. Fresh cool air assailed him outside. He closed the heavy door behind him carefully and took to his heels. Heading for the centre of town, he ran from Mäekalda Street in one spurt through Kadriorg Park. Between the hundred-year-old chestnut trees the road led to the tramline. He kept the silvery strip of the tramline in sight. The road passed along it straight toward town. It felt good to be running in the morning freshness.

He recognized the familiar streets and saw a greenish fence ahead of him. This surrounded a large yard which was the home of the cars. Beside the gate, on the fence, was a sign, in big red letters: "*Garage. Unauthorized entry forbidden.*" It was covered in barbed wire. In front of the gate was a guard-house. He pressed his nose against a crack in the fence and managed to peep in between the palings. He saw many cars standing there.

The boy was pleased. He tried to squeeze through a gap in the gate, but he heard the guard's stern voice: "Where are you off to? This isn't a playground – get going!"

The boy withdrew to the other side of the street. There was a good view from there. He hid behind a telegraph pole.

Soon a beige-coloured car came out of the gate, but

it wasn't a Pobeda, and some other, broad-faced man was sitting in it. The boy stayed watching disappointedly after it. Now he felt the cold north wind that he had not noticed as he ran earlier. He pulled up his jacket collar and buried his hands deep in his pockets.

A gang of boys was coming along the pavement. There were six or seven of them, of different heights and ages. They were moving in a quick rhythm, with large tattered rucksacks on their backs. *They might be the bag-boys,* he thought. His mother had once warned him to keep out of the way of the bag-boys. "They barge in everywhere and steal everything they can lay their hands on," she had said. He looked at them with mild fear, but interest. The bag-boys looked at him with steely gazes and stopped for a moment.

"*Ну, што смотришь?* Well, what are you looking at?" asked the tallest one. He didn't understand their language. He gave the Estonian greeting *tere* because he couldn't think of anything else to say.

The tallest bag-boy let his eyes roam over the boy's clothes. *I don't have anything to steal – I don't even have a kopek coin,* thought the boy. One of the smaller boys stepped closer and sized up his jacket. The boy took a couple of steps backward toward the gate.

The next car was starting to come out of the gate from the yard: this time a black one, the wrong colour and the wrong make.

The bag-boys went on their way. They continued walking at a fast pace, without looking back, like a pack of stray dogs.

Now the boy noticed a beige Pobeda moving toward the gate from the depths of the yard. He craned his neck trying to see through the windscreen who was at the wheel. It seemed to be the familiar man. The Pobeda was moving quickly toward him. The boy leapt out from behind the pole and ran toward the car waving his arms. The car stopped suddenly.

The boy was overjoyed. The man had noticed him. The boy saw him leaning over the front seat and opening the passenger door.

"This time I might really have run over you!" said the man.

The boy climbed in quickly through the half-open door.

"But you didn't!" He grasped the man by the neck and wouldn't let go.

"Well then, where have you been?" asked the man, patting the boy on the shoulder. "I went to visit you, but no-one was at home…" With a gentle movement he released himself from the boy's grip.

"Mummy took me to Auntie's place and went off," said the boy, in an accusing tone.

He stretched his hand out and keenly tried all the buttons, patting the dashboard as if to assure himself that everything was as before. The only button he didn't touch was for the windscreen-wipers.

The man shook his head. "First your daddy left you, and now your mummy… These parents keep slipping away! Maybe she went to the country?"

"We don't have any relatives in the country," said the boy sadly.

"Ah, so she went into the forest… picking berries," grinned the man. "Does your auntie know you've come to me?"

"No, I escaped from Auntie's place," said the boy proudly, looking the man in the face. "That's our little secret!"

"But which of us is going to work today?" the man paused to think for a moment, but then he winked conspiratorially at him.

"I want to stay with you," said the boy decisively.

The tooting of another car could be heard from behind. Somebody wanted to get out of the parking area.

"I can sleep in the car at night too!" persisted the boy.

The man selected a gear and the Pobeda moved away. "I know a place that's fun where you can spend the night…" he said thoughtfully.

The boy settled in closer to the man, to feel the warmth of his body. It felt so good to sit once again in the man's car, with its familiar smell. The boy turned on the radio. It sounded like church bells.

"*Вниманние, говорит Москва, радиостанция имени Коминтерна.* Attention! This is Radio Moscow, Comintern," echoed the rather solemn-sounding low voice of some man. The driver turned the Russian voice down a little. "Vnimanye, govorit Moskva, radiostantsiya imeni kominterna," said the boy, imitating the voice on the radio.

The man's expression became animated. "Do you know Russian?"

"No. But I remember everything."

"Interesting! Can you imitate your auntie's talk?"

He raised his head erect and pursed his lips: "Shtramm! Young gentlemen should learn to sit with a straight back from an early age."

Now the man burst out laughing.

"Splendid!" he said. "Go on!"

"Mummy's gone out and left me to look after you," he said, imitating Aunt Johanna's voice.

The car was passing along the narrow streets of the old town. The man drove the Pobeda skilfully and laughed at the boy on the sharp curves. But the boy noticed that the man's mouth was laughing, but his eyes were not laughing as they used to.

He must be a bit annoyed with me, thought the boy.

"From now on I won't leave you any more," the boy said.

The corner of the man's mouth was twitching. "Well, you're a real friend," the man replied.

*

The man and the boy were walking along a bleak empty corridor. From somewhere came the rhythmic tapping of a typewriter. They entered Room Two. It was empty and featureless. The man made the boy sit opposite him and left the door open.

He's only a brat, thought the man. *With a memory like that he'd make good Cheka material. A shame that he's the child of an enemy of the people. Otherwise something could be made of him… Still, we never know the level of a child's corruption. Perhaps they get it with their mother's milk. He should be sent to our system school – he might become a good worker.*

The boy was staring fixedly at him.

The man had never thought about being a father. Yet a boy like this might actually be nice. *But no, why not from my own sperm then? My own child.* But there was no time for that.

The man summoned up a radiant smile, meant to express enthusiasm. He also knew how to smile "heart to heart" or "innocent". Right now he needed to be enthusiastic again.

"You know what, boy – it's boring being alone. At home, in the car, on the woodpile… even in my office." He drummed his fingers on the table. "I've had a good idea…"

The man looked over his shoulder and shouted "Anna!"

Nobody replied. The secretary had disappeared again. Putting her lipstick on in the toilet? Chatting with the boys in the next room? They hadn't learned anything in high school. He would have to get himself a more mature, experienced worker. But there weren't any of those yet in Soviet Estonia. Yet you couldn't rely on the native Estonian ladies. Huge numbers of new cadres had been brought in – but they didn't speak Estonian.

The man took a long hard look at the boy and asked: "Did you manage to keep our secret?" This question came unexpectedly. He looked down and was silent for a moment, as if considering something.

Then he raised his eyes to the man again and nodded. "Sort of," he said guiltily.

The man was silent for a moment, without turning his gaze from the boy, and then began to laugh. *Nice boy… but a windbag,* he decided.

"Wait a moment," he said to the boy. He pulled his chair away from the desk and stepped out of the room.

Anna was in the corridor, whispering with a secretary from another department. Nobody had a sense of duty to build a new society. The man grinned, coming up quietly behind Anna. He said, half-aloud: "I have a boy in the preliminary investigation room. Send him to the Muraste children's home."

Anna was taken aback, and stared astonished at the man. "Another one! There are no places in the children's home."

The man placed his hand gently on Anna's shoulder. Anna's back became tense.

"Find one. Say that I sent him, and register the boy under another name." said the man. *Losing her cub drives the vixen out of her fox-hole.*

He gently stroked the secretary's shoulder. "And be motherly and tender."

The secretary blushed and chuckled: "I can't!"

The secretary from next door also pursed her lips and looked quizzically at the man.

The man struck his chest and said with piercing eyes: "How so, girls? You must be prepared for the future!"

He could see the future. In his mind's eye he saw both girls with big bellies. Their daughters with even bigger ones. Their grandchildren would one day live in an ideal society, where everyone had an identity code stamped on their skin, a personal number in a register; where all telephone numbers and addresses were mapped; where microphones and cameras tracked their every movement. And he could sit in his office and track them all. He stopped for a moment longer than necessary and let the girls look at him. He was aware of his own effect on the opposite sex, especially when his eyes flashed and he straightened his back. Then he turned around and walked with energetic steps back into the room where the boy was waiting for him, crouching like a puppy on his chair.

There was affection, trust and excitement in the boy's eyes. *So many emotions at once,* thought the man. *Conflicting and yet obvious.* He smiled broadly to the boy. "Our plan worked! Anna's going to take you to play with other boys!"

Now he noticed a little unease in the boy's eyes, but still excited hope as well. That hope had to be nurtured. It wouldn't do to make everyone's lives happy all at once. The man sighed. *First of all the enemies of the people had to be liquidated.*

*

Johanna knocked on the door of the sock factory on which the sign "Red Dawn" had recently appeared. The contours of the words "Iron Thread" on the previous sign could still be made out. A smell of cotton and the whirring of knitting machines assailed her from the room. She knew that her sister wasn't here. Perhaps, though, there was someone who could tell her where to look for their designer.

They looked at her inquisitively. Many more foreign workers had come in. The older machinists, though, recognized Johanna by sight.

No, nobody had heard anything about the designer. They spread their hands. She must be ill.

Johanna left a message in case the designer turned up. "It's urgent," she said, politely wishing them goodbye.

Where else could she look for the boy or her half-sister? At their home the door was locked and the windows closed, the curtains drawn. Nor did the boy have a key. Johanna shook her head. In the old days you could turn to the police if a child went missing. There was no point in talking to this new militia, though. You might vanish yourself. They would take you away and move into your empty house.

She had seen worry and trouble brewing in the air when they stepped in through her door with their suitcase. Now they had stepped out again, dragging Johanna's carefree citadel with them. Now it was too late to close or open the door to them and their common future. *Why were relatives brought into the world? You could choose your friends, and even those were mostly a burden. It was the same with love. It only brought heartache. If Alan ever does come, he'll see me troubled in body and soul. I haven't been to the hairdresser for ages and I've had my dress since 1939. Even a gentleman with the noblest feelings would stop loving the moment he saw a woman like me,* thought Johanna, looking at the grubby tips of her shoes.

Now about that boy. Sooner or later the mother will surely want to see her son, concluded Johanna. *I don't have to do anything but wait. Perhaps the boy will get hungry...* Johanna swallowed and felt the pangs of conscience. She went back to the tram-stop to go home again. Jingling its bell, the rumbling red tram with its wooden seats approached. "Number 1", said the sign: "Viruturg – Kadriorg".

*

The man surveyed the security guidelines on the desk:

"Information relating to the identification of criminals against the state needs to be collected constantly and actively. Since a large proportion of the anti-Soviet element keeps contact with foreign spies, these should be hunted with the help of secret checking of their post; they should be recognized, followed and tracked."

The man took up the letter, attached to its envelope with a paper-clip. The stamps bore the profile of the English king.

Dearest Johanna,

It is getting warmer and lighter in London now. It's easier to wake up in the mornings. Summer is approaching in quick steps, bringing with it memories of Madame Butterfly at Covent Garden on that unforgettable night.

The man thought, *Looks like a meaningless mish-mash of words. Is this a purely personal letter or does it contain a hidden code?*

He put the letter down, deep in thought. *Perhaps these letters should be let through? Maybe a correspondence like this would be useful for the English operations? Many enemies of the state had escaped to England and they would be carrying on their agitation. The boy, the mother, the aunt... perhaps some feedback there? Perhaps this correspondence should be directed, in case the woman or her half-sister is ready to collaborate. Perhaps even feed them some secret misinformation?*

Interesting – does Alan Hanley only read the news, or does he take part in choosing and editing the items? Perhaps he's involved in spying himself, the man reasoned. *I should get in touch with Counter-Espionage. But then they would take the whole project out of my hands. Better to do it myself at first, and later let's see.*

The man took up a pen and wrote in blue ink on a note accompanying the letter:

Section V

Let the letter through. Set up monitoring by secret postal checks and send copies of correspondence immediately to me. Process chemically to establish whether there is a secret message or coding.

*

Muraste children's home was a world in itself. At the top of a hill, near a graveyard, out of town. Neither world, of wartime or peacetime, reached this far. There was always war between the children here: for a better shirt, a bigger piece of bread, or a softer pillow. Half-starved children screamed and fought here in ragged clothes. They settled scores between themselves, because there were few carers, and even they were exhausted.

Hand in hand with Anna, the boy approached the old manor house. Anna didn't talk much. The boy observed her swinging gait and thought that she was almost as beautiful as Mummy, but she had thick pink lipstick on and black inky lines drawn on her eyes, which somehow made those eyes look very feline.

With Anna the boy stepped through the door of the children's home. The house seemed big and grand, although its paint had faded and plaster was peeling off the walls. There were big chinks between the floorboards. That seemed interesting to the boy.

It was exciting to arrive in a new place. The boy looked around inquisitively. The furniture in the teachers' room was old and worn. A beautiful picture covered in shiny glass hung on the wall, from which gazed a man with bushy eyebrows and a military face. Under his large hooked nose hung thick, dark whiskers.

In the room sat a gaunt, stern-looking lady who assessed them with a long gaze.

"Here's a new boy for you," said Anna, pushing the boy to stand in front of the orderly.

"Yes, I've already had a call from your office." The orderly leaned over the boy and studied him attentively.

"Do you want to join the bigger or the smaller boys' group?"

"Bigger," replied the boy without hesitation.

"We-ell," – the orderly shook her head – "I suppose you know best."

After filling in some papers she took a stamp, blew on it, pressed it onto a cushion of ink and struck it hard on the notebook. It did not leave much of a mark.

"Can I try to stamp it?" asked the boy helpfully.

"Ah, it'll do," grunted the orderly, looking at the boy distrustfully.

"I have to go now," said Anna, quickly taking her leave.

The boy watched her go, a little worried. The teacher got

up, and the boy noticed that a little trumpet was attached to her hip. *A strange instrument,* thought the boy. *But it's good that they play music here. It might be nice, being here.*

The teacher led him to a room where there was a row of many iron beds, and showed him his own bed. It had a striped mattress but no pillow.

The teacher took one from someone else's bed and put it at the head of his.

"We have our own system here. Before breakfast and before lights-out there's a roll-call," said the teacher, patting the trumpet on her hip. "When I blow the fanfare, everyone has to line up."

"I don't like standing in line," said the boy, looking dejectedly around the empty room.

"You'll soon get used to it," replied the teacher.

*

She was walking around the house, hoping to find traces of the boy. He might have forced open a window or broken in and come home anyway.

But there were no traces. Johanna had said that the boy had left early in the morning. *So where is he? Is he really hunting for me?*

She stepped inside from the street door. Her last hope was to see him crouched in the entrance hall.

But that was not the scene she found. The hall was cool and smelt of damp.

She sighed deeply and opened the door of the apartment. What greeted her in the room were open cupboard doors – a hasty departure. The apartment was as untidy as an uncombed head.

She stepped through the apartment, looked into the bathroom, kitchen and back-room, which still had a smell of smoke, a memory of the man. *Am I alone now?*

She went into the kitchen and started watering the flowers. The pelargonium had drunk its potful of water and the soil was as dark and dry as ash under her fingers. *What shall I do now?* she thought, looking out of the window.

Normal life was going on in the windows of the house next door. Now the neighbours could see her in the well-lit room, with the curtains opened. It was a sight they hadn't seen for nearly two years.

But no-one enjoyed the scene or applauded it.

*

Suddenly there was a knock at the door.

Perhaps it's the boy, she thought suddenly, as she rushed to the door.

With trembling hands she grasped the latch and pulled the door open. Behind it stood the man, still with his bright blue eyes and flashing white teeth. Still damned handsome. Even though she now knew that he could not be trusted. She slammed the door in his face.

She leaned on the door for a moment, tense in her thoughts.

I don't want to see him… but if he knows something about the boy? Hardly.

The man knocked again. She didn't answer. Time seemed to have stood still for a long tense moment on both sides of the door. "I came to tell you not to worry about the boy," came the man's voice from behind the door, and then she heard the echo of his slowly receding steps.

She opened the door.

"Where is he?" she asked in a hoarse voice.

The man turned around, hesitating a moment. His face still bore the same innocent smile. Then he stepped closer and stood facing her.

"I don't understand – what happened? Where were you?"

he asked, grabbing hold of her. That familiar touch was now alien.

"I'm not playing hide-and-seek," she said, pulling her hand free from his grip.

The man forced himself indoors and sat down on the sofa: where the boy usually slept.

"What did you do with my son? What game are you playing with him?"

"You have a remarkable son. Sharp, good-natured, brave." He crossed his leg over his knee. He had shiny new shoes on. "He came to me himself… We went looking for you."

She approached him, and stopped in the middle of the room. She was trying to stay rational.

"So let's go to him now."

"It's all right. He's with other children."

He got up and leaned toward her. She turned her head away. She smelt his cologne and didn't want to remember it.

"Let him play with the other boys an hour or so more," he said, looking at her candidly.

Suddenly he looked so sincere and benevolent. She was confused.

Did I imagine it all? she thought, suddenly not knowing what to believe any more. Grasshoppers started sawing in her head, driving her thoughts astray. Again she wanted the common sense to retreat to the haystack.

"Don't worry," he said, pressing himself against her for a moment. Below the surface she was trembling.

What a liar! she thought. *Or was he really more innocent than she believed?* At that moment she wanted to hope that all her fears were just the fruit of a tormented imagination, that it was not too late to wake from the bad dream. The stronger the man's embrace became, the greater the confusion she felt in her head. The grasshoppers were sawing even harder.

He pushed her against the wall.

If I could hit him with something… to make him disappear. A thousand thoughts whirled in her head at once. *I won't give in,*

I'll simply switch off the electric current in my body.

The man's grip was strong. He pressed his lips against her neck. She didn't respond to his kisses, but still he managed to get to her.

She wanted to escape, but she couldn't move.

I can't even control my own body. My whole will is sapped away. She felt everything within her starting to throb, against her will. All the horrors that had happened had not lessened the man's power of attraction. Again she sensed the entrancing effect of the cologne on the man's traitorous skin, and the touch of his hated hand was good.

This man was an intruder. *This is an invasion. It mustn't be sweet.* The grasshoppers were chirruping rhythmically and extremely loudly.

The man let out a roar. Against her will it touched the woman too. A shiver ran through her body and it shattered into a thousand pieces. With him she flowed into oblivion.

Everything in her life was wrong again.

She looked at him and thought: *a shame that this man is so corrupt. He has no conscience. He doesn't believe in anything that I believe in.*

A pity that we aren't like-minded, he thought. "I want you to help me," he said, drawing his finger over her wet face.

"How can I help you?"

"You are my heart and I am your brain. We are organs in the same system," he said, putting his hand cautiously on her stomach. "Together we form a whole. I want us to start working together."

Now it came – the moment of truth! she thought, turning pale. *It's all about security. He's going to recruit me.*

"I'm not suitable for this work," she said in a hoarse voice.

"You are. Everyone can learn," he said, adding a note of enthusiasm to his voice. "I'll teach you. You're clever and beautiful, you should use your talents. You're wasting yourself in the sock factory."

She shifted further away. *What a tirade. What night-school taught him this poetry? He needs a clever and beautiful informer. Weren't there enough of the new cadres? Masses of them were brought in.*

She turned her face away, stiffening.

"We need people like you, who are honest and trustworthy," he explained.

What trust are we talking about? she thought. The hoppers had stopped playing.

His hand was still on her stomach.

"Do you make a habit of recruiting in bed?" she asked, suddenly getting up. She walked naked across the bedroom to the bathroom to wash herself clean, not knowing whether she would ever be clean again. She had never informed on anyone before. Her conscience was still clean on that score.

The water was cold. *What has become of my husband?* She took a towel and dried herself so hard that it almost hurt. She grabbed her dress from the bathroom hook, put it on and stepped determinedly into the room.

Even this man must have a boss that he fears, she thought, feeling her fighting spirit re-emerging.

"You'll give me back my son straight away or I'll complain about you."

He grinned and said, without taking his eyes off her, "Where? It's your word against mine."

"There must be law and order somewhere."

"I am that law and order" – he paused slightly – "and justice."

Now an ironic expression appeared on her face.

"According to the law you get ten years' imprisonment on paper. I can also offer you the firing-squad," he continued, buttoning up his shirt. "You have protected an enemy of the people."

She flinched almost imperceptibly. *What does he know about us? What did my husband confess to?*

"You're only still here because I like you," he told her almost confidentially.

She lowered her eyes.

He got up, and lifted her chin, so as to look deep into her eyes.

"Think about it…" Then he let go of her and slowly started moving toward the door.

She went after him and grabbed him by the sleeve: "I want to see my son."

He turned around and again looked penetratingly at her.

"So you'll start working?"

Perhaps I should play along, to gain time, she thought.

He took a pen and a crumpled paper from his pocket. It had something printed on it.

"I'll need your signature. Believe me, our co-operation can be good."

He started unscrewing the cap of his fountain-pen.

He even has the paper printed ready, she thought, and said emphatically, "First I want to see my son."

He folded the paper and put it with the pen back in his pocket. Then he took a car key from his other pocket. His movements were measured and precise, like his steps, as he now walked out of the door ahead of her.

The east wind brought a coolness to the summer afternoon. The raw air seemed refreshing. Her head became clearer. Her world had collapsed again. An amorphous hope had filled her breast, only to fall to pieces again.

How many times will this happen before I learn anything – to curb my optimism? I let the system betray me, I want to believe their lies. I fly along with the alluring rhythm of their music, I sink into their lyrical promises. She shook away these thoughts. *Now I have to get hold of the boy. But then?* she thought in a panic. *If I don't start collaborating with them… Will he take the boy away from me again, put me in prison, have me deported, abandon me? Who will look after the boy then? Might Johanna adopt him?*

Feverish thoughts filled her brain. They were milling around like ants.

She sat down next to him on the cool leather seat of the Pobeda. *Cars like this were only handed out to Bolshevik Party leaders and Cheka agents.* How had she not realized that before? *And this man isn't a driver. Under his shirt he must be bulging with invisible epaulettes.* What did this security agent know about her? She tried to keep a sober mind, think logically, arrange the facts.

She thought about her friends, who were not even involved in politics, but were deported in 1941. Stalin wanted to deport the whole nation; only the war stopped his intentions. *Temporarily? Genocide can always be repeated.*

Does this man want me to compile new lists now?

*

Johanna was sitting once again with her ear to the radio, hoping that Alan had included a veiled coded message to her in among the news. He might say something about the Royal Opera House, Covent Garden, about which production was currently playing there. Then Johanna would get some idea of his state of mind. *Ah,* Johanna decided, *maybe not after all. All operas ended tragically! Better not make comparisons. The situation was dramatic enough.*

From the radio came Alan's voice: "We cannot close our eyes to the fact that citizens of many parts of the world do not enjoy the freedoms of the British Empire. In many countries dictators or oligarchs are exercising unlimited power through the political police…"

Again the station wavered off the frequency and the airwaves started crackling. Johanna twiddled the knob, but it was no use. Indignantly she switched the wireless off with a click and remained sitting by it for a moment. She gazed at her well-appointed room. At the beautiful antique suite, the old paintings on the wall, and was pleased still to have this oasis in the surrounding desert. She could still listen to Alan's voice on the wireless, browse through old magazines, escape into novels and gramophone records. It was sad to live alone here, but it was better than the GULAG. She glanced at the silent telephone on the bureau. It too had become an antique, left over from the passing of time. The telephone had lost its voice in the night when the city was burning, the lines were cut and the stage of the Estonia Opera was buried in ruins. There was no sense in racking your nerves waiting for the lines to be restored.

Johanna imagined Alan sitting on the sofa in his living-room, one leg over his knee, wearing well-pressed tweed trousers. One eyebrow cocked higher than the other on his otherwise neat oval face, as if he wanted to ask something. *But what?* Today she couldn't even hear his words on the airwaves.

Are you keeping well? Alan seemed to be moving his narrow lips. Johanna didn't know how to reply.

What will become of me, my sister and the boy? Johanna shivered at the shoulders and drew her kimono tightly around her.

*

"Your group is working in the field right now," said the teacher, moving toward the farm with the boy.

Outside in the field there were many boys, clustered around a smoking bottle. As the orderly and the boy approached closer, the neck of the bottle exploded and a cloud of smoke escaped.

The boys chuckled as they surveyed the orderly with rather guilty looks on their faces.

"What are you up to here?" she asked in an angry tone.

The tallest boy smiled slyly like a fox: "We were working here, but some sort of explosive came out of the flower-bed. We wanted to defuse it, but we didn't manage…" The other boys burst into a titter.

"Isn't it enough that Rein has lost two fingers!" shouted the orderly at the leader of the group. "Stop it immediately!" She turned to the others. "Is that clear to all of you?" Then she gestured to the new boy. "Here's another one for your group. Teach him to work, and not to make exploding bottles!" she said gruffly, and departed across the furrows with rapid steps.

Everyone's gaze was fixed on the boy. They studied him curiously.

There was a long, pregnant silence.

The boy wanted to ask about the explosive, but he took up another subject in a friendly way: "What are you growing here in the nursery?"

"Watermelons," replied the leader of the group, eyeing the boy's peaked cap. "Listen – let me try your cap on."

"Daddy gave it to me. I can't give it to you," he replied apologetically.

"We don't have our own things here, everything's in common!" The leader grabbed the cap from his head and put it on his own. He wiggled his head, laughing as he looked at the boys, as if seeking confirmation. They tittered and nodded that they agreed with him. The leader turned to the boy and conjured up a tough face.

"You see, it's like this: you do everything that I say around here."

"But you're not my mummy or daddy," said the boy.

One of them chuckled.

"If you had those, you wouldn't be here," exclaimed the leader, spreading his arms. "If you like, call me Dad… and if you don't, call me Mum."

Jeering laughter was heard.

The boy wasn't fazed: "So which are you?"

The leader's expression turned dark.

"And now I've got a boy here who's asking for a beating…"

The boys stayed silent and looked on, interested in what would happen next. All eyes were fixed on the leader, who stepped menacingly close to the boy.

He stopped for a moment and said slyly: "Do you want us to show you our bunker?"

The boy nodded enthusiastically. He felt as if he had been able to arouse a little respect in the leader.

The leader turned to the boys: "You stay here and do a bit of work, Chunky and I will show the new boy the bunker." The boys exchanged glances. He motioned to a square-shouldered smaller boy and they stepped over toward the brushwood. The boy followed them.

"The bunker is our group's secret," said the leader. "And telling tales about it brings the death penalty."

Fear and tension seized the boy.

"Let me try on your jacket!" said Chunky to him.

The boy felt awkward, but he didn't want to give away his jacket.

"I'm afraid it's too small for you," it occurred to him to say.

"Take it off anyway – it'll get dirty in the bunker."

The leader was now sizing the boy up with his gaze.

Perhaps I ought to meet trust with friendliness, thought the boy, reluctantly taking off his jacket. Chunky snatched it from his hand and started putting it on as he walked. The jacket really was too small for him. The buttons at the front couldn't be done up.

"The sleeves are too short too," commented the boy.

Chunky still kept the jacket on, as they moved deeper into the bushes.

The mouth of the bunker was covered with branches. Chunky bent down and rolled away a big stone with a groan. Underneath it appeared a hatch with rusty hand-grips.

The group leader pulled the trapdoor at the mouth of the bunker open and the boys squeezed inside one at a time. It was dark inside and smelled of soil. The leader drew a match and lit a paraffin lamp he called a 'snot-nose'. Now the whole contents of the bunker was revealed to the boy. There was everything that the lads had found on the battlefield. Equipment of both armies. The most highly prized seemed to him to be the old blue-white-and-black insignia of Estonia, pictures of which his father had shown him.

"Wow, great!" said the boy, unable to take his eyes off them.

The sound of the fanfare could be heard far away and Chunky moved towards the mouth of the bunker. "Evening snack, now we get a glass of sour milk," said Chunky, starting to climb out of the bunker.

"You're lucky," the leader told the boy, hauling himself up.

The boy would have liked to stay here longer, but he put the insignia down and followed the others.

"Think about being obedient!" said the leader, shutting the hatch in his face.

"Wait!" cried the boy, banging against the hatch. Then he heard the stone thudding onto it. He stretched out his arms and pushed with all his might against the trapdoor, but it would not budge.

"All right, open up!" cried the boy. "You can keep my cap and jacket!"

But nobody replied. Silence filled the whole bunker.

The boy looked around. It was dim in here, the flame of the 'snot-nose' flickered and made shadows. Although his heart was thumping with fear, he thought aloud: *I can sit here for a while, there are plenty of interesting things in here. Sooner or later they'll come back.* But his confidence was hollow. He was angry with the man for sending him here. Did the man really think that he would like playing with these boys here? *What a stupid idea! He should have known him better.* Yet the boy couldn't get too angry with the man, because he himself had broken their agreement, he hadn't kept their secret properly hidden. The pangs of conscience burned in the boy's breast. He talked too much… *In the future I'll have to be more careful.*

So this is how the Forest Brothers live. His father had talked about his former life in the forest. And his mother had replied: "How do you live there in the forest!" At that time the boy had thought that would be very exciting. But now he started to doubt it a little.

Looking around him, he saw a real grenade. It was notched and heavy. He took it carefully into his hand, surveyed it and delicately put it down again. In the corner of the bunker were empty bottles and a box of empty cartridge-cases. *Ah, so that's where they get their gunpowder.* He looked with concern at the trembling flame of the 'snot-nose'. *What will happen when it burns out? Will it be completely dark then?*

And then it happened. The whole bunker was plunged into pitch blackness.

Now he felt unhappy and alone. That moment lasted an eternity, until suddenly it seemed as if his father were sitting next to him. His father was sitting in silence, not even smoking a cigarette. But his silent presence was somehow good and encouraging. He was no longer afraid. He told his father about the grenade and promised to show him the Defence League insignia too, when the 'snot-nose' started burning again. "I didn't know grenades were so big and heavy. But in the photographs they were shinier," the boy went on. "Everything's different in real life."

His father didn't reply.

"You see, Dad, now we're Forest Brothers!"

This time his father seemed to nod to him.

A twisting gravel road turned off at the Vääna-Jõesuu highway toward the Muraste orphanage. The Pobeda entered the courtyard of the Muraste manor house.

"Your son is now a lord of the manor. You see, he's relaxing here at the old Muraste estate!" said the man with a smile, but to himself he was cursing his own pliancy: *On my desk there's a pile of a hundred files, detention orders, statements waiting for me… and I'm wasting time here on this woman's excursion. I hope it will be worthwhile.*

She looked out the window at the decaying manor house. "So you took him straight to an orphanage."

"Only until his mother turns up. I don't have a nursery," he said.

When the car was parked, she pressed on the door-handle and tried to open the door, but it wouldn't obey her so easily. The man put his hand on hers and showed her how to do it. They got out of the car and approached the main door. Her steps were rapid. Soon, soon she would see her son.

The orderly's room was empty. Only the radio was playing, and a plaintively read poem could be heard:

Hooray, the working bee! Here the hay will soon be cut in the thriving meadow.

Here comes the powerful coarse-fodder team.

Rewards will come for those who exceed the norm.

The hollow words resounded in this empty stone-walled room as if being intoned by an entire choir.

They went on down a long corridor. The noise of children could be heard from the rooms. Somewhere they were having a pillow fight, and somewhere boys were squabbling. The man went on restlessly. He was annoyed that there was no order here.

Finally they found the orderly, sitting alone and lost in thought in the Red Corner, where they kept the Party posters. She was smoking, her trumpet resting on her lap. The Red Corner was decorated with flags, slogans and Stalin's portrait.

"We've come about that boy that Anna brought you this morning," he said, turning to the orderly. "This is his mother. Let's fill in the papers quickly and hand the child over to the mother."

The orderly stubbed out her cigarette petulantly. "It's the Quiet Hour right now."

He turned to the boy's mother. "While the papers are being put in order, we can fill in your form and sign it," he declared.

"Before signing, I still want to see my son. Which room is he in?" she inquired of the orderly.

"Please bring the boy straight here," ordered the man.

The orderly got up reluctantly. The woman got up too, and followed her apprehensively.

The orderly turned around and faced her: "You can wait here."

"No, I want to see how they live here too."

"They live all right," snapped the orderly, dragging her slippers and swinging her trumpet in front of her.

The man followed the women. *I don't know what will be revealed there,* he thought.

They arrived in a room with big windows. One pane was shattered. Some boys were brawling, others were lying in their outdoor clothes and shoes on their iron beds.

"Order in the house! No outer clothes on the beds!" commanded the orderly.

One of the boys retorted: "It's cold today!"

The woman cast her eyes around the room.

"Where is he?"

"Where is the new boy?" echoed the orderly.

The boys exchanged glances and shrugged.

"He'll turn up for the evening roll-call," muttered Chunky.

Then she noticed her own son's jacket on the boy who spoke.

"Why are you wearing my son's jacket?"

"He gave it to me himself."

Now she recognized her son's peaked cap on the head of the group leader. The peak had been complemented by a Pioneer badge.

Her eyes were blazing: "Where did you get that cap?"

"You're a Pioneer yourself and a group leader. Aren't you ashamed?" interjected the orderly.

He shrugged and set about unfastening the Pioneer badge from the cap. "It was too small for me anyway," he said, giving it to the woman. She grabbed the group leader by the shoulders and shook him.

"What did you do to him?" She was losing her self-control.

"Nothing," replied the leader angrily, shaking himself free from her grip.

The man realized that something was wrong. He also stepped up to the group leader and looked him piercingly in the eye. "You're the biggest one here, but if you don't find your group member right now, from tomorrow you'll be in the labour colony. There you'll be the smallest one. That I promise you."

At this piece of news the group leader slunk away and beckoned almost imperceptibly to Chunky. Chunky understood the wordless hint and slipped out the door.

The orderly grabbed her trumpet, put it to her lips and blew. A very loud cacophony came from it. "He should turn up straight away after that call."

The boys gathered in the room for roll-call. The new boy was still missing.

The group leader took two steps forward and reported: "He was working in the fields – shall I go and look for him?" The man nodded. The group leader hurried out the door, the woman at his heels.

"Why this untidiness?" the man asked the orderly in a low voice.

"You see how many children we have; I can't run after them all the time. And you send me more every day…"

"Then call in more Young Communists, volunteers, to help you."

"There are no volunteers," said the orderly firmly.

*

Chunky rolled the stone away and prised the trapdoor of the bunker open. It was dark inside, and hard to make out the boy's silhouette in the corner.

"You can come out now, and if you blab a word about this,

you're a dead man!"

The boy climbed out of the bunker, and while Chunky was closing the hatch, set off rapidly deeper into the bushes.

"Hey, where are you going? Wrong direction!"

"No, I'm not coming back to you any more," cried the boy, setting off at a run.

Chunky started running after him, but he tripped on a rock and fell over.

"Come back here!" he screamed, sprawled on the ground, after the boy into the forest. "They're looking for you!"

But the boy had already vanished.

He ran fast through the bushes and didn't even feel the scratches of the alder branches on his face and hands.

It was so good to run. He reached the path that was cut through the bushes, and carried on along it. A horse had passed through it; he could sense fresh horse-sweat and the smell of dung in the air. He wanted to run as fast as a horse. His legs seemed to move by themselves. The cold left his body as steam from his mouth. He no longer needed the jacket or the cap. He put on an extra spurt. He could scarcely feel his heels touching the rough ground.

It felt so good to move forward, run away. When the flickering of the 'snot-nose' had been snuffed out in the bunker and darkness had come, it became very silent. The boy had heard only the beating of his heart, his own breathing in the surrounding void, and the echo of his own voice. Here on the path, even at dusk, there was plenty of light and sound. The soughing of the wind, the cracking of a branch and the chirping of grasshoppers filled his ears with their music. At the moment he didn't even need the Pobeda's radio.

The boy thought that he had better run in a fixed direction. Although it was nice to simply run, every path ends up somewhere. At the moment he didn't know where he would like to end up. *Perhaps at home? But there was no Mummy or Daddy there any longer. Or to Auntie's? But it was boring sitting indoors there.* If he found Mummy, she would take him to Auntie's place. If he found the man, he would be sent to the boys at Muraste. Or he might not be, if he told him what happened? But he couldn't betray the Muraste boys' secret. He'd get the death penalty for that. He'd already blabbed the man's secret. Or rather, half of the secret… and that was where all his problems began. Otherwise all three of them could be sitting in the Pobeda or eating chocolates.

The highway appeared straight ahead. *Isn't that the same road I took on the way here with Anna? Then it must lead back to town,* he reasoned to himself. *Which way to run?* He hesitated for a moment and trotted onwards. The road even seemed familiar. He remembered those farmhouses that appeared in the depths of the clearing.

The rumble of an approaching motor was heard in the distance. *That's a truck,* he thought. From behind a grove crawled a big old lorry. *An old Mercedes rattletrap,* he decided; *it must have been made long before I was born.* He wrinkled his nose, but still waved his hand. Now he could feel the soles of his feet, and the exhaustion in his body. The truck slowed down and screeched on its brakes. He ran up to the driver's cab, from which peered an elderly chap with a fag in his mouth and wearing a flat cap.

"Hello," said the boy; "are you going into town?"

The man eyed him for a moment and beckoned with his hand: "Climb aboard!"

*

They criss-crossed through the village of Muraste and along the Vääna road, looking for the boy, and even at his home. *Where else?* They had not yet visited Johanna's, but the woman couldn't go there with the man. The road narrowed. They had now come again to the familiar railway level crossing. At the narrow crossing a barrier obstructed them, with a red light flashing.

The warning whistle of a train sounded from afar. A big freight train rolled slowly through in front of their eyes.

"There certainly are a lot of wagons," he said, putting his hand on her knee. "He will turn up. Don't worry."

In her mind's eye the woman saw the cattle-wagons in which her friends were deported in summer 1941. They never came after her and her husband. They were living at a different address, and at that time her husband wasn't yet on the People's Committee. The boy wasn't even two years old. She was carrying him in her lap and thinking of where to hide with her little child if the next wave of deportations started. Now she had to think again about where to hide with the boy. But she could no longer carry him in her arms, and the invisible bond between them had vanished.

I should jump out of the car and find the boy myself.

She looked back over her shoulder. Behind them a large truck had stopped, and the lights of some other vehicle appeared. The man checked her with a look. She smiled, although her right hand was damp with sweat. *I should find the boy and escape with him. There must be a way out somewhere, because otherwise we will be mice in the claws of this tom-cat.*

Finally the last wagon had gone. The bell at the level crossing started to ring again and the red light to flash. The man took his hand from her knee, turned on the ignition and put the car in motion. The boom started to rise slowly. From the other side of the crossing a car was already starting to move slowly.

Now, she thought. Before he could move away, she quickly pressed the handle. She jerked the door open and jumped out.

The man also jumped out immediately, but the truck blew its horn. The driver shouted from the open window: "Where are you going – you're blocking the road!" The man looked quickly over his shoulder. Cars were coming toward him from the other side too, and it wasn't possible to turn around. The railway crossing was narrow and edged with a fence.

He watched her as she ran. *I'll catch her anyway. First I have to find the boy.*

*

She can't look for her son on her own, thought Johanna, looking at the panting woman sitting on a chair in front of her. *She's worn out,* she concluded, surveying her half-sister. *She used to be a fine girl.* Just a couple of years ago Johanna had regarded her with her professional eye and thought that if this young woman's cheekbones were put before the bright lights, she would even be suitable for the stage or a film. But what had her worries made of her? A thin, nervous, neurotic creature. Now she reminded her of her own mother. Johanna's father had left her for such a woman when the girl was ten.

"Horrible that the child has disappeared," declared Johanna about the sad spectacle. *How good that I don't have children,* she thought to herself. But even she was not so heartless. She was able to sympathize with others' troubles in every role on the stage, and sometimes in real life. *But life was always full of troubles, especially in the time of the Soviets.*

"I'd like to help you in some way," declared Johanna.

Tension appeared on the woman's face. "That would be nice of you," she replied with a cool stare. "But how?"

Johanna knew that her sister blamed her for the boy's disappearance. But it wasn't her fault. She wasn't a teacher. She didn't know the inner world of little boys. She didn't know what they would want or where they would run.

"I'll make a space for you in the cellar," said Johanna. "You never know when the goons will come knocking at the door."

"No, I'll go out and continue searching," she replied sorrowfully, getting up from her chair.

Johanna watched impotently. She wanted to jump off this merry-go-round of terror, *but where?* The merry-go-round seemed to be turning ever faster, at full speed.

Johanna opened her Baroque-style escritoire and took out again the letter she had received that morning from Alan. At last! Every fresh look at that letter was like a vitamin injection. She needed it again. On thick snow-white paper, adorned with Alan's golden monogram, were the impatiently written lines in that familiar hand. But the last sentence seemed to carry a special meaning: "Pinkerton is preparing for a sea voyage to visit Cho-Cho-San. This time he has serious intentions."

That's a reference to Puccini's 'Madame Butterfly', concluded Johanna. In the second act, Admiral Pinkerton visits his 'butterfly', Cho-Cho-San. But Johanna didn't want to think of the third act, which ends in hara-kiri for the butterfly. *It wasn't the idea to rush that far ahead. Alan only mentions preparing for a journey. Does that mean he's coming to see me? Is that really possible?* – the joyful thought ran through Johanna's head and sent shivers down her spine. Johanna grabbed her own solo record from the shelf and pulled it with her fingertips from its cover. Madame Butterfly's aria of yearning for Pinkerton was the second-last item. *I can't write back to him from Cho-Cho-San, because then it will be revealed that it's me... Better to choose an aria from Verdi's 'Aida' and let him interpret the princess of Nubia's suffering under the Egyptian yoke.* Johanna sat down quickly at her bureau, took some squared paper, the only kind whose supply had not run out, and wrote on it in her calligraphic hand:

Dear Alan,

Things are fine with me. Life is beautiful, as in 'Aida'. I feel like the Princess of Nubia.
Do you still have my solo record? Listen to the last aria on it. Isn't it wonderful?

Johanna worried about whether Alan would understand her reference. *He is quick-witted,* she consoled herself. *How good that we're united by the secret language of music!*

Johanna recalled how she and Alan had, after a concert, climbed up the dark winding stairs of Oleviste Church, which made her giddy with its sharp turns. The way upward had seemed endless, and Johanna had stopped to catch her breath. Alan's arms and chest had supported her from behind so that she wouldn't fall backwards, topple, perish, suffocate from her own emotions. In every kind of emotion there was a droplet of holiness, but here on the stairs also one of sacrilege. Their arms, bodies, mouths were united for a moment in that dark stone tower, in spite of their pounding hearts and breathless lungs. It had been a kiss in the dark unknown, before ascending another couple of stairways and emerging into the light. On the open ledge of the roof they were greeted by a sharp, rough east wind, their eyes were dazzled by the sunlight and the incomparable view. From up there the town of her birth seemed a miniature, doll-like, and the problems inhabiting its red roofs and narrow streets seemed tiny and insignificant. The cool easterly wind forced them into each other's embrace again, to seek shelter in each other.

When can I hide myself in that embrace again? thought Johanna, folding the letter.

*

The woman didn't know where to look for the boy.

She walked along the much-ravaged nocturnal streets of the town and listened for voices. Somewhere a door creaked, somewhere muffled music could be heard. Most of the lights were out, all the windows had drawn curtains. The cobblestones were ever ready to sprain her ankles, because the street lighting was not on. She moved in a criss-cross fashion, stopping at the church steps. Someone was coiled up there in a ball. *He wouldn't lie sprawling,* she thought, bending down. The toothless face of an old man stared back at her. She straightened up and moved on. *Shall I call out to the boy? No, it would attract too much attention.*

"*He was looking for me himself,*" the man had said. *Where might he work? On Pagari Street?* She moved along toward Pikk Street. There she could go up on the pavement, but even that was bumpy; some paving-stones were missing. *The boy is hardly likely to know the man's work-place... Or would he know more than I can guess?*

Some stray dogs ran around the corner. She recoiled against a wall. You could never know if any of them was rabid. Then she heard the distant echo of footsteps. She listened. They didn't belong to the boy.

The sound of the steps was cut by the rumble of a motor. A car was approaching around the corner. She withdraw into the shadow of half a drainpipe. This might be a militia vehicle. She had to find the boy before the man or his henchmen did.

A couple of hours later the sky started to lighten. Her feet were tired. Her blisters must be bleeding, but there was no time to think about that now. There were more people around, and new noises were heard from the houses. Suddenly an elderly woman ran past her on the street. "Don't go that way – bag-boys!" she shouted in warning as she ran past. The woman stopped for a moment and then moved toward the gang of boys. Perhaps they would know something. She surveyed the approaching crowd of lads, their bags on their shoulders. The band divided into two as they approached her. She screwed up her eyes in the early dawn light to see whether they were wearing any of the boy's garments. "Hello!" she greeted them. The bag-boys didn't answer, but hemmed her in.

"Have you seen a boy about this tall? Looks like me?" she asked, stretching out a hand like a yardstick.

"*Что, что*? What, what?" frowned the tallest of them.

"Ishchu malchika," she gesticulated. "Moy syn…"

The boys exchanged glances; there seemed to be something familiar about the woman's face. "*У гаража стоял*

83

мальчик, помнишь? There was a boy standing by the garage, you remember?" One of the boys mimicked the woman's Estonian greeting to the gang leader. He nodded to her and asked: *"А что мы за это получим?* But what do we get for it?" She opened her bag and took a couple of socks from the bottom of it. "Gde?" she asked, brandishing the package of socks.

One of the smallest boys grabbed her bag quickly.

"Подожди! Wait!" yelled the gang leader, and the boy gave her back her bag. The leader indicated the direction with his hand, saying: *"Гараж… машины… понимаешь?* Garage … cars … understand?" One of the boys made the sound of a car.

She understood and nodded. She gave the boy the packet of socks, saying "Thanks very much" in Estonian and set about leaving.

"Секундочку, дайте вашу шляпу. One moment – hand over your cap," said the leader, pointing to her blue beret. She took off the beret and handed it to the boy. Then she made a quick exit. She didn't look back. She only listened for the sound of anyone following.

"А мамочку ебать не хочешь? But don't you want to fuck the mother?" asked one of the boys.

She could hear the boys giggling and their leader berating them. The bag-boys moved on, in the other direction.

Garage, she thought. *Of course, the Pobeda is there!* She quickened her steps.

*

The man knew that his path was difficult. He had to open up the ground and turn over every stone. Identify every enemy of the people. Pursue, track down, trace. Find every enemy soldier in his bunker, drag every bandit Forest Brother out of his lair. Resistance was fierce, because, above all, it was in people's hearts, a learned practice, a trained way of thought. It was necessary to bring in new people, because you couldn't build a new society with the old ones.

He sat in the car and lit a cigarette. A simple cheap Soviet one: a 'Belomorkanal'. Even though it was the aim of international imperialism to sell him foreign cigarillos, flood the country with American Coca-Cola or the rivers with French wine. Estonian boys had already got to ride in German cars and fight in the German army. But they were sent to the front line, without the fanciful greatcoats or fine guns. Basically they were burned as cannon-fodder. The international arms industry had, in the course of less than thirty years, conducted two world wars, trying to annihilate everything of value and every surviving culture. The arms industry had to earn money and sell its products like every other capitalist enterprise.

He was proud to be able to sit in a Soviet Pobeda, not serving some rich English family owning Rolls-Royces or Jaguars. He had seen a beautiful life in bourgeois Estonia only in newspaper advertisements, and not known it himself. His childhood passed without a father, as he was in a prison in the Republic of Estonia, and his mother had the hardship of earning a washerwoman's wages for herself and her son. He had grown up in penury on the wrong side of the tracks and looked with longing at the passing freight trains. Only when the war broke out did he get onto a train, which took him to the state higher security school in the town of Pavlovskiy Possad.

Now his day had dawned to build a new society – a more equal, better, more humane one. To do that he had to struggle for every soul, for the consciousness of every little boy. To sit here in the garage and wait for the coming of that day. He stretched out his arm and looked at his watch. It was nearly eight o'clock. He was sure that the boy would come. *This boy might be made into something if he's trained. Who should do that? It was harder with the mother,* he decided. He didn't like the way that she had run away a second time.

The morning was cold. He switched on the engine and twiddled the knob on the radio. The whole interior was flooded with sweet music. He smiled with satisfaction. The ministry's car was supplied with a radio made to special order. Nothing was lacking in this car that was found in foreign cars. Only the rear bearings were installed dry, without a smear of grease. *Everywhere there were vermin, with no sense of state property, no desire to create a better world.*

Now he saw a familiar face beyond the gate. *There's always a scoundrel,* he thought. He put the car in gear, drove out of the gate and opened the passenger door. The boy rolled onto his neck like a big snowball. He had no jacket, and his nose was blue from the cold night, but he had a smile on his lips as always.

"Isn't the night a bit too cold for hiking?" asked the man teasingly.

The boy snuggled up beside him to get warm.

"I didn't like the Muraste boys," the boy stated laconically. "The only car they had was an old truck they just used to carry potatoes and cabbages."

The man grinned and turned the radio up. Some rhythmic swing was coming from it.

*

She arrived panting at the garage at the moment when the familiar Pobeda was turning out of the gate.

She stopped to catch her breath and focused her eyes. The top of a little head was visible next to the driver. Yes, that was her boy. *Alive and well! Thank God!* Intoxicating joy overcame her. Instinctively she started running after the car and waving at it. But then she stopped. *If he picks me up now, he'll demand my signature again or put me in prison. But what would the boy do with a mother who was a traitor or prisoner? I'm never going to turn informer.* She swallowed and let her hand drop. *Let them go for now. He will take the boy back to the children's home and I'll try to get him from there.* She stuck to the spot and watched the receding Pobeda's rear lights as it braked for a moment.

I don't know if he noticed me, it occurred to her.

*

The man saw the woman emerging from a side-street in his rear-view mirror. He turned to the boy and asked: "Have you seen your mother?"

The boy shook his head.

The man glanced again at the woman who had started running after the car but had stopped. He stepped lightly on the brake pedal and thought about whether to pick her up or not. In the morning light she looked beautiful, even when exhausted, but he didn't want to trust her any more. *She's run away from me twice. She'd certainly do it again. Let her run after me now. I have the bait!*

He looked at the boy and said: "I haven't seen her for ages either."

The boy is made of better material, he decided, looking once more at the standing woman in the rear-view mirror. *Interesting – does she think I noticed her?* Then he flashed the indicator and pressed the accelerator.

*

She saw the flashing indicator and then the brake-lights going on, as the car decelerated on a bend and disappeared from view. She sighed heavily. She had only been a couple of minutes too late. Now the boy had gone again.

She sank down breathlessly beside a board fence.

"You have only two options," Johanna had said, "- to turn to the militia or look for the boy yourself. Both options could have the same result: the hunter is found sooner than the hunted, arrested or forced to snoop for others. You can be blackmailed."

I'm already as good as dead, the man had said. "You've sheltered an enemy of the people. The minimum sentence for you would be ten years' imprisonment in a corrective labour camp. I can also offer you the firing squad."

She knew that she had no professional future, she could only live in hiding in someone's back room, a cellar, or a forest. Autumn was not far off. *How would it be to live with the boy through a long winter in a bunker? How long could we hold out there? Can that be called life?* She and her husband had thought that their life couldn't get any worse.

Even in the dim room behind the curtains we had had a life, one that we weren't able to appreciate. We could have loved and cherished our little boy more, played with him more. Felt the joy of human contact, each other's lively glances, thoughts exchanged, old books, crackling radio broadcasts. Enjoyed a cup of chicory coffee, a mouthful of mashed potatoes, a gulp of smoky air, the simple knowledge that blood is coursing through our veins, even if it is weak and almost useless… We couldn't. We hadn't appreciated the unity of our own family. The shelter that had been given to us. We had just angrily blamed the world, each other and ourselves. The water that shimmered at the bottom of an imperceptibly emptying glass. Could I do that now? But now it has vanished like the tail-lights of the disappearing Pobeda.

All that is left is myself. A woman on the run. With no yesterday and no tomorrow. For I can't sell my soul and my conscience. Not on any account. The son of a freedom fighter doesn't need a traitor for a mother.

She raised her eyes from the black asphalt to the sky. Carefree white early-morning clouds were moving across it. They were simply moving on a blue background. Moving. *Perpetuum mobile.*

*

"Have you ever travelled in a train?" the man asked the boy thoughtfully.

"Not yet," he replied.

"Trains travel quickly and quietly," said the man. "And the conductor brings you sweet biscuits and tea with sugar."

"A shame that there are no biscuits in the car," said the boy.

"You can't make tea in a car either," grinned the man. "I like driving in a car, but it's even more exciting in a train. The locomotive puffs out smoke as it goes along, it has plenty of power. And when it gets up speed, the wagons just whoosh along the rails."

The man shook his head and smiled to himself. "It's great speeding through the forests and villages. In a warm carriage, with a biscuit in your mouth…" Then he turned to the boy: "Wouldn't you like to go travelling?"

The boy looked at him with interest.

"It would be so exciting to see new places. Different sorts of towns and people," the man continued dreamily.

"But what does my mummy say?" asked the boy.

"When your mummy turns up, I can send her after you," said the man kindly.

That might work, thought the boy hesitantly.

"Maybe your daddy also went to Russia, many people are going," said the man meditatively, and shrugged.

It would be great to see Daddy, reasoned the boy. "Do you really think he's in Russia?"

"There are plenty of people going there now who don't like it here." The man patted the beige steering-wheel with his hand: "The Pobeda is from there too. There's a big factory that will make a thousand of these in a year."

The boy's eyes sparkled. He would have liked a car like this for himself.

"I'd be pleased if you'd learn a little Russian," said the man.

"Then you could help me."

The boy nodded.

"When you come back," winked the man, "we'll start doing some exciting work."

*

Alan's car had stopped in front of the theatre where a charity concert in aid of war veterans was soon to begin. The door of the old Jaguar opened with a quiet click, as if it were concealing its movement in the night. Alan extended his leg cautiously, so as not to step into a puddle, but on the Strand the rain gurgled uninterruptedly into the gutter, without causing puddles. There was no sense in opening his umbrella, because the entrance to the theatre was protected by an awning lined with lights.

Alan stepped onto the damp red carpet and entered with rapid steps through the well-lit, beckoning doors. He searched in his jacket pocket for the invitation, printed on a white card. A doorman in black livery led him to his place in the furthest box and quickly closed the door behind him. He seemed to be one of the last to arrive. People were sitting in a fug of perfume and wet clothes and clapping. The lady in charge of the charity appeared on the stage in a splendid scarlet dress, which seemed to symbolize the congealed blood of the wounded. She began in a melodious voice: "Ladies and gentlemen, welcome to our annual charity honouring the men in uniform who were fighting for King and Country…"

At such moments it was comfortable to recall the war and donate with the generosity of a bad conscience. It didn't stink of the trenches in here. Alan had been a young front-line reporter in the final years of the First World War. The meat-grinder had spared him, he got out with just a couple of scratches and slight concussion, caused by a collapsing roof. Unbelievably quickly the world's memory had extinguished all the terrifying images of war, such as amputated limbs and men blinded by poison gas, and rushed into the next war. Now that too had ended. True, with an atomic cloud over Japan, but that did not affect the air of England. Perhaps that too would be rapidly forgotten. Alan joined in a round of applause. The dazzling lady glided off the stage. The heavy velvet curtain revealed, in front of the grand piano, a female singer in a considerably airier costume, and a piano accompanist in a tuxedo.

Perhaps it would be possible to arrange some charity performance like this for Johanna too? Competition to take part in an event like that might not be so tough as for the roles at the opera house, thought Alan. He would have to speak to the director of music at the BBC, who must surely know some agent. But it was now six years since Johanna had performed here. The war had wiped away cultural links with Estonia, and the audience's musical memory. The pre-war world had been blown to smithereens by bombs, and those jigsaw pieces could not be put back together again.

Alan listened to the diligently mediocre trills of the soprano and thought that if the situation in Eastern Europe had really become so crazy as Simon's security reports would have you believe, then he should rescue Johanna. One person at least. If England did not manage to rescue a whole country or nation, then at least one soul could be saved. Would that be Alan's contribution, a new mission for a confirmed bachelor?

Alan liked orderliness, his nicely furnished terraced house, where his peace had not been permanently broken in half a century. He liked his world, where the cares and the winds of war could be obliterated in a sound-proofed studio. Problems could erupt on the air, but not in his private sphere. And yet that had now happened. He had to make a decision. It had been so comfortable to meet for fleeting trysts, entering each other's lives, and then return to domestic peace. Even in love, Alan needed rest, his own private territory. That suited Johanna as well. Her radiant performances sometimes needed their backstage moments. Peace, relaxation, the restoration of reserves of strength. Despite the reach and outgoing nature of their work, they were both introverts, loners, egoists. A confirmed bachelor and spinster. Oh misfortune! And now they felt the lack of each other. At least Alan thought so now; he didn't want any more solitude.

The music rolled in waves through the hall. The singer was replaced by a quartet. Mozart by Elgar. *Can feelings vary, as music does? No,* he thought. His feelings had been put to the test by the war and by the German and the first Russian occupation. Then at least the letters started to move and telephones to ring, which were certainly monitored. The new Soviet occupation threatened to cut through the last communication channels, the last sublimation of love. Some decision had to be made before it was too late. This rare and unexpected ray of sunshine, bringing him love at a mature age, so wounding and painful, was being eclipsed.

On the stage the music reached a crescendo and the violins were sawing Vivaldi to pieces. Alan decided to cast his fate to the winds and make preparations to travel to a cold country. Tomorrow he would ring the Foreign Office, the British Council, a charitable organization, the Soviet Embassy, talk again with Simon…

*

At Johanna's home it was a bridge evening. The hostess and her friends sat around a big mahogany card-table. They all smelled of mould and mothballs, because Johanna had ordered them all to put on their good old clothes for the evening's card game. As if it were still 1939. *In this house there were no checked shirts, and they didn't drink tea from glasses, getting the aluminium spoons in their eyes. The dictatorship of the workers and peasants had not reached here yet,* thought

Johanna – although she already had a fugitive in the cellar.

Johanna peeped at the gallery of her friends as if in a hidden distorting mirror. Her partner for today's game, her long-standing colleague from the stage of the Estonia Theatre, the baritone David, was glowing with his usual charm, despite his bulk. The artist playing in the opposing pair, however, looked as though he had already been through a couple of unsuccessful suicide attempts. Johanna turned her gaze on her literary friend. Villem the writer had absent-looking myopic eyes, as if he spent most of his time somewhere in another, better galaxy.

"Make your bids!" – the baritone interrupted Johanna's train of thought. His lively brown eyes tried to arouse Johanna's desire to play. But Johanna was far from enthusiastic. *Should I defend myself or make a false manoeuvre?* she thought, eyeing her cards. "You're so absent-minded today, my dear," remarked Villem opposite her, teasing her affectionately.

"Oh, it's hard for me to concentrate today," Johanna excused herself, slipping the queen of spades from between her fingers. "Bad hand, but I'll back you." "Well, what's going on in your pretty little head? What's making you restless?" the artist chimed in.

"Ah, I'm worried about my nephew. The child has gone missing. I don't know where to look for him," explained Johanna, sizing up her guests with a suspicious look. *Could any of them help?*

The men sighed sympathetically. "Everywhere is full of homeless children," remarked Villem the writer, who knew what homelessness meant. He was still, for the umpteenth year, living with various friends.

"Don't you have someone you know in the militia?" asked Johanna cautiously, raising her eyes and, like a spider, extending her feelers out among the flies in her web.

"None in the Red Militia at any rate," replied the writer, turning to the silent artist: "Hasn't State Security ordered a few portraits from you?"

The artist's eyes widened in astonishment: "From me?" After a moment's pause he replied: "They wouldn't commission me; they have their own Socialist Realist school... the ones whose pictures never used to make it into the exhibitions." He turned his long-suffering gaze on Johanna: "... but a child disappearing is a terrible thing."

"But listen – talk to an old stagehand of ours," – a possible solution occurred to the baritone. "He's now our Political Instructor and deputy director... that admirer of yours!"

Johanna made a face as if she didn't realize which admirer it was. *Did they really promote Aksel to deputy director?* she thought, and asked: "So who has now moved from stagehand to the Red Corner?"

"Aksel! He was always doing everything for you!" the baritone gestured with his cards. "You remember, he made you your very own steps for *Carmen* and he carried your train in the dress rehearsal of *Eugene Onegin* so it wouldn't get dirty."

Johanna just shook her head. "Carpenters are now leading the troops and the former leaders are in the forest."

I will not start singing their song, thought Johanna, *but I can pay a visit to admire the procession of vulgarity and the spelling mistakes on the posters.* Yet she didn't want to leave the ancient protective bosom of Kadriorg Castle Park. The symmetrically planned park here created an illusion of elegance and culture. As if someone were still playing baroque music in the castle and people were readying themselves to go to a ball wearing magnificent clothes. But Johanna knew that that didn't happen any more, even on the *Estonia* theatre stage. The costume department had received a direct hit. Instead of costumes there was only bomb-dust. *Maybe the ghosts of Carmen, Tosca, Madame Butterfly and Tatyana are still standing in the vacant lot, waiting?* Johanna shook her head. No longer could you hear the rustling of Carmen's dress. She had been with the theatre troupe on trench-digging work in 1941. Even then, in place of the costume designs, on the corridor walls they had put reproductions of Dzerzhinsky, Molotov and Daddy Stalin.

She didn't want a new daddy; her heart was still weeping for her old fatherland.

Johanna looked at the slightly worn Art Deco cards in her hand: "I can't make anything of this hand!"

"It won't work today, you see," shrugged the baritone.

"Bridge requires imagination, but during the bomb attack in 'forty-four even my imagination ran out," remarked the writer, and started counting up the score.

The baritone took a screwed-up paper from his jacket pocket: "Look at the leaflet I got today!"

The players' eyes lit up and the leaflet was passed from hand to hand. On it was printed:

"Estonians!

All over the world the movement against the Soviet plague is growing. We will not be left alone! Rescue is not far off!

The Liberation Committee."

The players' mood became tense and an imperceptible ray of light passed onto each of their faces.

"It must be from the Forest Brothers. Seems to be a potato-print," declared the artist enthusiastically on its composition.

"Good that the liberation movement isn't dead," offered Villem the writer. "Somehow it feels as if Churchill and Roosevelt have sold us down the river."

"No!" exclaimed the artist with a shake of the head. "According to the Atlantic Charter, we should get back our pre-war independence and borders." He jumped up from the table and continued indignantly: "The world community can't close its eyes to us!"

"Maybe those men in the forest get better information from radio broadcasts than we do," ventured the baritone.

How good that the men have got some life in them again, thought Johanna. She too felt a racing pulse. "The west won't abandon us," she interposed in the men's talk.

"We need help urgently, because every day someone is arrested," the artist declared irately. "Newcomers are being brought in to replace them, though, to mix with the population!"

"Yes, they're hoping that a mixed nation will have no identity, then it's easier to rule us," agreed the writer. "But they don't know us."

The hope had filled the room with an unprecedented electricity. The air had started moving and swept away even the smell of mothballs.

*

The man was sitting in his office and browsing through arrest and search orders sent to him by other departments. There were many of them, according to different sections. Some could expect execution, some imprisonment or recruitment. *Amazing that there are so many enemies of the people. What are they hoping for? Some charter or treaty? A change of dispensation? How do they not understand that the world has been redistributed. Every victor has received its own share. And Estonia is such a small share that no-one will start fighting over it again.*

He looked at the leaflet on his desk.

Liberation Committee? They certainly are idealists! They print leaflets in the forest and carve wooden stamps with pocket-knives. They collect information, they twiddle the dials of their secret radio receivers. Why? The west only needs them for subversion. The curtain has been drawn down unnoticed on them. Now the times are different, and one must move with the times.

He lit a cigarette and took a deep puff. Once again he read the leaflet on his desk and filed it under its letter with a form attached. Signatures from others had to be collected on it too. *A handful of men in the forest listening to western propaganda radio and thinking they're forming their own division! Where will they fight with that – what hillock or lake will they besiege? Behind the next hillock is great wide Russia. If you don't have a*

Pobeda 1946

*globe or a map, then at least take a look around. The Soviet Union
stretches from horizon to horizon. And outside it all the borders
are now closed. Let it be understood that their battle is over.*

He raised his eyes from the papers, meditatively. *Enemies
never begin a war again in the same place,* he thought. *They
definitely look for new lands to attack. In Asia, Africa ...* But for
him it was now mainly internal enemies he had to battle with.

Anna appeared at the door and interrupted his train of
thought.

"What will I do with your boy?" she asked. "Prisoners'
transport, like the others?"

He grinned, lapsed into thought, and fixed his blue eyes
on the girl.

"You know what," he decided: "check our railway sub-
division and find out who's working on the Moscow train. Send
him on a proper train, with a ticket for a reserved seat."

Anna raised her sharply lined eyebrows in surprise and
nodded.

After a pause, he continued, without taking his eyes off the
girl: "Nice boy, isn't he? We're raising the future cadres! Maybe
we'll make something of him!"

"Good," said Anna and vanished through the doorway.

Do I have a weak spot too? thought the man. *Lenin loved
children as well.*

*

Johanna opened the door wide. She still hadn't learned to
peep through the door. On the threshold stood her harassed
half-sister. Her eyes were burning and under her eyes the
shadows had grown even darker.

"He isn't at the children's home."

"Stop it now. You can't keep looking for him in children's
homes forever," said Johanna, taking her by the hand. "I'm

pleased that you yourself are still free to walk around." Johanna led her sister by the hand into the kitchen. "Come on, I'll make you a cup of hot tea."

"I only want a glass of cold water," she said, sinking into a chair in the corner of the kitchen. Now her strength was utterly exhausted.

Johanna took from the sideboard a tumbler apparently of cut glass, turned on the tap and let the water run. *She's doomed to die if she wanders around like that,* she thought. Now the cascade of water had passed through the pipework and turned cold. Johanna put the glass in the column of water and turned to her half-sister: "You've got to understand that if they find you, you'll have to start snooping or you'll go to Patarei prison." She stretched out her arm and passed the glass of water to her. "Drink the cool water. You've got to have a cool head."

She grabbed the glass and gulped greedily.

"I have to go and find that bastard," she said, sputtering water. "I know where he keeps the Pobeda."

"Bravo! And that's just what he's waiting for," Johanna said, theatrically clapping her hands. "Then you're in their hands. And after that he'll pass you round for the pleasure of his whole security regiment." She gave a significant pause for thought and raised her arms heavenward. "And then you'll refuse to work for them and you'll be shot. And what is the use of that for your vanished son?"

The woman pressed her lips together and looked at her wide-eyed. As if believing her and yet not wanting to. She sobbed.

Johanna sighed deeply and gazed out of the window. The lilacs were coming into bloom outside. Their blossoming was as fleeting as fireworks. All the more startling in the midst of a terrible time. Johanna took a deep breath, as she did before a decisive aria.

"I'll start to look for the boy myself. You, though, are going to sleep. And as long as you're heading for the prison, you can practise sleeping down in the cellar."

*

The Baltic Station in Tallinn still bore the scars of the war, and only part of the building had been renovated. There was a draught and a nervous hurry about it. There were those who were awaited and those who were being despatched. There were tears, germs, viruses and love that had stood the test of time. There were beggars, homeless people, bag-men and party functionaries in suits, who were hurrying to the train. Since Moscow had abolished the travel permit system on 13th April, a convoy of immigrants was heading for Estonia. Now everyone could move around within the Soviet Union, wherever they wished.

Firmly holding Anna's hand, the boy walked through the waiting-hall of the Baltic Station. He studied with interest the vast station building, where people with large suitcases and bags were bustling.

They moved forward to the platform, where people were hurrying to find their carriages, embracing, crying and waving from half-open train windows.

"The man fixed you up a seat on a good train," said Anna, bending her head down and boring her eyes into the boy's. "You're not going to run away again?"

The boy looked at her and shook his head.

"You listen to the conductor's instructions," continued Anna severely, "but if you disappear, you'll be caught and sent off like a prisoner."

"But if I don't like it there?" asked the boy.

"The man has big plans for you. If you want to be a hero, don't ask yourself if you like it or not. You'll simply be studying. All children have to go to school. You've been lucky, you can go to a special school – a Colony."

A station master in a red cap rushed past them. The conductors were standing by the doors, checking tickets.

They headed for carriage number 4, from which stepped

a large, stout conductress, wearing a uniform and with red-painted lips.

"Is this a carriage that goes to Moscow?" asked Anna.

"Yes. At Petseri we'll be uncoupled."

"I've brought you a boy who's travelling alone," said Anna, tugging at the boy's sleeve.

"Yes, I got the order," replied the conductor briskly.

"Announce it when he gets there. Keep an eye on him, please. He has a habit of running away," said Anna, pinching the boy's nose. Then she waved and headed off. The boy looked after her for a moment sadly and then turned to the broad-shouldered conductor.

"Can I have tea with sugar and a biscuit?" the boy asked.

"But of course, I've got the samovar boiling!" replied the conductor, pushing the boy aboard. "First we'll load the travelling citizens on, we'll get going and then we'll have tea." She shoved the boy ahead of her through the narrow corridor and stopped in front of a door. "This is my compartment." She took a key from her pocket and opened the door. A burst of hot air rushed out of it, and a real samovar appeared.

"Today we have *barankas* instead of biscuits," said the conductor, taking from a drawer with a flap a round *baranka* rusk on the end of a string.

"Are they sweet?" asked the boy.

"Very, with tea," said the lady. "You can have your *baranka* sooner if you sit down nicely now."

People were blocking the passageway, settling into their seats. The carriage had double bunks. The conductor showed the boy his seat by the window.

"You sit there now, later you'll climb up to sleep." The train jerked and set off. People outside the window started running alongside the train, waving.

Although the boy had nobody to wave to, he waved happily to everyone left behind.

*

The man sat in his dim office playing with the tip of his pen. His finger became inky and he reached for some blotting paper. He rubbed the pen-tip, covered with black liquid, as well. It was made in some fine factory. Almost hand-crafted. The girls were tittering behind the door. The secretary was not in a working mood either. Anna hardly ever was. Yet there was plenty to do. They had to infiltrate the Forest Brothers, provoke the writers in the capital, find vermin in the factories. And if there weren't any, they had to create them. Vigilance must not dissipate. Terror.

The man wriggled in his chair. Despite the velvet cover, it was hard. Everything felt hard, even his prick.

Invite Anna into the office, feel her silk stocking, slip your hand over her knee. Everything about her is slack, like her nature. Not like the boy's mother, who is still missing. Why am I thinking about her, wondered the man. *There are plenty of women, and most of them I could seduce sooner or later. Why can't that woman get out of my mind? Is it because she ran away? Took off faster than the others. Gone far? How far? No, that woman had the smell of a snowdrop. There was something cold and pure about her. She didn't bloom like lilacs or roses, ready straight away to drop her petals and wrap you madly in her scent. That woman didn't want seduction, she didn't have the sweetness and juiciness of an overripe strawberry. Not the syrupy quality either. She was a snowdrop, which blossoms modestly in spite of the cold weather. She had given birth to the son of an enemy of the people, concealed an enemy for several years and finally lost him. And yet she was ready to bloom again. If men were greedy, then women were incomprehensible in their immortal romance. Or were they subconsciously seeking protection, security in the world where it didn't exist? Hope is the last to die – how did that go?*

The man pulled open the lower drawer of his desk and took out the woman's file from among the binders. At the beginning there were just handwritten notes, without stamps or numbers. *Give the material to Anna to type? Then it will be registered and officially in order. Then to catch her, interrogate her, process her properly… No,* he decided, *I'll wait a couple more days.* It had already been reported to him that the woman had searched for her son in a children's home. Ultimately she would have to come here to look for her son. Her own nice clever son. By that time the boy would be far away. He imagined the boy on the train travelling through the Russian wastes, his eyes glowing from his new surroundings. And he would get a cold shower too. Not bad. Invigorating. Learning discipline. Becoming a man.

"Anyusha!" he cried.

A moment later Anna appeared at the door.

He peered at her for a moment, unleashing a mischievous expectation in Anna's eyes.

"If the boy's mother should turn up, send her straight to me," he said firmly.

Anna raised her eyebrows thoughtfully and coughed.

"I'll bear it in mind," she said disappointedly.

*

"How many times do I have to tell you: don't go out any more," Johanna told her sister.

"Never?" she asked.

"You'll go out when another regime comes in."

"When?" she sputtered.

During your lifetime, I hope, thought Johanna, eyeing her sister, and said: "Soon."

She was a bad liar, but good at telling white lies. The woman shook her head incredulously and started putting her shoes on.

She won't listen to me anyway, thought Johanna; *it doesn't matter what I say. I might as well say something optimistic, positive.* "I don't think the west will abandon us," said Johanna, fixing her eyes on her sister. "And Alan won't leave me here to vegetate. First he'll come through the radio waves, later he'll materialize. He'll simply step out of the radio set." Johanna's voice had moved into a major key. Her sister's face seemed to become even sadder.

The worst thing is baseless consolation, Johanna realized, as she grasped the toe of her sister's boot.

"Let me deal with it. I'll go for a chat with the political instructor at the theatre; he might have connections. You sit here. Rest, listen to music. Read books. Educate yourself."

"You mean I'm stupid." A pause cut the air. "I am, too. Falling into a trap," she said, turning her head away.

Johanna looked at her with sympathy. But the consolation was as grey as the mousy woman in front of her.

"No, now you're in hiding in your hole. But the traps are in front of the hole. Everywhere we're not looking."

She released her foot from Johanna's grip. She got up, put a scarf on her head and stepped out of the door.

Ahead of her lay yet another trip along the nocturnal streets. A search without a goal.

*

The boy looked with excitement out of the window at the scenes flashing by. These town slums he had never seen before from this angle. The rail embankment was higher than the town streets, and he could glimpse strange courtyards, even look into some strange lady's room where there were no curtains in front. From time to time his gaze was veiled by smoke from the locomotive, which glided in puffs past the window, as if white clouds had descended from the sky and were now racing with the wind. *The Pobeda man was right: it's*

103

nice to travel by train.

"Choo-choo-choo!" wheezed the engine, if you pressed your ear to the window.

"Chayku! Tea, hot tea!" shouted the conductress, walking astride the swaying train, clinking glasses of tea in her hand. Her fingers were placed through the iron handles of the glass bases, and so, like a centipede, she splayed out her limbs in every direction. In each hand three glasses of steamy tea were sloshing.

The boy's face lit up even more. "Me!" he cried in his resonant voice, adding: "Now with a biscuit, please!"

"Three roubles," teased the conductor, revealing her gleaming gold tooth. She put a glass of tea on the table by the window in front of him, but no more *barankas. Three roubles,* thought the boy. *Where do you get those?* He examined the flaming-nosed scrawny passenger opposite him, who was unrolling dried fish from a newspaper. The man tore off the head of one of them and tore the fish to pieces. Then he smacked his lips at the boy.

"Хочешь воблу? You want some vobla?"[*] he asked.

"Don't you have any biscuits?" asked the boy, smiling awkwardly.

"Возьми, возьми. Take, take," said the man, putting a little piece of fish in his hand. The boy put it in his mouth. It was hard and salty and smelt of sea-water, which had once got into his throat when he was swimming. He didn't dare to spit it out and let the fish swim around his mouth.

"Вкусно! Tasty!" sniggered the man, putting the next piece of vobla in his mouth. *Is this Russian food, which I will now have to eat?* thought the boy, not knowing that his luck was in; he was sucking on a real delicacy.

The train slowed down and almost came to a stop. Somewhere far away a red signal glowed. *Maybe we're letting an oncoming train through.* Suddenly a thud came from the roof. As if someone's feet were running over the ceiling of the carriage. *What animals can they be,* thought the boy. *Are there cats or dogs travelling with us? Or has a lynx jumped from a branch of a tree onto the train? Squirrels wouldn't make such a loud noise.* The footsteps came and went. Even the man with the vobla and the other passengers turned their eyes toward the roof. "Bag-boys," someone suggested.

Really, bag-boys again? thought the boy, recalling their quick steps. *The same ones I met on the street, or new ones?* Here in the train he felt safe and secure. He knew he was very lucky to be sitting in a warm carriage. Although he would have liked to be running with other boys up there on the roof, breathing in the coils of smoke that were blowing out of the engine's stack.

The train jerked. Choo-choo, shrieked the engine's stack, setting the iron wheels in motion. The engine let out a loud whistle and the footsteps on the roof stopped. The boy reasoned that the bag-boys would now be lying on their sides or backs, because they couldn't stand up any more; the wind would sweep them away. For the wheels were thumping ever faster on the rails and the distance between sleepers got ever shorter. The train shook as it gathered speed on the smooth tracks. The boy took a sip of sweet sugary tea and thought about the bag-boys on the roof. *That's how they get to ride on the train and no-one drives them away. The conductress is hardly likely to want to climb up on the roof of a moving train in the midst of this dark forest to grapple with the boys.*

Outside the window it was getting dark and the engine was puffing thicker and thicker clouds into the wind. The train was swinging in a pleasant rhythm, singing its choo-choo lullaby. The carriage was full of the hum of a foreign language and the window was getting damp from the passengers' breath. Here it was warmer and brighter than home or the children's home. The forest changed to fallow fields and burnt stubble. Ahead in a meadow, two thin cows and a nag were chewing. For them, too, a happy new time had come, when the grass was sprouting, no more shells were exploding and summer was getting ever closer.

The boy's eyelids sank down, his head jerked, and he saw a golden clearing, over which flew dragonflies with glittering wings. One of them flew up to the train window. It said: "If you get sad, think of us. Then you too will grow glittering wings and you can rise into the air and look at the world from on high." The dragonfly whirled with pleasure outside the window and chirruped: "High in the sky everything looks very beautiful. The world spins and glows like a top. You just have to be able to spin with it. You mustn't stop!"

*

Alan was sitting outside the door of the BBC Director of Music. He had brought Johanna's records with him from home.

In the morning he had rung the British Council and several musicians' agencies. He had found no help anywhere.

At the Council they just shrugged regretfully. There were no co-operation agreements, exchange stipends or any sort of cultural contacts with the former Baltic states.

"We should help the cultural workers in those countries," Alan had said, "because during the first Soviet occupation, in the course of one year, many musicians, writers and artists were banned and sent to camps in Siberia."

Unfortunately the Council has its own regulations in its work, it was amiably explained to Alan. Directives had to be followed for implementing cultural diplomacy. There were rules about how the British taxpayers' money should be spent. The Council's co-operation with Russia was being broken off, too, to say nothing of its so-called satellites.

The musicians' agencies complained about the bad economic situation. The war had ruined both the concert halls and the public's pockets. There was not enough work even for domestic musicians, to say nothing of foreign ones. The city was full of homeless musicians. "And what was the name of the singer you know? Johanna who? Sorry, don't remember, never heard of her –"

I'll have to do some publicity for Johanna, market her name, Alan had decided. *There are few singers who can perform both Puccini and Wagner expressively.*

Finally the door opened and he was invited inside. Alan stepped energetically over the threshold and smiled charmingly.

"Dear ladies, I've brought you some magnificent music for broadcasting," he said, brandishing Johanna's gramophone records.

"And do you have the licence to use them?" asked Mrs. Hughes sceptically.

"Yes, I have the musicians' consent," replied Alan almost convincingly. *A little white lie in the service of the cause,* he thought.

"But from the record company?" persisted the shrewd department employee. "Before we let anything out onto the air, we have to clear the rights."

"The record company no longer exists," declared Alan.

"Oh, that war," remarked Mrs. Hughes sympathetically. "I hope the company's successors didn't get hit by a bomb? Perhaps the rights have moved on?"

Alan shook his head sadly. "There's no record company and no legal successors. Everything's been blown away by the winds of war. The whole state, the whole country."

The ladies looked at Alan in bewilderment.

"Let's put it on and listen. Free music!" Alan enthused the musical ladies. "Let's save the BBC money."

Mrs. Hughes shook her head, but stretched out her hand.

*

"Before we hear a report on the Czechoslovakian elections, let's have a little musical interlude. Here to sing for you is a remarkable voice from the Estonia Opera House, which was unfortunately demolished in the war. It is still in ruins in Tallinn, with its beautiful Gothic architecture," Johanna heard Alan saying.

Bursting onto the airwaves came Johanna's voice – her sad appeal from *Madame Butterfly*. Johanna's heart stopped. Alan had not forgotten her. She had waited for a hidden secret code, but now her voice echoed openly on the radio from England. What a miracle, a gift from fate, thought Johanna, feeling choked with tears.

Johanna heard herself sing: *Un bel di, vedremo levarsi un fil di fumo**, and at once the Iron Curtain melted away.

And then, however, her heart was filled with worry again. She was singing on imperialist radio. What would happen when it was heard by the Central Committee of the Bolshevik Party, the KGB, the Kremlin in Moscow? With that thought she heard the tolling of funeral bells in her ear.

Would she be called now, or sent straight to a prison camp? Could she even sleep tonight? Or stay up to wait for the rumble of the Black Raven's engine, the squeak of its brakes in front of her door?

She couldn't sleep anyway, from excitement and love. *Why did Alan choose just that aria? Smoke on the horizon? Is his ship on its way here?*

Enchanted, Johanna pressed her ear to the radio speaker and felt its pulsations through the fabric covering.

For a moment, it would not even have been a shame to die. Her fading aria melted into Alan's voice.

They had met, after all.

*

On waking, the woman gazed at her half-sister, whose transformation had been complete. She looked again like a prima donna of the opera theatre. Her cheeks were rouged and one eye was covered by a gauze net from her hat.

"I have to pull myself together to prepare for negative emotions today," said Johanna, self-consciously adjusting a silk scarf around her neck.

"Think of it like the opera stage," recommended the woman. She felt embarrassed to need her elder sister's aid again. Her father had abandoned Johanna before her sister was born. Now her father was in Sweden and evidently angry that his daughters had not followed him. But his daughters were grown up and they had their own lives, which just now had run on the rocks. Maybe their father had been right, but they couldn't talk to him any more. Letters weren't getting through.

"For the sake of your boy Aida is now going over to the plunderers," announced Johanna in a theatrical voice, emphasizing the greatness of her own merit, and stepping majestically out of the door.

The woman stared after her with a worried look, mixed with a droplet of hope. A cloud of scent lingered after Johanna. The woman stood for a moment as it faded and shut the door. She had to wait and send her half-sister into battle. *Maybe my sister's contacts will be useful.*

Johanna had to step once again out of the protective walls of her home. She only did that in cases of extreme emergency, for in the lower town she only accumulated depression. Johanna surveyed the polluted Kadriorg Park. *What sort of gulf separated Peter the First and Catherine from today's Leninists and Stalinists? Power has been taken over and culture demolished. Everything was built in the worst possible taste.* Instead of a world in pastel shades had come garish colours and patterns,

109

where every colour competed with another and nothing fitted together. Where they were printed onto rags on the streets, called by the grand name of 'slogans', the shabbiness of the material made them dull, as if they had been smeared with dust and mud from the start. Johanna viewed a strip of cloth buffeted by the wind near her head, on which was daubed in red, in crude letters, "Under the banner of Lenin, led forward by Stalin – to the victory of Communism!" It seemed to Johanna that the writers of the slogans had lost all touch with reality. In compiling their five-year plan they had mixed up actuality and illusion. *They only need to produce vodka to sink their failed utopias. But there wasn't even enough vodka; even that smelled of turpentine and the necks of the bottles came off with the caps.*

Johanna hummed to herself: "The moon belongs to everyone –"

At the scaffolded theatre it was not easy to find the offices. The theatre office was temporarily placed on the stairs of the former entrance. *Am I now climbing voluntarily into a wolf's lair*, thought Johanna, knocking on the veneered door of the deputy director and opening it slightly without awaiting an answer.

Sitting under a portrait of Stalin was Aksel, a big shaggy man, his tie on crooked. He raised his eyes from a newspaper and they were radiant.

"Well, just look! I was only thinking of you today!"

Johanna smiled appealingly. "Really? I'm pleased to hear that –"

Aksel straightened his back and said with slight pathos: "I'm pleased that you're fighting for the building of our opera house." He paused slightly, and continued accusingly: "I've already had a call from the Party Central Committee complaining that hostile western radio is criticizing the slow rebuilding of our theatre." Aksel shrugged. "But it's being built by German prisoners of war, and those Fritzes are no longer in any hurry anywhere."

He fired a look at Johanna and grinned: "Good, of course,

that you're putting your shoulder to the wheel!"

Johanna shook her head. "Not my shoulder, my voice. How my old record came to be on English radio is a mystery." Johanna spread her hands theatrically. "My records are still being played. They still remember me –" *How quickly the jungle telegraph spreads,* thought Johanna with horror. *Like wildfire.*

"Of course they do. And we're glad you're here to refresh our memory," said Aksel with politeness or irony. That was an inexplicable nuance for Johanna.

"Am I in danger now?" asked Johanna suspiciously.

"We're all in danger always," replied Aksel. "I used to think that it was dangerous to move around stage scaffolding or hammer a nail in, but –" Aksel left the sentence incomplete. He fumbled in his pocket and offered Johanna a grade-one *Pobeda* Russian cigarette.

Johanna shook her head. "I thought you were out of danger now."

"Did you come to tell me that?" His former friendliness now seemed to have deserted Aksel.

"No, I came to ask you for help. My nephew has vanished… and I thought you might have contacts."

Aksel grinned bitterly and lit his cigarette.

"Come and sing for us," he said, furtively sizing up Johanna with his gaze. "We're having a little closed concert the day after tomorrow for a Party clique. The Minister of Security is invited. He's a great lover of physical education and culture." Aksel moved back and forth, putting out his match as he did so.

A match would go out by itself, because the air here contains no oxygen, thought Johanna, and asked, "And what would I have to sing?"

"You were always a divine Tatyana."

Farewell Brünnhilde, farewell Diva, thought Johanna, *welcome Tatyana… Damn brat of a boy!*

*

The man entered the library. He went up the stairs with their grubby carpet. The man hoped it would not leave marks on his shiny shoes. People had been wiping their dirty feet after spring rain. Ahead of him, beyond the doors, towered the shelves of books. They were half-empty, since a large number of creations of capitalist wordsmiths had vanished from the new shelves, and there had not been time enough to translate the works of Soviet penmen. On the shelf for Scientific Communism there were copious new volumes. No-one had even tried to touch them. He took from the shelf a volume of Lenin, smelling of the press, its pages still stuck together. *On a shelf like this, away from sight, it is hard to create a burning desire for the new ideology,* thought the man. Actually he knew that most of the texts were hard to read and boring. There was plenty of ideological rhetoric and repetitions like machine-gun fire. He had also found it hard to read them and repeatedly put them down, but the party required a knowledge of them. Those long wriggling chains of bullets had to explode in your head even in your dreams.

He stepped up to the woman working at the information desk, who looked like a lady, but he addressed her as a comrade. He drew her attention to the fact that Lenin's works were on an inner shelf where they were hard to find.

"Shall we turn the shelf around," asked the librarian, "or drag the shelf over by the door?" There was an unpleasant note of sarcasm in her voice.

He thought that this woman's name, too, should be noted down. They had already begun making new lists. Deportation of unsuitable elements had been halted because of the German occupation. It was now planned to continue it. Lists of the intelligentsia were being compiled, and the kulaks were being indexed too, so that settlement of the collective farms would go more smoothly. But Rome wasn't built in a day. The new society had to be built methodically, but not hurriedly.

"Have you read those works yourself?" he asked, turning on the charm. "Perhaps you could recommend to me the volume that discusses the unification of the world's proletariat?"

The librarian was a little confused and cast down her eyes. She started rummaging in her files.

"Unification of the world's proletariat is discussed here and there," she replied evasively.

"Every kind of unification is enjoyable. May I ask your name?" he said, driving her to even greater confusion.

"In what sense?"

"Every sense" – he paused and smiled fatuously, "I have to work on my dissertation and I need your help, Comrade –"

"Comrade Kokk," she replied dubiously.

Cock, not hen, he thought. He sized up the woman with an appreciative stare and decided: *I won't start a cock-fight with you, you're not so tempting. But we'll get you to lay in a new nest.* From his top pocket he took a notebook and wrote the woman's name in a column headed "FOR DEPORTATION".

The man was still concerned about the Englishman's correspondence with the boy's aunt. He had to break the code. Make himself familiar with the enemy's figures of speech.

"Comrade Kokk, I need a book with synopses of the librettos of operas."

Now the librarian was in complete confusion. "Operas about unification of the proletariat?"

He waved his hand wearily. "I'm thinking of a survey of proletarian classics, like Verdi's *Trovatore.*"

"We don't have information like that yet," said Mrs. Kokk, shaking her head. "There is one book about Italian operas."

He followed with interest the way Comrade Kokk climbed the ladder to find him the book on the highest shelf.

"We have only one Reading Room copy."

He summoned a smile to his face, took the book and headed for the reading room. Walking past the desks he surveyed what the readers were perusing. *Still those old* *books and pictorial magazines from the bourgeois period.* There wasn't anyone reading *Pravda* or *Rahva Hääl.*[*] At least in the bourgeois magazines some parts were censored and blacked out! Books required editing of the text or some of the pages to be ripped out.

Time would make its corrections. To everything.

*

When the boy woke up in his bunk on the train, the world had changed again. Outside the window there were hazy chimneys, endless dark grey factory walls, then again little wooden houses with sparkling blue window-frames. He liked the lively colour of the frames, distinct from all the grey tones. Alongside the train moved a motor-cycle with a side-car, as if racing with the boy's carriage. But the train was faster than the side-car, and the motor-cyclist in his goggles disappeared behind a fence. Then the train went over a viaduct, under which was an enormously wide street. The boy had never seen so many cars and buses before. There had not even been this many in the Pobeda man's garage, and here they were all moving around without crashing, like ants. Buses with antlers were moving on the streets, seeming to be attached to wires by ropes.

Great, thought the boy. The houses here were big, the streets endless and full of people. Everything seemed to be in one beautiful grey monotone, except the red flags and slogans. Here everything was different, exciting and a little frightening. People here wore quite different clothes, they walked around as if in old costumes.

The scene was again interrupted by fences and parallel railways with trains going in the same direction. One train came so near that you could look in its windows. Sitting in it was a girl with plaits and big floral rosettes. The boy waved to her. The girl noticed and waved back. Then she stuck her tongue out at him. But the plaited girl's train was faster and soon she was gone. The boy thought it would be nice to see all this with Mummy and Daddy or the Pobeda man. He was sorry that he alone saw all these inspiring scenes. He looked at the man with the vobla, who had started packing up his bag, and asked: "Are we nearly there?"

"*Москва-Москва*, Moscow-Moscow," said the man without raising his eyes from his suitcase.

The boy climbed down from the upper bunk, jumped into the corridor and went to find the conductress. The lady was wearing her uniform jacket and was fiddling with a big key with its end missing.

"You're in no hurry. You're going onto another train now. Let's let the citizen passengers off first, and then I'll put you on the next train."

"Is the next town even bigger?" asked the boy.

"Nothing is bigger than Moscow," mumbled the conductress, starting vigorously to release the bolts of the doors.

"Then first of all I'd like to ride on one of those buses with antlers here in town."

"You'll have time enough to wear antlers. You can ride a trolleybus some other time," she said angrily. "Go back and sit in your place like a proper passenger."

Maybe I should still get off with the others, thought the boy, turning his face to the window. But the houses rushing by had signs in Russian, and maybe everybody here spoke that incomprehensible language. *Perhaps it's better to stay with the conductress after all. If I find Daddy, we'll come back to Moscow,* he decided. Outside the window there now ran a ribbon of grey platform, on which porters with trolleys were waiting, and people coming to meet the train with colourful flowers wrapped in cellophane. The man with the vobla opened the window and sultry air rushed in, the smell of iron and axle grease, pleasantly tender and good.

"Citizen passengers," cried the conductress in a strong chesty voice, "we are about to arrive at Leningrad Station. Moskva, Leningradskiy vokzal. Priyekhali, pora vykhodit!"

*

The Gloria Palace cinema was full of visible and invisible epaulettes, new *nomenklatura* of the new era. Faces rushed past Johanna's eyes, like a gallery of Goya grotesques. She saw them and didn't see them. In her mind's eye she just had to picture her neighbour Eugene Onegin, to whom Tatyana was writing a letter. Actually she was singing and writing to Alan. It was easy to use the substitution technique of acting practice, because she actually had a correspondent. It was still exciting to be once again the beauty Tatyana, glowing with love, to sing Tchaikovsky to piano accompaniment on the narrow stage and project her voice into the hall, where there were poor acoustics, because this was a silent cinema built in the twenties.

"Пус-кай по-губ-ну я, но преж-де я в ос-ле-пи-тель-ной на-дежде, let me perish, but first in blinding hope" – Johanna sang Pushkin's deathless words.

Her voice did not roll out into the hall as it usually did. Was it because of the voice itself, or the old piano which the pianist's fingers were pounding furiously so that the keys touched the little hammers and they in turn drummed on the strings of the piano? Johanna did not lose her confidence. The more challengingly she viewed the audience, the more proudly she held her head. Johanna knew that the audience should not be begged, it should always be conquered. From her first step onto the stage, from her first look, turn of the head, they should be taken possession of, otherwise they won't respect you. They will look at you or they won't. They will listen or they won't. You must capture their attention completely, captivate them like a good-time girl, primary-school teacher or Sunday-school preacher. They will either believe you, follow your invitation, or just yawn.

Now it was Johanna's turn to conquer them.

Soviet officials, attention! KGB members! Silence! Now you'll look at me and listen!

"What an-xious wave of thought is sei-zing me, I drink the poi-son flu-id of de-sire –"

Even during the piano solo Johanna moved her shoulders slowly, made an unexpected sweep of the hand, so as not to dissipate the audience's attention.

Johanna's voice had gone out and reached its full range even in this narrow hall.

"Full of con-tempt you may strike the blow, po-wer over me is in your hands -"

Now she knew she had the audience in her grasp. For a moment the KGB men were sitting between her fingers and following the heaving of her bosom in the light of the projector. She was sending them her own wish: *I want to find the boy! I want to see Alan! I'm thirsting for freedom, for love! They belong to me.*

"May it come, what is des-tined for me, I take cou-rage and o-pen my soul to you," echoed Johanna's voice from seat to seat, from row to row, until it reached the last empty chairs, where two security men were sitting, each alone at either end of the row. Tatyana's plaintive trill reached even their conspiratorial ears: "Shame and fear o-ver-whelm me, but my ho-nour is his gua-ran-tee, I bold-ly en-trust my-self to it."

Then came the applause. Strong, unanimous. The new rulers did not stint when they were offered a good performance of a national classic. Johanna bowed slowly and deeply.

As she raised her head, she let her gaze roam over the rows of faces. *Unknown stern visages*, she thought. Then she also saw a scarcely perceptible satisfied nod from Aksel, the political instructor.

117

*

"May I introduce one of our prima donnas," Aksel presented Johanna to the head of state security, a major-general. Johanna smelt strong alcohol on the corpulent man standing in front of her. She summoned up her veiled gaze and her captivating smile.

"A wonderful Tatyana – how do you know the Russian soul so well?" The major-general bored into Johanna with his sharp little eyes.

"In love all souls are the same," replied Johanna, casting her eyes down for a moment. "It is so easy for me to sing of the pain of love, since my ward, my sister's little son, has vanished."

She lifted her worried eyes toward the major-general.

"Life inspires art," concluded the major-general, who paused and then displayed his charity. "When and where did your nephew disappear?"

*

The woman stared in amazement at her sister. God had granted charisma to Johanna. She was able to turn it on and off like a table-lamp. But when she turned it on, it shone with a strong neon glow.

Did she really manage to get support from the security general? Wasn't this just another empty promise, a senseless hope?

"I had them eating out of my hand – and they still liked me as Tatyana! In my age group I could soon be singing Queen of Spades," her sister told her with pride. "The general promised to investigate the boy's case personally. He said there's some new law, *postonavleniye,* whereby relatives can get temporary rights to raise a child." Johanna was still in her element, with her sails up. "I have another bit of news!"

From a drawer in her antique bureau she sought out an envelope with an address in Russian and drew out a letter in English.

"Look," she said. "Alan's handwriting, but posted from Moscow. Could this be a provocation?"

The woman inspected the letter with interest. It was written on good strong English paper and put in a shabby yellow Soviet envelope. "Seems genuine," she shrugged.

"I've been comparing the handwriting with his other letters to see if it's genuine," explained Johanna with the secretive excitement of a little girl. "And the letter doesn't seem to have been resealed. I recognize the traces of their steam-kettle and cheap glue! Alan is inviting me to Moscow to a secret rendezvous!"

Her sister's enthusiasm was infectious. And yet the woman couldn't raise more than a strained smile. She so wanted to empathize with her sister's joy at the imminent meeting, but her mind was paralysed by one and the same fixed idea: the boy. *What will happen if the major-general seeks out the boy, but she's in Moscow?* she thought. *I can't command her not to travel.*

"I have to reply to this address in Moscow. Do I dare to go?" asked Johanna anxiously, although her face reflected the flush of a first kiss. "Who will look after you for those days?"

"Oh, don't worry about me," countered the woman, "I might travel to Tartu."

"Really, at the moment no-one can help you here. Just wait for the major-general's answer. But isn't it dangerous to make a journey like that?" Johanna pondered. "You must put on my dark brown wig!"

"And I can put on your coat with the mink collar and your hat with the hair-net. Become a version of you."

The woman gazed at her older sister, who had always seemed alien to her. She took Johanna's hand in hers. They looked each other in the eyes and suddenly burst into uncontrolled laughter. They had never laughed together before. Not even in peacetime. Now they had come together in an invisible trench.

"Stalin and his ilk…what terrible times…" sighed Johanna. She drew breath and wiped a tear of laughter from her eye. "Yes, go to Tartu; in that university town there might still be a scrap of glory, of old culture… Maybe they haven't had time to destroy everything, paint everything red…".

A peculiar glow had again appeared on Johanna's face, one which only a dream could bestow. "Ah, I want to sit in Werner's café too and debate Baudelaire's poetry…".

Then Johanna took her sister by the waist and became a Joan of Arc. "Go and hide in the shrine of the spirit, as long as I do battle with the Red Army… I don't want to worry about you being here in the cellar."

The woman stood in her elder sister's embrace and thought with sadness about Chekhov. To Moscow! To Moscow! To Moscow! was written in clear letters on Johanna's flushed face. *But what has become of my child?* That fixed idea would not leave her alone.

*

The boy was standing naked in the dressing-room of the bath-house; his hair had been cut away to nothing. The orderly was checking him for insects. Bedbugs, fleas and lice were not welcome at this educational institution! The orderly was satisfied with the results of her check, and handed the boy his worn dark-blue trousers and a jacket that was a bit big, which had once been the same colour as the trousers.

This colony had been created with the support of the already disgraced founder of the secret police, Dzerzhinsky, and was based on the principles of the educator Makarenko. Repetition was the basis of the teaching here. Over and over again the children had to repeat the correct ideological slogans, beat their ideas into a fixed form. Discipline, control and vigilance were supposed to train them into new cadres. Every day one had to exceed the planned target. It was hard for little boys to do.

"But I'd like another jacket. This one is too big for me," said the boy in Estonian, extending his arms.

The orderly looked at him in amazement. The boy was gesticulating energetically, but the orderly didn't understand him. The boy opened up the front of his jacket, hopping around among the lockers.

"This is like a kite, you can fly with it," explained the boy.

"*Ничего*, it's nothing," answered the orderly, finally understanding the message of the boy's dance. "You'll grow into the jacket soon." She knew herself that the children were not getting enough to eat. They grew in height, but not in girth.

*

The civil defence instructor whistled and the group of boys ran to their places. It was time to start another war game. He divided the boys into two groups: our side and the fascists. Everyone wanted to be on our side and no-one a fascist. The latter group was made up of the youngest, the stupidest and the weakest. And the boy too.

When the fascists had got a good beating and the game was over, the instructor gave a political speech. He said several times a word that was familiar to the boy, *pobeda*, which only made the boy sigh as he examined his chafed hands. Finally they all had to chant in unison the slogan "*Коммунизм – то есть советская власть плюс электрификация всей страны,* Communism is the Soviet state plus the electrification of the whole country." When the lesson was over the boy would have liked to ask what the instructor had said about the Pobeda car, as everyone was running away.

Nothing can be that hard, thought the boy. *I don't need anyone's help.*

He didn't understand anything. He didn't know anyone. Everything went on in a foreign language. Everything was different. Only the trees outside the window were as green as in Estonia. Even the leaves were a little different, some even with beautiful white trunks.

The Pobeda man wanted me to learn Russian. Here I can really do that well, he repeated to himself.

But it was chilly.

As soon as homesickness overcame him and sadness invaded his soul, he pressed his tongue between his teeth and nibbled it. If you bite your tongue, tears won't come into your eyes. Those two things were very closely connected.

The boy hummed a Pioneers' parade marching song to himself. It had a happy, energetic melody. He had even learned the words by heart, though he didn't understand a single one of them. *What is there to understand? The main thing is to sing and speak,* the boy decided. *It's better not to understand it all. Then you can think for yourself. For instance, that this song is about the Pobeda.*

*

The signal for supper was a drum-roll. Onto the aluminium plates of the boys standing in a long line were put one potato, a little piece of fish and one piece of strange-coloured bread. Everyone sat at tables and started on their food quickly. In the time that it took for the boy to look around for a moment and gaze at the endlessly long tables, his potato disappeared. *Did it simply roll away?* When he turned his gaze on his neighbour, that boy looked at him in surprise and then appeared to hunt under the table. The boy looked under it too. There was nothing there. Now when he returned his eyes to his plate with a shrug, the piece of fish was gone too. This was no great disaster, as the food didn't seem appetizing anyway. Nevertheless the boy got up with his plate from the table to go and ask for another potato. But a whistle that pierced flesh and bone stopped him in his tracks with one leg in the air. The boy put his foot back on the floor and stopped in perplexity.

"Садись обратно на свое место! Get straight back to your seat!" commanded the orderly's admonitory voice. The boy raised his empty plate toward him and shook his head inquiringly. Now even the orderly understood something and bawled in Russian at the boys sitting next to him. There was a momentary exchange of words which the boy didn't understand.

Finally they all rose with a clatter from the table and headed for the dormitory, where there were several layers of bunks as in the train. The boy liked this. He climbed into his place in the upper bunk, closed his eyes and imagined that he was back in the train and that it was speeding along on silver rails. But the floor didn't jolt with the familiar rhythm of the wheels and the varying lights outside the window didn't reach his eyes through his lashes. Nor did the shadows run along the wall. Only his stomach rumbled. The boy opened his eyes again and stared in the darkness at the ceiling, from which plaster was crumbling. He wondered whether plaster might fall on him in the night. But that didn't seem terribly frightening, since his knees and elbows were aching from the war game. 'Our side' had jumped on top of the fascists and forced them onto all fours.

The boy felt tiredness throughout his body, but he wasn't able to fall asleep. Everything was new and different. It even smelt strange here, not like at home. He thought of his mother and father and would have liked to be back with them. He was ready to forgive his mother for taking him away from home. He was no longer angry with his father either, who had also left home. His parents sometimes behaved incomprehensibly.

Everyone who was bigger than him took no account of him. The boy decided to grow up quickly. *Tomorrow I'll ask for two potatoes for myself and I won't look away,* he decided.

*

The man was sitting opposite the major-general in the former Laidoner office,[*] looking at an old press and inkwell, made of some precious bone or imitation of it. Relics of the bourgeois world, left to rest as trophies on the desk of a KGB major-general. The major-general himself exuded a dignified gravity, as if reconciling himself reluctantly with the overweight of his own imposing body. Even his cheeks were plump, in contrast to his strong-willed stern eyes.

He raised his gaze to the man and stared at him for a moment, which seemed too long to the man.

"So you're swanning around in your new car. How does the Pobeda feel?"

"Good for operations," he replied briskly. "It gets attention and catches up with enemies of the people."

"Not too much!" growled the major-general. "We're not masters in this country quite yet."

He turned his gaze from the high windows to the medieval façades of Pikk Street and declared: "If we don't bring order to this buffer zone within the border area, how will we achieve the Communist world order?"

"Every day we're winning new friends, even among children and young people," the man responded to his pessimistic thought; "we're paving the way with each individual mind."

"Not all minds are suitable for the new society," replied the major-general pitilessly; "we have to get rid of dissenters. We have to clear the ground for new settlers, but your figures are poor."

"We're doing what we can, Comrade Major-General.

Increasing the speed."

"Yes, Major – increase it. Don't just cruise around in your new car," said the major-general, with a warning note, as if he had detected some joy-riding.

The major-general fixed his sharp gaze on the man again.

"At yesterday's concert, the Tatyana in *Onegin* attracted attention. A really spirited performance. But in the Party Central Committee they think that she's not opening up her soul to us, but to British intelligence." The major-general left the question hanging in the air.

Damn woman, thought the man about the boy's mother, *she still hasn't turned up.* "I'm dealing with the singer's correspondence, processing her half-sister, and I've achieved a confidential relationship with her nephew, through whom I even found his father, an enemy of the state, who supported the Tief government* and who was presumed dead," he reported optimistically.

"Very good. The singer feels the loss of her nephew. Where is he?"

The man felt that he was in a fix and summoned up a very concentrated expression. "I sent him to a colony in our system to study. The boy has a brilliant memory. Good prospects."

The major-general's face sank into a sulk and his jowls hung like pears.

"If you have a confidential contact behind enemy lines, why did you send him away?" asked the major-general, shaking his head indignantly. "Do we have so few boys to re-educate in colonies? All the streets and railway stations are full of homeless boys." He craned his neck forward confidently and gave a clear order: "Bring the boy back immediately according to the new decree which gives relatives temporary custody. The singer is to be informed about it."

"Yes, Comrade Major-General," said the man, losing his bold bearing for a moment.

"And no excesses with the singer, just surveillance," warned the officer, turning his head toward the door and casting a glum look at the death sentences on his desk. The audience was over.

The man got up more quickly than usual. He went to his own room and pulled the drawer of the filing cabinet open with a snap. Angrily he took out the woman's file and wrote: "Urgent! Pursuit!"

Now he had waited long enough.

He turned to the door and shouted to Anna: "I have something for you to type – also –" he paused – "connect me to that colony where we sent the boy."

"Are you missing him?" Anna's head, surprised, appeared around the door, as if hoping to detect some human feelings in the man.

"There is no missing in our work," replied the man, extinguishing the momentary glow in Anna's eyes.

*

The boy was marching in line and singing a marching song. He was phonetically imitating the words without knowing their meaning.

"*Lehko na serdse ot pesni vesyoloy,*" his voice rang out boldly amid the cacophony of other voices. *Am I still lifting my leg at the right time and high enough?* he wondered.

The trainer commanded: "*Раз… раз… раз… раз, два, три! Отряд стой!* One, one, one two three! Company, halt!" He turned to the boy and said: "*Хорошо поёшь! А ну-ка вставай в первый ряд!* You sing well! March, into the front row!" The boy didn't understand him and smiled awkwardly. His neighbour in the company shoved him out of the line. The boy stood perplexed. The trainer grabbed him by the shoulder and pushed him in front of the line. He shoved aside a dark-haired October child* and pressed the boy into line in his place. Then he straightened the boy's shoulders, stuck his chin out and commanded: *"Отряд, песню начинай! Company, start the song!"* The line started singing again and stamping on the spot. The boy joined in with a lusty voice. The trainer stood in front of him, conducting: *"Громче! Louder!"* He sang with all his might and felt proud that he had got into the front row of the company. Only the drummer and flagbearer were in front of him now. If he made a little more effort, they would soon let him carry the flag. *If only the Pobeda man could see me now, he'd be proud of me.*

Mixed in with his singing, though, was the sound of an orderly who entered the yard, booming something over their marching song.

"Отряд, стой! Company, halt!" The singing stopped abruptly. The orderly and the trainer were looking at the boy. His new neighbour in the ranks pushed him out of the line again.

"Давай, давай, тебя к телефону! Telephone for you!" commanded the orderly, taking the boy by the arm. *Telefonu,* repeated the boy, feeling his heart beating faster. *Who could it be: the man, his mother or his father?*

The boy pressed the damp black receiver to his ear.

"Well, bus driver, how did you like the train trip?" said a familiar voice in Estonian.

The boy's face spread into a broad smile. The man hadn't forgotten him!

"The train was great! But they've cut off my hair here, although I don't have lice," said the boy, all in a rush. "Now we're marching and singing in Russian. Are you coming here?"

"Don't you want to come back home on another train?"

The boy's eyes widened like locomotive wheels. "Yes, I do!" He pressed the receiver even closer to his ear.

"The Pobeda is missing you too," came crackling down the line.

Tears came into the boy's eyes, although his smile didn't leave his lips. "I miss it too. A lot."

"Then I'll arrange the trip for you. We'll meet soon."

Joy grew in the boy's breast; it swelled even beyond his oversize school shirt. The man was missing him! *Business between drivers. Not everyone understands that,* thought the boy with a gulp.

*

In Johanna's living-room the gramophone was playing and laughter could be heard. As if in a time-warp, the guests were once again dressed in splendid formal clothes, only in the fashions of former years. Johanna served the wine from a crystal carafe, because she didn't want to display the label of the bottle. It had been hard to prepare for the party, now that there was no more Imavere butter, Kawe coffee, English Lipton tea, French Pommery champagne, not even Latvian Ligatne toilet paper.

Johanna was wearing a dress decorated with ostrich feathers, and a diadem glittered in her hair. Only she knew the reason for the party. She was celebrating her imminent reunion with Alan and the possible return of her nephew. She had been allowed to write a claim to gain custody of the child. Let others share in her joy unknowingly! She had not dared to tell anyone a word about her secret meeting with Alan in Moscow, in case the security services hindered his journey, or she might be tailed. Her late-evening soirée was now in full swing, and her guests' vocal cords were resonating. But the subject had not changed.

"*Pravda* wrote in the spring of 1941 that Peter I made a big mistake by leaving the original Baltic peoples in the lands they inhabited," said Nikolay, a journalist on the defunct Russian-language newspaper *Severnoye Slovo*. He was known for his gift with words, and he liked to spread his erudition around. "But now they're arresting not only native Baltic people but all real and imagined opponents of the new power," continued

Nikolay. "Even the administration of Russian speakers' affairs has been declared anti-Soviet."

"Yes, even you, former Russians of Estonia, are among the weeds that have to be uprooted," said the writer, pouring Nikolay some champagne.

"But I, a Jew," asked the baritone – "I hardly managed to avoid the German concentration camp. Must I be prepared for the next one?"

Nikolay rolled his eyes helplessly: "We're all on the way to Siberia."

"Those times are over now. You're giving me the shivers," said the lady on Nikolay's arm, shaking her shoulders in her décolleté dress.

"They're not over. We are simply blind. We're letting ourselves buy promises that will never be fulfilled."

The baritone shook his head and added: "They say the security services are preparing a new list of cultural workers."

Cultural workers, thought Johanna. *What a fate befell the creative geniuses Meyerhold, Mandelshtam and Bulgakov! Now we hear that Akhmatova and Prokofiev are in disgrace. How the country treats its composers, writers, stage directors! No matter what nationality, no matter which town they're from…*

Carefully, Johanna stepped over the kitchen floor so that the carpet would not slip out of place, as it covered the hatch to the cellar where her half-sister was sitting – another defender of the democratic government of Estonia. *Should I put aside a slice of tart and a glass of sparkling wine for her too?* thought Johanna. She had bought them in exchange for her last pearls.

A little group had gathered around the artist. They all gasped as they listened to him talk, describing the atmosphere at home: "My studio is already full of new settlers, and the bedroom, where I now work, is reeking with the smell of oil paint and turpentine fumes," he said.

"That's why you're always in an elated mood these days!" the author interjected. "Maybe it's not so bad!"

"So let's enjoy a feast during a plague – fiddle while Rome

burns," declared the baritone, sitting down at the piano. He opened the lid of the keyboard and let his fingers run through the opening bars of 'Mickey at Sea'.

"I've just been commissioned to do an ode to the navy," said the author, and sang in a mellow voice: *"Now Mickey's leaving Pirita in a little white kayak".*

The baritone filled his nostrils with air and put on an ominous expression. *"Oh-oh, what's bobbing there on the waves – that horrid sea-monster, ah-ah-ah-aa- aa-aa-ah-aa –"* He laughed as he reached the bottom notes. *"Hiuli-hi, hiuli-hi,"* the Mickey choir of guests sang the refrain. *Here we are singing now,* thought Johanna, *because singing is better than crying. Today I want to be happy.*

Down in Johanna's cellar, the woman had time to think. To hear the clacking of heels overhead, the dance steps, the music, the vibration of the floorboards. To imagine the lights and the joyful glow of the party guests, who had been blocked off from her in the darkness of the cellar. Wartime had taught her that happy times last only a moment. They would have to end soon. Beloved friends could be sent to their deaths tomorrow, and a bomb attack could be expected at any moment. Nothing was lasting, except the hidden pain, which would never leave you.

She listened to a familiar melody coming through the hatch of the cellar and wondered who she would now like to dance with. Her own arrested husband? Yet what appeared before her eyes was the alluring glow of the other man, the grip of his hands and the touch of his skin. She screwed up her eyes, and with her palm wiped away that filthy image from her eyes and mind.

Were women at their most vulnerable when their men had left them? Abandoned? Had she felt lonely, or simply fallen for that handsome package of the opposite sex who unexpectedly roused her from sleep when he stepped in through her door? Was this simply a subconscious cry for help, a wish to forget? There were more questions than answers. She couldn't unmake her own mistakes.

Had she subconsciously anticipated the moment of separation from her husband? Had they only been bound together by common ideas, a child and a linked fate? The intimate moments between them had become fewer and fewer. It had taken just one apparent benefactor to appear in her life, with his flashing eyes, his box of chocolates and bunches of flowers, to knock her off her feet. Like those cut flowers, which were already dead without knowing it. Without admitting it to themselves, still fragrant, still attractive in their beauty.

So she hadn't understood it. She hadn't recognized the iron grip of the system in the strange man's touch, which wanted to rob her of family, child, her elementary humanity and freedom.

Suddenly she felt that it was good for her to be sitting alone in this cellar. She was not longing to get out, she wanted to hide away in here. She was no longer suited to the world above the floorboards. She just wanted to see the boy. That was all that was left to her. *Was even that left to her?*

*

The man was sitting once again in the reading room of the library. He saw with satisfaction that Comrade Kokk had disappeared. In her place sitting at the issue desk was a young girl, an Estonian from Russia who had recently arrived from Leningrad, traces of the blockade in her gaunt figure. The bookshelves had been rearranged, and the spines of Lenin's works glowed red in a place of honour in the foreground. Yet there were still no crowds in front of that shelf.

He surveyed the skinny new librarian for a moment and pondered how it would be to sleep with her. He liked women of all shapes and sizes. *Even thin girls like that can have their own charm. It's interesting to lie on top of them and bruise them.*

You get the impression you've broken them, but usually you haven't. They're easier to lift up and turn around. It's interesting to wake up sleeping beauties, too, to pump life into their dry bodies. Bodily juices. But for now the man would not go into that wasteland. He'd had enough experience of seducing bodies. Actually what he liked was seducing minds. Breaking spirits. Taming reason. Changing a person's beliefs. Recruiting disciples. He had always succeeded, but not with Snowdrops. Even when he had conquered a Snowdrop woman's body, he hadn't broken her mentality. *The die hadn't yet been cast,* he thought. But actually he had come here to the library for the sake of the woman's sister. *What a family of vermin,* he thought, shaking his head. *The principled ones are the worst.*

He was browsing through a book on Italian operas. It was haunted by old photographs, coloured theatre posters, costume designs, excerpts from the scores. Portraits of Verdi and Donizetti. More illustrations than contents. Here one could dip into only the frills of costumes and the finer details of make-up. Everything was grotesque and decadent. *The rampant juicy fruits of a dying society,* he thought.

"Pinkerton is preparing for a sea voyage to visit Cho-Cho-San" it had said in an earlier letter from the Englishman. Now in a fresh letter he had written more about Pinkerton's travel plans, that he would soon be heaving anchor and setting sail. The man opened up the index at the back of the book and ran his finger through it. P for Pinkerton. There was no Pinkerton, only Puccini. Then he turned the pages back to the letter C. And lo and behold! Cho-Cho-San, page forty-seven.

His fingers rapidly flipped the pages of the book. Teatro alla Scala staged *Madame Butterfly*! His eyes devoured the text with interest. Now he found Pinkerton as well. *Of course, Lieutenant Pinkerton, not just any ordinary Pinkerton. The Lieutenant is preparing for a voyage.* Ideas were rushing to and fro in his head. *Is this a case of a real landing, or is the spy being sent under the code name Pinkerton on an ordinary motor-boat to our shores? Or will he be dropped by parachute?*

He turned his attention back to the book: "...to return to Japan and visit his beloved Butterfly...". *Might there be a connection with Japan in all this? Unlikely. The atomic bombs have already done their job at Hiroshima and Nagasaki. That enemy has surrendered. Its song has been sung.*

He stopped to think: "...to visit Cho-Cho-San?" He knew of nobody with that code-name. It was a message to the singer. Is Cho-Cho-San Johanna? Now even his boss, the major-general, had been captivated by the singer's performance. This Cho-Cho-San was a dangerously fast operator...

He took out his notebook and wrote down: "Find out if Johanna L. has played the role of Cho-Cho-San." *Maybe the singer is also the contact? Is the courier arriving from London?* He had to trace the singer's movements and eavesdrop on her sister. The boy would have been summoned urgently by now too. *So grab him!*

He raised his eyes from the book to a little couple amusing themselves in the corner of the reading room. *What if all this is just the cooing of two lovebirds, senseless baby-talk? You never know*, thought the man – in his job, no-one was ever accused of too much vigilance.

*

The boy lay on the bed with iron springs and a deep hollow in the middle, in the colony's isolation room. He coiled up in the hollow even more, to keep warm. It had rained in the night and the room was clammy. Shivers ran down his back, and he was worried that if he was shaking like a leaf in this way, they wouldn't let him go home. He wanted to get out of bed and run or squat. Then he would get warm. Instead he was now curled up on his back, starting to swing his legs at marching pace under the covers. He sang along in a whisper to conserve his strength. So that the joyful rhythm would carry him forward.

I want, I want, I want, he sang.

I want to turn the steering-wheel and drive past.

I want to send out fumes and go whizzing past.

The boy's legs moved in the air faster and faster. The springs of the iron bed creaked in time to his singing.

It seemed to him that the Pobeda man was sitting beside him, and singing the same song. His song. The car was bouncing along to the same rhythm.

I want to wear black tyres and a beige coat.

I want to flick my winkers, peep-peep, to give a signal.

I want to be a car. Speedy, bouncy and splashy in the puddles.

In the boy's head the words started to form rhymes and get mixed up with other songs.

My name is Pobeda and merry is my mood.

When I get up some speed, then get out of my road!

Peep-peep, I'm always out in front, in front of the rest,

The man in front, he's in my way, I'll prove that I'm the best.

I'll fight for the comrades...

The door of the isolation room opened and the orderly stepped in, a thermometer in her hand. She pulled the sheet off the boy, because during the march the blanket had fallen off the bed, and stuck the thermometer under his armpit. The orderly gave the boy a stern look and then wrapped him again in a cocoon made of the sheet and blanket. Now it was hard for the boy to move.

He had a new worry. *What will happen if the silver streak in the thermometer rises too high?*

When the orderly left the room, he wriggled out of his cocoon and let the thermometer under his armpit fall onto the mattress. Now it would be good if Mummy's cold compress was put on his forehead and he could drink some raspberry tea to get his fever down quickly. *Wherever did Mummy go without me? Is she back at home now?* thought the boy. *How do you get a temperature down?* He thought of the snowfall and imagined himself sliding down rails on the icy roadway back home.

Cold shivers shook his shoulders again. Now I'm getting too cold again, felt the boy, hearing the chattering of his own teeth. *Best to put the thermometer back under there,* he thought, searching for it in the hollow of the bed. He had scarcely stuffed it under his armpit when the orderly came in again.

"Ну, покажи. Well, show me," - she put her hand on the boy's sweating chest. She lifted up the thermometer and narrowed her eyes. *"Нормально.* Normal," she nodded.

The boy nodded back, trying not to let his teeth chatter. He felt his whole body being invaded.

"Tomorrow you can go to roll-call," the orderly encouraged him.

He started to feel better. He knew that now he would definitely get well. The Pobeda and the man were waiting for him!

*

Johanna's morning began with visitors at the door. Johanna knew that in these new times, visitors didn't always bode well.

"Perhaps about the boy – really, so quickly?" asked her sister, her eyes burning with hope.

Johanna raised the hatch of the cellar in the kitchen.

"First of all you're going down there." Looking at her indecisive state, she urged her: "Quickly!"

Her sister descended the ladder and Johanna lowered the hatch on her vanishing head. Then she pulled the kitchen carpet swiftly over the hatch. The doorbell rang again.

"Coming! Patience!" she cried over her shoulder, moving toward the door. Passing the hall mirror she glimpsed her own image in the mirror. *I look like a bug from the cellar myself,* she thought. *Who can this uninvited guest be, so early in the morning?*

She straightened herself up and opened the door. There stood a stout woman with a confident expression in an ill-fitting outfit, and a colourless flunkey of a man.

"How can I help you?" asked Johanna amiably.

"We're from the housing administration. May we step in for a moment?" asked the woman. Without waiting for an answer she manoeuvred like a mother-ship past Johanna. The tugboat on her tail.

They don't seem to be deporters, thought Johanna, weighing up the situation. *Yet who knows their distinguished job-titles these days?*

"Please step inside." She indicated the living-room with her hand.

The housing administrator took an inquisitive look around the room and then opened her briefcase. She took a printed paper from it. "Johanna, daughter of Alfred?" she read from the typewritten sheet, and raised her eyes to Johanna.

"Yes, that's me."

"You are entered as 'single' here," she checked, and then demanded: "Who else lives here?"

Johanna considered how to reply. She couldn't tell the truth and it was dangerous to lie. She smiled hesitantly and said: "I'm waiting for my foster-child here. I've just made the application."

The housing administrator let her eyes roam around again and indicated the bedroom door: "How many rooms are there in this house?"

"Three including the living-room… but I'm an honoured cultural worker and I need a room to work at home."

The administrator took a pencil and made notes on the sheet.

"I know who you are," she stated drily. "You have too much surface area. Creative work can be done in the theatre as well."

As if she didn't know that the theatre is in ruins, thought Johanna. She smiled and assumed a persuasive tone: "We take new roles home with us. We do voice rehearsals, we learn the words, we analyse the libretto, we practise the scores…". She indicated the piano, breathed in and sang a scale in a powerful voice that resonated throughout the house. "Do-re-mi-fa-sol-la-ti-doooo…".

The security man was taken aback, but the administrator only raised her eyebrows in surprise.

"Well, you see – who could put up with the voice practice, apart from me?" asked Johanna with bravado.

"I'd be pleased to listen," said the administrator appreciatively.

Terrible, thought Johanna. *Does she want to move in as my neighbour?*

"Thank you, but my work demands concentration and peace."

"Our comrade refugees who lost their living space in the war are also looking for peace."

"My cacophonous practices are hard even on my nervous system," explained Johanna, letting out a loud trill in a high register.

The security man was in shock again and clutched at his ears.

"Never mind – war refugees are used to bombs exploding," stated the administrator. "Soviet people are used to difficult conditions."

Where are these war refugees coming from – the war was over long ago, thought Johanna. *This is colonialism in disguise.*

The administrator wrote something more in pencil in her notebook and looked beyond Johanna toward the bedroom door.

"Please understand me," Johanna tried to convince the lady in panic, "I need space to concentrate – artistic work has its difficulties too…".

"I do understand you," interrupted the lady in a resolute tone. "Otherwise I would be redirecting you to a smaller living area in Kopli." Without asking permission, she stepped into Johanna's bedroom and cast her calculating gaze over the walls and corners of the room. "A room like this has enough space for both rest and work."

"May I offer you a little cup of coffee?" Johanna changed her strategy to get a little closer to the lady.

"No, no, it's time for me to move on," said the administrative officer categorically, and started heading for the door. The security man followed in her shadow.

"Oh, I would have liked to show you my costumes," said Johanna ambiguously. The administrator lady looked Johanna up and down, and then looked at her own imposing bosom. Both women knew that all of Johanna's wardrobe would be a couple of sizes too small for the administrator.

"Come and have a look at a wonderful Japanese kimono." Johanna encouraged the lady toward the wardrobe. *If this were wrapped around her in a non-Japanese way, maybe it would just about fit,* thought Johanna, opening the wardrobe door. The smell of a better world came tumbling out. She grasped Cho-Cho-San's silk kimono, of which she had had a copy made, from the wardrobe, and held it out to the lady with a smile. "Try it on, this material is quite soft… there's enough room in it."

The administrator took the hem of the rustling kimono between her fingers and measured its breadth. The kimono glistened like an enormous sea in its silky blue lustre.

"Where would I go in this?" said the lady, with a chuckle in her voice.

"It's nice to slip it on in the mornings. Good for sitting around in. Natural silk is warm in winter and cool in summer."

The administrator shook her head.

"Please take it, as a souvenir," said Johanna; "you know how to appreciate music. It's from Puccini's opera *Madame Butterfly*. You should come to the theatre when the building rises from the ruins again."

The administrator turned her broad back to the security man, obscuring his line of sight, opened her briefcase and put Cho-Cho-San in it.

"Not much depends on me," she said quietly to Johanna,

looking her in the eye. "We don't have anywhere to put people. I'll do everything to see that you don't have to move out of your house... but you won't be left alone here."

"Even with a boy?"

"Even if you had ten children."

The woman clicked her briefcase shut and muttered to the security man: *"Пошли!* Let's go!"

She strode through the living-room and opened the street door without looking back.

"Please come again, we'll have a little cup of coffee together, we'll have a chat –" Johanna called after her.

"You'll be contacted," declared the administrator, opening the garden gate. Her companion followed her without closing the gate after him.

Horrible business, thought Johanna. She rushed into the kitchen, pulled the carpet away from the cellar hatch and pulled the hatch open.

A wave of coolness confronted her.

"You can't stay even here any more," said Johanna anxiously, extending her hand to her sister on the cellar steps.

"We're lost. We won't be left alone here any more."

The gates of the house were guarded on both sides by chestnut trees. Their buds were coming into flower. In a couple of months they would be forming green prickly balls, with which to attack intruders – if there was enough wind and patience. But neither they nor the woman who was emerging from their protective grasp had patience. She stepped out of their shade to the creaking of the gate, looked anxiously in both directions, as if searching for a visible or invisible enemy. Having established that the coast was clear, she stepped rapidly, suitcase in hand, toward the setting sun. The crepuscular trees and gardens

cast criss-cross shadows across her path, so that she did not
at once notice the moving contours of a bent, shadowy figure.
The shadow had been invisible, hidden in the greater shadows
of the wall of the neighbouring house, and was now moving
along behind her.

It was a man in a grey raincoat, though it had not rained for
a couple of days.

The woman's feet were walking in a stranger's shoes; she
wore a stranger's coat, to reach the territory of her own people.

But the journey there was long. She had to get, unobserved,
from among the chestnuts of Kadriorg into the shade of Tartu
Toomemäe. Actually the coat was not a stranger's; it belonged
to her half-sister, who had become ever closer to her in the
past few days. They had actually become real sisters, so she
was sorry they had to part.

She speeded up her steps in the alien shoes that were now
her own. She thought that perhaps her former world awaited
her ahead, bewitchingly, and for a while she would escape from
the searching, and the fear, that had become her everyday lot.
She had a strange presentiment that her sister would manage
to find the boy and do what she had not succeeded in doing.
For in other ways, too, her sister's pace had been lighter, her
flight higher.

The faster her steps moved, the more rapidly she was
followed by the silent shadow in rubber-soled shoes.

The road led first to the bus station. In front of the station
stood a row of red buses. She thought of how the boy loved red
buses. If he only knew that his mother was about to board one,
he would come out of hiding. The boy would take his mother
by the hand and they would climb together up the steps of the
red bus. Although it was a veritable sin to travel alone on a bus,
she stepped up to the cashier and bought a ticket.

She had to wait over an hour for the Tartu bus. She simply
had to blend in with the crowd of passengers. She had to be
part of the expressionless waiting mass. For in each of them
was hidden a hope that their eyes did not express. They were

all waiting to get somewhere.

The shadow crept among the standing crowd and moved into the long corridors of the bus station. Somewhere a door creaked and somewhere a voice was travelling along a telephone line.

*

Harrods was full of people, like the Christmas rush. Now there was a press of tourists, incomers and Londoners, simply wanting to see a better life. The counters showed the proud displays and the lights shimmered, as if there never had been a war. Alan wanted to buy Johanna something from London, from this, the most expensive store, as if the Harrods trademark would prove the strength of his feelings, the value of his love.

Actually this bachelor was a miser; at least he didn't like spending money – not even on himself. Did he think he wasn't worth it? No, rather it felt like senseless waste. He could get the same things more cheaply elsewhere. You couldn't carry a package bearing a Harrods label around everywhere; the value of something had to appear in the thing itself. Not in the packaging, not in the place, not in the cost of the purchase. In that sense Alan was an outright Marxist, and he might just as well have done his shopping under the vaulted ceilings of the GUM store in Moscow – except that there was nothing to buy there. Not, at least, for Johanna. They had walked through Harrods together before the war, and she had gazed with interest at the Egyptian motifs on the ceiling and walls. In those days she had been singing Aida and wearing the dark stage make-up of a Nubian princess. Egyptian soldiers had imprisoned Aida and thrust her into slavery. Here in Harrods he was back in Egypt again, but on this stage she could act as Cleopatra, whose majestic eyes surveyed her vain treasures. *What am I allowed to buy for you?* Alan had asked. *Nothing,*

141

darling, Johanna had replied, with feigned indifference. She was carrying everything she needed with her, within herself, like Schopenhauer.

So whatever gift shall I buy her? Alan was thinking, letting his eyes roam over the expanse of the women's clothing department. He cautiously fingered a silk scarf. A turquoise scarf picked out with gold filigree attracted his gaze. A singer had to look after her voice, and Johanna wore a scarf even in summer. Alan asked the price of the scarf of the trim young shopgirl, who self-consciously pouted as she uttered the excessive noughts. *Stiff prices,* thought Alan, reluctantly drawing his wallet from his jacket pocket. But then he recalled Simon's admonition: if you have women's clothes in your suitcase, you will be asked by Soviet customs who they are for. Alan quickly withdrew his hand from the soft, slippery silk, as if the smooth coldness of the material had singed him. Better to take something that might be for personal use. *Perhaps a gramophone record?* But where would a tourist play it on his travels? There were no gramophones in hotel rooms, not even in America.

Perhaps a gentleman might get through a book on his travels? Again the bass voice of Simon admonished him: they leaf through books very carefully, looking for anti-Soviet literature. Since most of them don't understand English, they might simply confiscate a book.

Such intolerance of everything alien and unknown, mused Alan. The Soviet Union had once promised its Western allies that it would form coalition governments in all the countries in its zone, tolerating diversity of ideas. Now, though, dissidents were disappearing everywhere; only one ideology was favoured in Eastern Europe. Alan turned his steps toward the grocery department. *Surely I could take chocolate or shortbread with me? Or are even they signs of imperialist taste these days?* Among the dazzling Harrods counters, Alan looked around and felt he was losing his way in the gilded expanses. He felt a flush and a slight giddiness coming on.

"A box of chocolates, please," he said to the permanently smiling attendant, pointing to the dark red box with its nocturnal view of Harrods. On the lid glistened the façade of the store with its great glowing window-dressing, where one could make out mannequins in fashionable dresses which were no longer available in Estonia. *Would Johanna like it, or would it only make her sad?* Alan could not answer that question now. He wanted to get out into the fresh air. His temples were throbbing. He still had to go to a solicitor to get his invitation certified. *Was that piece of paper perhaps a better gift for Johanna? Or just another empty gesture?* That was for the Soviet officials, the authorities, to decide – yesterday's friendly allies, today's enemies. Life was strange.

*

The closet in which she had been placed was less than half a metre wide and even shallower from front to back. At first she had stood up, listening to a man's heavy breathing. Time had passed very quickly, and then stopped altogether. Only when plaintive muffled screams had emerged from somewhere beside her – "I can't breathe any more! Open the door!" – had time started to move again for her. *How long will I be trapped in this cupboard?* she thought.

"There's no air in here!" screamed the woman's voice again. The tramp of the guard's approaching boots could be heard, but not the creaking of the door. *Or did the doors have well-oiled hinges? Unlikely,* she thought, and cried out: "Open the cupboard door! What are you waiting for?"

Someone else was starting to rap on the door.

A heavy thump could be heard, as if someone had fallen against a door. "Stop knocking!" resounded the rough voice of the guard, "or do you want to get knocked yourself?" The knocks stopped; only the low wailing of the neighbouring woman continued as a writhing echo.

She felt menaced by an oncoming panic attack. *Warm air rises,* she tried to think logically, *so I should try to squat down.* She slid her back slowly down the closet door, but her hunched knees hindered her movement.

Not even the gravitation of the earth will help me. She tried to turn around in the cupboard and get down to the other corner. Now she managed to hunch her knees hard against her chest and start to slide slowly down the side wall. *Edgeways or flatways – which way did Kalevipoeg's boards go when he was fighting with the sorcerers of Lake Peipsi?* * she thought, for something to think about. It was important to keep her brain working.

Free downward movement continued slowly, until her bottom felt a cool stone floor under her. This brought a moment's relief, although the pressure of her knees on her chest seemed to reduce her lung capacity. *It's better to breathe shallowly,* she reasoned. *Then the air will last longer.* Even so, she wasn't sure of this, and at school she had been weak at physics. *At school* – she repeated the phrase nostalgically; that was all so long ago. In the autumn it would be the boy's turn to go to school, but what could they teach him there? She had heard of the mass dismissals of schoolteachers. The new teachers, however, just had primary-school education themselves. You only had to know a couple of dozen words and praise Daddy Stalin. She and her husband hadn't talked to the boy about politics, so as not to shorten his carefree childhood. Maybe that was a mistake. Maybe they should have spoken freely about it, to get the boy prepared for imminent reality. But nobody even knew how long this would last. Realities and ideologies had changed rapidly in the war years. They had hoped that this absurd reality would be temporary. Were they mistaken?

She took a deep breath, although she seemed unable to get air into her lungs. It was hard to breathe without oxygen. Her breathing turned into panting. She had become a fish, gulping air. *But no-one hears the cries of fish,* she thought. *They simply vanish and die.* She lifted her hand and started drumming on the cupboard door.

"Call the man who drives the Pobeda!" she screamed.

*

She was shoved in through the door.

"Where is my boy?" she asked the man, staring fixedly at him.

The man looked deep into her eyes. "Your son has always found his way home, but you haven't."

"Where are you keeping him?"

"He's at a boarding school. He's joining the first grade. The boy's clever and smart; he'll grow into a fine man."

Her shoulders relaxed from the tension and started to shake, as if a high tension had been turned off and an electrocuted body was freed from stress, still trembling from the inertia. "A man like you?" she asked, through her tears.

"He's inherited his mother's intelligence and beauty. Her will-power. He has to be guided." He stepped closer to her and clasped her cautiously to his chest. "Why are you breaking up our relationship? We had it so good, the three of us."

She stiffened and stopped crying. "Let me go!" She turned her reddened eyes on him. Even now a dangerous magnetism could be felt between them. Even after all the horrors of this house, the woman was spellbound, as when a poor rat sees a cobra about to strike. Where did it come from, this physical tension between two such different souls, in spite of their two clashing worlds? What were they supposed to do? They didn't know. For neither could step out of their own posture or give up their own principles. The man, too, felt troubled by this knowledge, but he tried to control himself. It was not a general or an important guest standing in front of him, only

145

a mere prisoner. Yet this woman was somehow able to arouse him and take him out of himself, disturb his equanimity. He took a long look at her and shook his head.

"It's too late now. An investigation of your case has begun. You're a part of the system here." He paused. "The question is – which part? On which side? Apparently free on the street – or here in this cellar, this closet… It's still in your power to make the right decision."

*

Quandyk, the Bringer of Joy, looked at his wife and little Botakoz. *Aren't they cold again,* he thought. Here everything was so different. The clouds, the people, the houses. In the back of the truck there was no protection from the wind. The wind blew on the steppes too, but this was icy, damp, marrow-curdling. *You seem to be sitting in cold water all the time and a warming fire you can only dream of. In this country the Almighty distributed the cold rain with a generous hand, more than the plants needed.*

Quandyk didn't know whether he had made the right decision in leaving his land and village. But hunger and poverty had gnawed at his soul like his wife's plaintive singing. Would she start singing here at all? Even plaintively, sadly? The journey had been tiring. Sleeplessness was draining. Botakoz only cried and coughed. They had been promised a better life, work, money and an apartment. They were coming to build a secret site, numbered factory V-8817. When it was ready, they would build a kindergarten for their children and a recreation park for the whole family, by the sea, a sandy beach. So they had been told. *If God grants it and Comrade Stalin allows it,* thought Quandyk, narrowing his eyes to the cold sun.

The truck turned into a narrow street, lined by wooden houses and their front gardens. Around them was a planted forest and lawn. Only the trees didn't bear fruit, there were no apricots or pomegranates. It was called by the name 'park'. *Why were those trees planted at all?* The truck's brakes creaked and the wheels stopped in front of a little pale green house.

"We're here," said the escort, and the administrator also climbed out of the cab. The Bringer of Joy looked anxiously around the little house on the hillside in the shade of large leafy trees. *The sun won't shine here,* he thought. *The trees should be cut down, sand put in front of the house.* Everything here was different to back home. There was no space. Beauty here was useless. *Will we get used to it?* wondered Quandyk anxiously. *Can we grow things here, make it our own?*

The rear hatch of the truck was opened and pushed down. His wife adjusted her headscarf and got up curiously. Little Botakoz in her lap started whimpering again.

Johanna had appeared at the front door and couldn't believe her eyes. She had rung the political instructor at the theatre and hoped that this blow would not strike her. But the issue of immigrants seemed to be out of the hands of all circles of power. This issue was not within anyone's competence. They kept being brought in and housed.

"I've brought you a proper family," said the housing administrator in a low voice. "People from Central Asia are modest and undemanding." Failing to notice gratitude in Johanna's glance, she added: "If you could only see all the people who are arriving… You won't have to give up the living-room for them. We'll put them in the bedroom."

Johanna looked with dismay at the exotic trio and their bundles tied with string, which the driver started to hurl down from the truck. The father was alarmed by the thudding and stretched out his arms toward the box to catch the bundles. *"Осторожно, там чайник, фарфор!* Careful, there's a teapot, porcelain!" "I hope they're moving in here temporarily?" Johanna appealed to the administrator.

"Just for the time being," muttered the administrator. "Until the new suburbs are ready. The city government has already drawn up its five-year plan."

The administrator led the woman with her infant over the threshold. Johanna stepped away from the door. *One more suckling, as well as the boy.* After them the large bundles were hauled in, taking up most of the living-room floor.

Johanna noticed the newcomers' bashful looks, as they surveyed the room she had furnished with such care and love. *They don't appreciate antiques, they'll probably be looking for a place for the large rolled-up carpet,* thought Johanna anxiously. *Where will I put my own furniture to make room for them?* Johanna understood that the wave of moves in her life had not ended. Her sister and her boy had opened the door, and more and more visitors were coming. Some were sent away, others were brought in their place. They were taken, brought, and sent. What sort of manoeuvres did Fortuna, the chess-master of fate, still have in store for Johanna? She had already bought a ticket for the Moscow train. *Perhaps I should move in with Alan? Where else?* Now the new society had burst in through her closed door. Life in the citadel was over.

When somebody missed a line in a performance, you had to carry on over the error, improvise, so that the scene didn't crumble to fragments. Johanna tried to pull herself together.

"Perhaps we should have a little cup of tea to begin with?" she offered, putting on her best smile and trying to put on a good face in a bad situation.

Tea seemed to be a magic word for her uninvited guests from the distant steppes of Central Asia.

*

Choo-choo-choo, went the steam locomotive once again. This time the boy was travelling in an especially exciting train. It was a cattle-wagon, but now, unfortunately, there were no animals in it. He would have very much liked to travel with some animal, patting it or curling up at night beside it.

His mother had once taken him to the Kadriorg Zoo, and that had been one of the best days of his life. All the innocent robbers – the bears, wolves, and lions – were lovely, and the monkeys, hanging off the bars of their cages, were the funniest.

There were other boys and girls in the wagon. Some had been travelling for more than a week. Now they were all going from Siberia and the Urals to their aunts and uncles in Estonia. Since their parents had died there.

There was only one window in the wagon and that was covered with a grille. When it got dark in the evening, and no light shone in through the little window, they told each other horror stories, to give themselves goosepimples. Next to the boy, on a bunk, lay a skinny boy from Urzhum. He chatted to the boy about how he had been stealing potatoes and how his father and mother had finally died of hunger. Now the boy understood that he'd been lucky in life. He'd never seen actual starvation. Not even in the war.

The wagon was large and spacious. In the middle of it was a common toilet without walls, from which you could see the rails flashing past. A drain hole, where the boys could check their precision, but the girls went to quietly crouch.

A girl with long red hair, looking out of the window, cried "*Smotrite*, how many horse!" She had forgotten her Estonian. But it was good to talk even to her, because the boy now understood more and more Russian. '*Smotrite*' meant 'look now!' Everyone gathered like cattle around the window. Indeed the whole field by the edge of the window was full of sheep. Behind them ran a dog and a shepherd with a crook.

"If some sheep ran down to the train now, maybe we could get roast lamb," said the boy from Urzhum, smacking his lips. But the boy didn't want any of those sheep to die under the train's wheels. They were so pretty with their bleating heads and bright shorn bodies.

The train slowed down and gave a whistle. *For the sheep?* thought the boy. *Perhaps the train will even stop and load the sheep on to keep us company here in the animal wagon?* But the train didn't stop. It merely jerked a couple of times and carried on.

The boy imagined himself sitting next to the Pobeda man and steering it through the streets of Tallinn. Soon he would see Mummy again, and by now Daddy might have come home. His heart pained him that he didn't have a single gift to bring. Only the many sounds and images that teemed in his ears and eyes. He would have liked to bring big marigolds and a corncob, but the departure had been hurried. At least he had got his own clothes back. And socks with holes, where the toe poked out even more.

The boy hummed the home song of the colony: "*Sluzhu, sluzhu, sluzhu Sovetskomu Soyuzu* – I serve, I serve, I serve the Soviet Union," and let the rhythmic rumbling of the train wheels rock him to sleep.

The sun shone golden and the horse moved forward rapidly under the boy. Music was playing, a joyful march. The boy noticed he was riding over and over again past the same piece of forest, the same field. They seemed to be painted onto a large canvas. Was he riding on a circuit? Nor was this an ordinary horse, it seemed to be made of wood. It belonged to a sort of herd or a system and was tethered to other wooden horses. Sitting on them were the man, Mummy, Daddy and Aunt Johanna. It was nice to ride ever forward around the circuit with the repeated refrain of the music, swinging up and down. Then the horses slowed their pace and almost stopped. But before the boy had time to jump off, the horse started running backwards. Still on the circuit. All the other horses were now galloping backwards. They ran past the same stretch of forest, the same field, in the other direction. The sunlight dimmed. A cloud had appeared before it, from which rain began to fall. The boy and the horses got wet. The boy felt cold. He took a firmer hold of the wooden horse's bridle and yanked it, but the horse didn't feel anything, just kept going backwards and swinging up and down. The music playing was the same old refrain, which started to bother him. The sky got even darker and instead of rain it started to snow. The horses took no notice of the snowfall. They kept rushing backwards in the same rhythm, without noticing that the snow was covering them more and more. They couldn't stop, because they had to run in time with the music. But the music didn't stop.

The boy opened his eyes. The train had stopped at a station somewhere, and the same music was sounding on a megaphone from the platform. It had been switched on for the morning, like an alarm. The boy was glad that he no longer had to ride that circuit.

*

Splat! A hurrying passer-by spat on the tip of Johanna's shoe as she stepped down from the Moscow train.

That wasn't a pigeon, observed Johanna, noticing plenty of spit-blotches on the platform. *Good that I didn't put on my suede shoes. Ordinary leather can be cleaned more easily.*

Johanna looked around curiously and a porter with a wheelbarrow noticed her immediately. "Taxi," said Johanna to him, somehow dubious as she handed him her little suitcase about whether she would ever see it again. The porter went a couple of hurried steps ahead of her and then stopped again, to load someone else's suitcase onto his barrow. *Collectivism,* thought Johanna. Finally a whole group of travellers was scampering behind the porter's fully loaded barrow, all of them accelerating so as not to be left behind by the speeding barrow. Johanna was walking as fast as she could in her high heels, taking in new images and sensations. *Every town has its own smell,* she discerned; *here it smells of cheap tobacco and factory smoke.* Her eyes were caught by baggy trousers and colourful floral chintz dresses. People were swarming and scurrying like ants. Nobody gave way to anyone else or kept their distance.

"Sorry," said Johanna to a man who had bumped her. *He wants to simply step through me.* She had never in her life seen as many people as were waiting at once on the square in front of this station. *Aren't there enough trains or aren't there tickets?*

Her way was blocked by a little trolley moving on bearings, on which sat a legless war invalid. His hands pushed his wheeled platform forward rapidly and skilfully. Then he stopped abruptly in front of Johanna and stretched out his arm. *Poor thing,* thought Johanna; *good that he has gloves on.* Their colour had become an indistinct dark grey. *To each according to his abilities or according to his needs, how did the slogan go?* Johanna opened her handbag and gave him a rouble. She tried not to let the baggage barrow out of her sight.

"Don't keep your handbag open," a friendly older woman warned her; "there are plenty of thieves here!"

Johanna thanked her and grasped her handbag closer under her arm. Before her opened a square bounded by three railway halls. Lining it was a long queue of taxis. Although every sort of vehicle was rolling past, none of them stopped.

Finally a taxi with a checkerboard pattern approached, which did stop at the queue. The vehicle was filled with cases and people. *A taxi is public transport too,* observed Johanna with interest, *so the queue really does move faster.* The porter unloaded Johanna's suitcase and looked inquiringly at her. She had to cautiously open her handbag again, hiding its contents from the greedy eyes of possible pickpockets.

"Excuse me, where are you going? Maybe we can share a taxi?" a man with a suitcase in the taxi queue behind her asked Johanna. Johanna eyed the aged man suspiciously. Yet the stranger's friendly look inspired a certain trust.

Johanna took Alan's envelope from her handbag and recited the sender's address: "Sivtsev Vrazhek pereulok".

"Arbat," the man nodded, tugging his bags; "my journey takes me past there too. Did you know that Bulgakov lived there?"

Devils again, this time from Bulgakov, thought Johanna, shaking her head. "I've heard about him," she said.

"Then it'll be interesting for you to walk around there … on the literary circuit," commented the man, tugging on his bags.

The queue had moved forward a millimetre and sizeable ladies were pushing the man from behind.

"Where are you from?" Johanna's new taxi companion asked her curiously.

"Tallinn," she answered reluctantly.

"Ah, Pribaltika!" said the man approvingly. "Our new western border."

The man took a Thermos flask from his bag and twisted the cap off it.

"Want some coffee?" he asked generously, and poured some brown liquid into the cap for Johanna.

Johanna eyed the cap suspiciously, but still sipped a mouthful of coffee, more accurately chicory soup, containing no caffeine. "Here they make headache pills from caffeine," explained the man. "There are plenty of headaches, though."

"Why?" asked Johanna. The man just shook his head. *Because there are invisible dangers in this city that everybody fears?* Johanna had also known fear in Tallinn – of the Nazis and the Soviets too. Here in the Soviet capital, fear seemed to be part of the oxygen. You could breathe it in and out, but it didn't leave your bloodstream.

So this is Moscow, thought Johanna, looking around. Three large railway halls bounded the open square. One big trinity through which an endless mass of incomers flowed.

They had got to the front of the taxi queue. An old, long-bodied taxi soon appeared, with a belt of checkerboard below the windows.

*

Alan had come into a new world. Strange, exciting, impenetrable. Here the laws were different, the principles, the customs. The buses were red, the flags were red, *but the people?*

They looked at Alan out of the corners of their eyes and seemed to take no notice of him at all. Or weren't they allowed to? They had different clothes, they were rushing somewhere, pushing each other from behind. It was intimidatingly exciting to walk among them, moving along with the pulsing crowd, his only point of support the consul from the Embassy, a lanky tallish man with ever-laughing eyes. Even his English gait was not like a Muscovite's. Nor did he give way respectfully to others or beg their pardon.

"Sorry," said Alan to a woman who was rushing across his bows. The woman was carrying a string bag with the holes woven together, and inside it her products on display to the world. A cabbage, a bottle of milk and an angular black hunk of bread. It was all appetizing, as was this female citizen rushing toward the future with big fat lips, but she didn't stop or react to Alan's 'sorry'. Alan's utterance was dissipated among the hooting symphony of sirens and was of no importance. Nor were the woman, Alan himself or even the Embassy's consul. The mass of people rushed forward; they too blended into the identical grey torrent and were simply swallowed up.

Alan anticipated his imminent meeting with the woman he adored. The alluring, captivating and always elegant Johanna. Had the lady of his dreams remained the same or changed into an alien under the merciless pressure of the oppressive times? *Will our eyes recognize each other, will our hearts and bodies meet?* wondered Alan, feeling a peculiar excitement. Or rather a natural anxiety of anticipation. *We haven't seen each other for so long.* He mentally excused his rapidly thumping heart under his coat. He had seen Johanna as herself and as others, as a blonde, brunette and redhead. Even as a black-skinned Aida. He had seen her both on stage under the spotlights and in the discreet darkness of a badly-lit hotel room. No light had dimmed her glow, no wig had framed her face badly, for that beauty was programmed for Alan's eyes.

The consul looked back over his shoulder for a moment. His gaze slid over Alan, keeping pace a metre behind him, and looked for someone else. Might there be someone hidden, tailing them?

"We can't go in the Embassy car right to the door of the journalists' house," he explained to Alan. "One of our staff got a beating in the street from a 'casual drinker' straight after visiting a local Russian writer."

"What about diplomatic immunity?" wondered Alan.

"Diplomatic immunity is only apparent. This has happened to staff of other Embassies when they look for local contacts."

"Maybe it would be better to meet at the Embassy then?" asked Alan.

"We're well guarded. The militia check everyone's documents and local visitors who haven't been sent officially on Embassy business are quickly taken away. Before we get a chance to make inquiries. You'd only get in the door with me." The consul slowed his pace. "We're here. You have to remember that there are eyes and ears everywhere."

The flow of people along the boulevard carried them to the stone steps of a grimy beige-plastered house. The dark brown door to a staircase opened with a creak under the consul's hand, and a stench of damp and urine assailed Alan's nose. Inside the house looked worse than outside, or the cleanliness of the corridor wasn't very important to the residents. The consul stopped at the door of an apartment, with doorbells in four different colours down the side of the frame. He hesitated for a moment and then pressed number three decisively. A loud ring was heard from behind the door. Like in a theatre. The interval would soon be over and the curtain would rise.

Someone's heavy steps could be heard. The door opened

cautiously and a friendly man's face with alert eyes peered into the dark expanse. On recognizing the Embassy consul, a hearty smile lit it up.

"Welcome – come inside," he said with enthusiasm, firmly shaking the consul's and Alan's hands.

He led them down a long corridor into the depths. The door of someone else's room was half-opened curiously behind them and then closed hurriedly, leaving just a whiff of cabbage-soup smell. The friendly man led them to his own room at the end of the dark corridor.

Let there be light, said God. The silhouette of Johanna was revealed in the frame of a high window. She stood erect, her face toward Alan. It had not changed. In it glowed a welcoming smile, but it not move from the spot, did not rush toward Alan. Almost stiffly, it awaited Alan's approach.

*

The woman had been brought into the interrogation room, but the man wasn't there yet. She sat alone and listened to the guard's footsteps outside the door. Below the ceiling was a small barred window. There was nowhere to escape from here. There was nothing else to do here but think.

The man stepped through the door and looked at the woman hunched up before him. Only in her eyes could he still read traces of her former lustre and defiance. Her back was hunched, her legs were flecked with bruises. Her nose was red, her greasy hair was matted and her lip was chafed.

What's happened to her lip? thought the man. *Did she fight with a prison guard, get a painful kiss from someone or bite her lip?*

"Wouldn't it have been simpler to come with me in the first place?"

The woman turned her blank stare on him. "Where?" She

shrugged. "You would have brought me to this building anyway."

"You could have come here of your own free will. You could have collaborated with me without even visiting this building."

"The building and these stones are of no importance."

He looked at her and thought: *If she were washed clean, her hair combed, with new clothes on, could she still be a beautiful woman? Would I want her again?*

His sensitive nose picked up the woman's aromas, which no longer smelled of snowdrops. It was a mixture of nervous sweat, vomit, excrement, the smell of the prison cell. It reminded him of the compost that is put on flower-beds.

"You said you liked me," said the woman, with a scowl at him. "Why do you make those you like sick? Did I injure your male pride by running away from you?"

"So why did you run?"

"I was running away from the horror that surrounds you and that you no longer notice. You too are a victim of this system, but you don't know it yet."

The man adjusted his posture on the chair and straightened up. "Life is sometimes horrible."

She stretched out her neck and turned her head almost dreamily to the window. "Don't you ask yourself sometimes why you're here? What are you doing? Do you look in the mirror in the mornings?"

The man would have liked to grin, but the conversation had taken an unexpected turn. The interrogatee had begun to interrogate him. Her questions affected him somehow, even when they were silly. It was good if someone asked, and good to hear someone speaking of the purpose of life, even if seen from the wrong perspective. He crossed his arms under his chin and took a long look at her. *The enemies ponder the meaning of life and our side rushes into tomorrow without thinking of anything, without understanding anything.* He knew that not even he could seek justice and truth in every directive, every signed resolution. For life was moving onward on iron rails like Lenin's armoured train, without stopping, without counting the victims, without asking forgiveness. *Only this way will we reach the future, achieve power, break the resistance.* He got up from the chair and leaned over the table.

"You should tell me about your sister Johanna, so that she won't repeat what happened to you. You could still help her." He tried to find any perceptible reaction in the woman's body or face. But there was none. "How long has she known Alan and worked for British intelligence?"

Now the woman's face curved into a smirk. "Why don't you want to understand that women also have feelings? That women also seek love and that is more important to them than spying games." She looked him critically in the eyes. "The world isn't made only of political ideas."

"Then her love is simply being exploited."

"Exploited – what? For what?" She raised her eyebrows. "She thinks only about her music. Her costumes – she lives the life of her operatic heroines. She's never been interested in politics, or lived in the Forest Brothers' trenches or photographed your military aircraft. She can't even play her gramophone properly."

Is she telling the truth or lying? He pondered. *She's too smart to be innocent and silly. Everybody always denied everything here. Yet the woman still had a chance to choose.* He had made his choice, by entering the higher security college. That was the last time he had a choice. Since then the system had made all his choices for him. There was no way back. He simply had to go forward. Striding toward a bright future. Carrying his horizon with him and always shifting it forward before his eyes. Involuntarily or self-assuredly believing in it. Self-assuredly was easier.

He stepped closer to her and placed his clean hand almost reluctantly on the dirty sleeve of her dress.

"Don't you want to go home?"

She shook her head. "I no longer have a home among you people." Then suddenly she raised her pained gaze toward him in silent appeal.

He understood the meaning of that look, but couldn't oblige her. It was too late for that now.

"Please understand," he said almost sincerely, "if I don't make progress with you, you'll be transferred from the operations department to the investigation department. And other men will start interrogating you. They'll talk quite differently."

*

Alan was enervated by the sun. He was sitting in the old Arkangelskoye park and full of beauty. Beauty in and around him. Burned by the summer sun and the touch of Johanna's hand. The former manor park was now open to the public and Muscovite women in colourfully patterned chintz dresses were walking past them. Among the men's clothing one could still pick out sailors' shirts or soldiers' trousers. Bodies glowing with sweat under their singlets, sometimes wooden legs too. The war had left its traces, but in the heat of a summer Sunday all problems and losses seemed to have evaporated. He looked at these people, who were strangers, but not hostile. Certainly not enemies. Only their leaders made them into enemies, and those who got rich and fed on hostility.

Johanna was like a mythical goddess among them, in her pastel pink summer dress. Even in a relaxing moment in the middle of the day she had not lost her poise, her carriage, her self-conscious bearing. As if she were about to be called on stage at the next moment. Or to be photographed. Perhaps she was never really completely relaxed? Or did the newness of the environment and Alan's presence create an almost imperceptible tension? Yet her looks radiated tenderness and her smiling lips invited amorousness, even happiness. The touch of her skin and her scent were the old familiar ones. Even her perfume. She had to have a stock of extravagant Parisian scents. That perfume was hardly likely to be sold in the Soviet

159

empire. Or was it the unique fragrance of her skin that made all scents similar?

Alan lifted his right arm and placed it on her neck, a little damp from the sun, drawing her in a little closer. Johanna let her head sink onto Alan's shoulder.

So good just to be silent, thought Alan, but he did say: "So here we are now."

"Yes," whispered Johanna into his shirt. "I didn't know how many years, how many wars, would pass before I saw you again."

Alan stroked Johanna's hair with his fingers. "Let's forget it all. Here we are again, the two of us. I've felt a hunger for you for so long."

Johanna put her hand on Alan's chest and said: "Hunger and thirst."

I suppose it's to do with the war years, thought Alan. Their longing was cosmic, recognizable in every slim-waisted dress and every tattooed arm with the word 'Masha' etched in ink under the skin. It was recognizable in every body, every wooden leg and prosthesis. For the war had disconnected nearly everybody. Nearly everybody had been tortured by hunger. Everybody had thirsted for life, for the almost forgotten peacetime. And happy were those who could taste it today in the midsummer sun here in the Arkhangelskoye manor park.

The fountain babbled happily and sprayed its wet lustre into the sun. "Kru-kru-kruu" said the battered pigeons on the edge of the fountain and slaked their thirst in the constantly circulating turbid water.

My journey was worth this moment, thought Alan. *This sensuous closeness here on a park bench.*

He took Johanna's hand and sent an invitation to her eyes. He wanted to be even closer to Johanna. A hired Intourist car with driver was waiting outside the park gates.

They got up from the bench and walked hand in hand slowly toward the park gates. A brand-new freshly painted grey Pobeda pulled up outside of them. *Quite a nice car,* thought Alan. *Something of the Oldsmobile, something of the Opel Kapitän and something of Soviet mechanics. A little rounder and more spacious.* The designer had preserved the Art Deco principles, but found a modern streamlining solution. *A successful hybrid,* Alan decided, *like Johanna and myself.*

*

The National Hotel was located on the corner of Manezh Square and Gorky Street, with a view of Red Square. Here, in the heart of the city, there was a majestic spaciousness. The proud façade of the building dated from Tsarist times, but it had been renovated in the thirties. Under a roof on the façade a Socialist Realist fresco had appeared, and microphones had turned up in the rooms. This hotel served only guests of the Intourist system, foreign tourists. Soviet citizens were not allowed into the hotel.

Alan and Johanna entered the hotel's antique-looking foyer and stepped past the red carpet toward the marble staircase. Alan had left the metal key with its velvet tassel in his pocket, to avoid dealings with the administration. Yet the evening porter materialized straight away before them and cut off their progress.

"Your document, please," said the porter, looking at Johanna. Johanna cast him an innocent smile and looked to Alan.

"The lady's with me," said Alan, fishing in his pocket for his room key.

"I'm asking for the lady's document. She's not registered at this hotel," declared the porter in an imperious voice, without moving from the spot.

I mustn't show him anything, thought Johanna, feeling herself freezing from within. A cold wave was coming over her body. She smiled nevertheless through lips numbed by that inward frost.

Alan grasped Johanna by the hand and wanted to move forward, but the porter stretched out his hand without taking a step backward. "Your document, please," he repeated in a firm voice.

Better not to say anything in Russian, thought Johanna, and said in English: "Oh, where did I leave my passport, maybe in the Embassy?"

"No need to show him anything," declared Alan in English and turned to the porter with polite resolution: "This lady is my guest. We're going upstairs just for a moment."

Suddenly a man in a militia uniform appeared at the bottom of the stairs. He stepped closer and turned to Johanna: "Come with me."

Now it seems to be happening. "Excuse me," replied Johanna, feigning incomprehension.

Alan would not let go of Johanna's hand. She felt as if his hand was holding her in its iron grip, not letting her slip down through the ice.

"If you have some claims to make, address them to me," interjected Alan.

"You can move on, while we check the female citizen's papers," declared the militiaman.

"I'm not moving anywhere," declared Alan. "If you wish to talk to the lady, talk to us both."

The militiaman and the porter did not budge.

"First of all I want to ring the Embassy," Alan announced.

Johanna feigned boredom and grasped Alan's sleeve with her other hand. "Darling, perhaps we'd better leave," she said. She tried to draw Alan back by squeezing his hand. Alan obeyed her hand and turned around. They moved back toward the door.

"One moment," came the militiaman's voice behind them.

"This woman is my bride, we'll bring you the paper," said Alan over his shoulder and pulled Johanna forward toward the outer door.

Just so long as the militiaman doesn't blow his whistle and call a police car, thought Johanna in a flash. She felt a shiver running through her legs.

"Let's go for a little walk," said Alan in a carefree way, steering them out through the hotel door. Luckily the door was open and the doorman at a distance, on the hotel stairs. "Taxi?" he inquired.

"No," Johanna shook her head. "Let's go on foot."

Johanna didn't dare to look back and see whether the militiaman was following them. She moved forward as if in slow motion, expecting a fusillade from behind.

"A shame that we just let the hired car go."

"What do we do now?" whispered Johanna.

"Let's go to the Embassy, even if it is a long walk."

Even there they might arrest me, thought Johanna with alarm. *Bride, he said. Really a bride? Might that be helpful?*

"What are you going to tell them?" asked Johanna, walking quickly, looking straight ahead.

"I'll say that you're my wife," said Alan, quickening his pace and squeezing Johanna's hand. "I'll say that we're planning to get married, all right?" He cast a furtive inquiring glance at Johanna.

Johanna caught the glance, but didn't slow down. Right now she wanted to sit down or to fly. But she kept bravely walking at a rapid rate.

"This must be the fastest proposal of marriage ever. At running pace, even?" said Johanna, clinging even more tightly to Alan's hand. *Is this a temporary reprieve or a prediction of the future?* Johanna kept looking at Alan.

"Yes. No time for getting down on one knee," replied Alan, looking backward. He saw a man in a grey coat following them, frowned, and said: "Just in case, I brought from London a statement sworn before a solicitor proving my marital status – or rather, lack of it."

Johanna quickly pressed her lips to Alan's cheek.

"You're better than Pinkerton," she said, panting slightly

from the exertion, the fear of the militia and the extraordinary news. Now she wanted to sing, scream, whistle, clap or dance, but she just strode silently onward towards an unknown future.

How vulnerable we are in love, thought Johanna. *Here we are talking about marriage, and we don't know where to go. We don't dare to sit in the car, because we don't know if it will take us where we want to go. They won't let us into the hotel, where our bodies could entwine.* For the sake of love they were suddenly homeless. *Will I be taken to some dark prison cell even before I can taste love,* she wondered. Relations with foreigners were forbidden. *When did the English become foreigners, but the Estonians didn't? Just a few years ago Estonians were also foreigners here. Where does the foreigner end and your countryman begin?*

Alan pressed Johanna's hand more firmly again and said: "We're just like Adam and Eve, driven out of the Garden of Eden. You have betrayed your Communist paradise by touching my hand, and I'm not allowed in the door, though I've paid for my room there." He looked quizzically at Johanna. "You don't look like a prostitute who would spoil the hotel's high morals."

"A prostitute would get a lighter sentence than a traitor or a western spy."

"Which of those would you prefer to be?" asked Alan.

Johanna grinned. She had played all those roles on the stage already. Now Alan reminded her of a naughty little boy. But Johanna's head was troubled by a new worry. *What will happen if the British Embassy won't let me in and I'm arrested? There's bound to be a militiaman at that door too, defending the Embassy from Soviet citizens.*

Just ahead was a telephone booth with cracked window panes. Johanna stopped. Alan understood her body's signal. "Let me ring ahead to the Embassy."

The door of the booth opened with a creak. Now he had to look for a coin that fitted in the slot of the telephone. Alan rummaged in his pockets and found something. But the coin was too big. Johanna opened her handbag and put her hand in her collection of kopecks. One of them was the right size, and the telephone gave a long uninterrupted tone. An invitation to a rescuing call.

Alan narrowed his eyes and looked for the number in his notebook. The street lamp cast both light and shadow among the poplar leaves. He could just make out a number written in blue ink among the shadows.

The dial squeaked as it reluctantly turned.

Don't let it be cut off or not get answered at the other end, Johanna mentally prayed. Alan's finger helped in the dialling, back and forth. And then the inviting peeps were heard.

"Good evening! British Embassy," came the night watchman's voice to arouse hope.

*

The consul surveyed them with weary eyes.

"You should take your announcement to the registry office tomorrow morning."

"Would you come with us for support?" asked Alan. "So that the militia don't take us away from the Palace of Happiness?"

The consul screwed up his nose thoughtfully. "Tomorrow's pretty busy." He opened his large leather-bound notebook. "Maybe around eleven o'clock?"

Every number is a lucky number, thought Johanna, nodding.

"Suits us well," replied Alan.

"I'll do the paperwork myself." The consul looked thoughtfully at Johanna. "I'd recommend that you get your birth certificate translated into Russian. Or whatever identity document you have."

"I've already been given a Soviet passport," said Johanna. *Just as well I accepted the new grey passport.* Nobody actually wanted to get them. They were proud of their old, foreign,

165

Estonian passports. But the new government had hastily declared them invalid, so that no-one could leave the country.

The consul coughed and then said hesitantly: "Do you have any memento with you? Some souvenir? That might come in handy." Alan and Johanna looked at each other curiously.

*

Time didn't move in the cell. She stretched out her arm. Like her sister in the mornings, to get the circulation going. *Johanna's somewhere in Moscow now. Exalted by the smell of flowers, the touch of her sweetheart.* That is what she wanted to think. *It's better if Johanna looks after the boy. She'll create a better life for him, teach him to read music.* Yet this system seemed interested in Johanna as well. *Will they leave her in peace? How would she behave here?* She couldn't imagine her sister here in her veils and kimonos. Although she had seen her sister as a prisoner in *Aida,* the stage was something else, even in the most tragic opera productions. *Johanna shouldn't end up here.*

She sat for a moment on the stool. She rested her swollen feet. Before the guard looked through the hole in the door, saw her sitting, knocked with a key on the door and made her stand up. She felt that, sitting here on the stool, her pounding heart was getting back its calm rhythm. She didn't know if her heart was simply tired of this torment, or had become sick, as in childhood. Her aching muscles were exhausted by sleeplessness and mental torture.

Is my husband sitting in the next cubicle, has he already been shot or sent to a camp? Perhaps he's breathing the same musty cellar air? At this moment the thought of the damp smell of the cellar in the Pagari Street KGB seemed almost sweet.

She should have let her husband go to the forest. To live in the fresh air. *But the air is not much better in an underground bunker,* she reasoned. *How long would he have held out there?*

How long must men hold out now? The independence of a small country was a mote in everyone's eye. Members of the People's Committee and their allies had been pursuing the Hitlerites and now the Stalinites. One by one they had all been caught. Her husband was saved only by an unconfirmed report of his death: disappeared without trace. She had forbidden her husband to go into the forest and let everyone think he was dead. And then he died slowly in a back room. They couldn't have known that he would be in hiding so long. *Armies and powers had come and gone. Surely this absurd system couldn't last? In this house it seems that this utopia will last a long time. They're building a new network of informers here, they're recruiting new snoops. Dissenters are being liquidated. Reason is being murdered.* It doesn't matter how fast these Pobedas go, or how hypnotic the recruiter's stare is, they wouldn't lead her astray any more. *I shouldn't have drunk the wine, put the chocolates in my mouth. What's the cost of a moment of weakness,* she thought, knowing at the same time that there would have been more such moments. Sooner or later she would have been arrested, once she was on their radar.

*

The registry office was like every other building in the city of Moscow. Bleak, with a high ceiling and a portrait of Stalin on the wall. A uniformed lady with plaits piled in a bun was engrossed in the papers presented by the consul from the Embassy.

"If anything is still missing, I can get it for you from the Embassy," said the consul grandly.

"Can you register our marriage straight away?" asked Alan.

"It's not permitted," replied the uniformed lady only after thoroughly examining the declaration and documents presented to her. "We have a queue. Up to two months."

Johanna rolled her eyes and Alan sent an appealing look to the consul from the Embassy.

"Perhaps you have a possibility of making a special exception," said the consul in a soft voice, giving Alan a sign with his eyes. Alan fetched from his briefcase a packet of coffee with an English brand name on it and a box of chocolates with the image of Harrods, which Johanna hadn't yet had time to open. She had planned to enjoy them with her sister and nephew in Tallinn, when the boy eventually turned up. They would all have to do without that tasty morsel. But were Johanna's horizons now brimming with milk and honey? A midsummer night's dream?

The official nodded her head, accepted the gifts without a word and put them quickly in a drawer of her desk. Then she started silently leafing through the notebook full of written names and dates. *There must be microphones here too,* thought Johanna.

"The first opportunity I can find is in a week's time."

"Not any sooner?" asked Alan anxiously.

"That's the best I can do. Filling in and checking the forms takes time."

A thousand different thoughts passed through Alan's head. "My visa runs out in four days," he said with a smile. "Please help us. I would be very grateful to you."

The female officer with her bun who guided people into the harbour of marriage, looked at her notebook again with a severe expression. She took an eraser and erased someone's name. Then she took a pencil, browsed a couple of pages ahead and made an entry on a new page. Then she turned back the pages in her ledger and wrote Alan's and Johanna's names onto the page smeared by the traces of the eraser.

*

Alan and Johanna walked hand in hand past Revolution Square, thronged with people. Despite being from different worlds, from inimical political systems, they talked of marriage, of the union between two people, which is fragile even when it is supported by a common home town, family and society. They were thinking in different languages, carrying memories unknown to each other, venturing into reference systems that weren't from the same universe. How was this meeting between two souls here under the red star of the Kremlin even possible?

Johanna didn't know where to go with Alan. She noticed Alan's clumsy efforts to be a gentleman in a strange city, where a myriad of people was milling around, but there was a shortage of cafes and restaurants. The consul had warned them that in the better Moscow restaurants, such as Aragvi, there were microphones under the tables. The Soviet Union was ahead of its time in terms of listening devices. But even in the most modest restaurants there was a queue standing at the doors. Standing indeed – not moving from the spot. A few would get in that were known to the doorman.

On the other side of the street Johanna noticed a canteen with an open door with the name Молочная, where people were filing in and out. "Perhaps we could drink a cup of coffee there…" – she pointed to the milk-bar.

They crossed the street and entered a spacious room smelling of greasy *pirogi*. At high, round bar-stools people were drinking weak milky coffee or light cocoa and eating doughnuts.

Here they could stand close together and taste chicory coffee. At least it was sweet and warm. Alan sipped his coffee and turned his eyes discreetly to the ceiling.

"Listen to me carefully now," he said, taking Johanna by the hand. His gaze was serious. "Nothing is ever that simple, even when they let us get married. They might try to recruit you – and that would poison our life in London."

Johanna's eyes widened as she shook her head. "I would never agree to become their agent."

"Then they wouldn't let you out, or they'd arrange something else unpleasant," Alan's voice went on in an undertone in the hum of the milk-bar.

Johanna paused to reflect, her tongue against her upper lip: a bad habit from childhood that always came to the surface in tense moments.

"They've already tried with my sister…".

"And what became of your sister?" Alan asked, without taking his eyes off Johanna.

"She's in hiding. At first in my cellar, now somewhere in Tartu… Her son was in my care, but then he went missing…". Johanna lowered her eyelids and looked at the doughnut on her plate, which was chipped at the edge. "I didn't want to burden you with my problems."

"Sooner or later you would have to." Alan turned his gaze out into the depths of Gorky Street. The symmetrical massiveness of the Stalinist architecture had a chilling effect. "We're no longer allies and I'm now working for enemy radio."

"Yes, we've become official enemies, though neither of us believes it."

"There are plenty of those who do, who get swept along with every new ideology," said Alan without rancour in his voice. He cast a glance at the guests eating their uniform doughnuts next to their cups of milk.

"The people want to believe the propaganda; they can't all be bothered to think for themselves."

Will I tell him everything, thought Johanna, *or will I frighten him away? And yet… There are so many secrets around us, I can't create them between us,* she decided, grabbing Alan's coat button.

"After a performance I was introduced to the head of security," she said meaningfully. "So far we've only talked about the boy who disappeared and about music."

"Are you sure that he's the senior officer?"

"Yes, I was told that. Minister of Security. A major-general. I even have his telephone number."

"Is it the right number?"

"Yes. I rang him about the boy. At first his secretary answered, later I was put through to him."

A crafty twinkle appeared in Alan's eyes and he hungrily bit into a piece of sugary doughnut. "Give me that number. I can ring him and ask about your welfare. At least leave a message that there's a call from BBC radio…".

This idea shocked Johanna. "I don't know if you should …". She suddenly felt that the man with glasses on the next stool was listening to them talking. "Perhaps it'll make things even worse…" she said in a lowered voice.

"Believe me, there's power in the press. The head of security wouldn't want us to make him a radio news item. In case they start processing you, like your sister …" Alan didn't finish his sentence, and the three dots hung in the pregnant air of the milk-bar. His gaze had become anxiously intense.

"If they put pressure on you, threaten them with an international station that half the world listens to."

"You might be right, but do they care about any radio? Or anybody's opinion at all?" wondered Johanna. "In the past five years all sorts of horrors have been unleashed on the world … and nobody is amazed."

"Everyone cares about their own name, at least, their own personal reputation. Nobody wants to be the victim of slander. And they don't talk about public secrets."

Johanna sighed: "They're not afraid of anyone."

"Everyone has a boss they depend on for their welfare. Even generals," asserted Alan.

They sipped their milk drinks in silence. *I see that he's a bridge player; he's thinking of his next move,* observed Johanna, squeezing her husband's hand in admiration.

*

The boy was standing in an identity parade at the Tallinn distribution point for minors. Some of their relatives from the country were surveying the line. They were supposed to recognize the right boys. The wrong child must not be handed over to them at the distribution point. The boy pulled horrible faces, so the old bewildered couple wouldn't want to take him. *How terrible,* thought the boy, *if the Pobeda man doesn't recognize me, now that my head is shaved. They're sure to put me back in the line when he arrives.*

But they didn't. After lunch the door of the boys' room was suddenly opened and there he stood: Uncle Pobeda, in all his splendour and power. The boy ran toward him eagerly. The man bowed down and swept him up in his embrace. It was so nice to hang around the man's neck and sense the familiar fragrance of cologne on his cheek.

"My travelling man is back again!" laughed the man and asked: "Shall we take a little spin in the Pobeda?"

The hum of boys in the room had stopped. Now they all ran in a cluster towards the window and gazed on the beautiful beige car down on the street. The boy felt proud when he saw the envious looks of the other boys. None of them had a tall and genial young uncle who owned a brand-new Pobeda.

"Let's go and check over the car," said the boy importantly, grabbing his own tattered shirt. The two of them strode through the boys' room, past the guard, out of the door of the distribution point, without anyone saying a word.

He knows how to get things done, thought the boy as he sat down in the familiar Pobeda, which smelt slightly of petrol. How good it felt to sit again on this leather seat and look at the familiar town through its windscreen.

"Shall we go home to your place now?" asked the boy.

"I have a small apartment and I'm not a relative of yours. You have to go to your auntie first," said the man.

Disappointment overcame the boy. *That was bad news!*

"I don't want to go to Auntie's," he pouted; "she won't let me out of the house."

"This time she will. Your auntie filled in an official paper to look after you."

"I'd rather go to Mummy's."

"I don't know where your mummy is." The man drew him closer and put his left hand on the wheel. "We'll be meeting often and going for car rides together," he consoled the boy. He grasped the boy's right hand too, and pressed it onto the wheel.

"Let's go, bus driver, I need your help!"

The boy took a firmer hold of the wheel and started steering the car. They were travelling along Narva Road toward Kadriorg. The man pointed out a brown five-storey building on the right-hand side.

"If you want to see me, you come to that building, second floor, flat 6. I'm there every Tuesday and Friday."

The boy looked intently at the house, to commit the right door to mind.

"We're going to play a new detective game. It's very exciting. You have to listen to and remember everything that Aunt Johanna says. I have a feeling your auntie has a secret that you don't know about yet."

What secret could it be, thought the boy. "Is it a good secret?"

"That's for you to find out. Maybe we'll go on the track of the secret together," said the man with new enthusiasm. "If you remember everything well, we'll go to the zoo next time."

To the zoo, thought the boy. *I'd really like to go there. I've got to train my memory properly.*

"Don't say anything about me to Auntie. Otherwise she won't let us play the detective game together or go for car rides."

The road rolled through Kadriorg Park. The ancient chestnuts waved their branches in welcome in the wind. The old castle appeared behind it. The two of them turned

173

the wheel, to enter the familiar Mäekalda Street. Behind the wooden fence Aunt Johanna's pale green house awaited them.

"We're here," said the man with a wink. "See if you can get in the door. Say that you've been brought home, but don't mention me."

The boy squeezed his hand in a manly way and jumped out of the car.

"I'll come to your place…" the boy counted the days on his fingers: *Wednesday, Thursday, Friday* … "the day after tomorrow," he said, carefully closing the car door.

"Okay!" the Pobeda man shouted from the car.

The boy trotted to the garden gate, slipped in through it, and crossed over the lawn to Auntie's oak door. It was not locked. He pulled the door ajar, looked back and waved to the man.

The Pobeda moved smoothly away and disappeared into the depths of the street.

"Auntie Johanna!" cried the boy from the entrance hall.

Not hearing an answer, he entered the living-room, but the room was empty. He stepped past the piano into the bedroom and pulled the door fully open with a bang, to surprise his aunt. But now he was surprised himself. Sitting on mattresses in the middle of the room were strange foreign people. The bedroom furniture was pushed against the walls, there was washing and a child's blanket hanging up.

"Hello, where's Auntie Johanna?" asked the boy when he had got over the shock. A man with a broad round face and narrow eyes looked fixedly at him. He asked: *"А ты кто?* But who are you? Where's my Auntie… tyotya?"

"Тётя уехала. Auntie's gone." *Even Auntie's gone away,* thought the boy. *Everybody's just disappearing.* Then he decided that Auntie's disappearance maybe wasn't so bad after all. *Now I can go outside and play. But what about Auntie's secret? My important detective game?*

A woman in a scarf asked him gently: *"Чайку хочешь?* Want some tea?" *I could drink some hot tea,* he thought.

"With sugar?" he asked. Not getting an answer, he said in Russian: "Sahar, you understand?"

The woman nodded, gave the infant bundle to the man, and took the lid off a round plastic canister. At the bottom of it, real white sugar was visible. Now the boy's face spread into a smile. He sat on a mat astride a bare mattress and stretched out his hand for a cup of tea.

*

Johanna seemed to be sitting on her childhood swing again. She felt slightly giddy. Everything was going up and down, she was standing on her feet, then on her head. She didn't even try to get it clear in her present state of mind. She only hoped that this state wouldn't end. That reality in its tin boots wouldn't step onto her doormat again. It was so easy to exist. And her mind was so easy.

I mustn't love him, she thought. *For there's no hope in this love. There's no future.*

"Our future is Communism," read a framed Supremacist poster above her head in the National Hotel. Johanna chuckled like a little girl who knows she's causing trouble and will keep causing it. *I mustn't get used to him, for afterwards I'll feel his absence. My thoughts will wander beyond the sea again, where the wind will blow them back. And my feelings will drown in the waves. Then I'll be like a modern-day unhappy Cho-Cho-San, sitting in my tight kimono and listening to the neighbours' pentatonic wailing. And crying over Lieutenant Pinkerton, who will not cast anchor again on these shores. For they won't let him do it. And he won't take me with him across the waves either, because they won't let me out of here. Our love will shrivel, evaporate, turn into an old legend. I can go back onto the stage of the Estonia opera house, when it's ready, and weep my kimono wet before the audience. The audience will applaud my spirited singing, without knowing that I've been crying my heart out. Simply a woman driven mad by the pain of love. One who's of no use to anyone.*

And yet I don't want him to take his hand off my knee. I don't want him ever to release me. I want to be a magnet clinging to his side. And I could die with him. Right now. Right here. That's how I am. Broken. Spoiled. Tormented by the winds of war and mauled by the pain of love.

Johanna adjusted the sheet and put her hand on her forehead, as if these outward gestures might call her thoughts to order. But order and decency had been swept out of her mind, and even the Soviet order could not force her to rise out of this foreign enemy's bed. She drew her fingers over the forbidden man's now roughened cheek and pressed her mouth again to his lips.

I mustn't love you, she thought. *I'll get dressed straight away and run away from you before it's too late. I'll do that in a moment, when my legs can carry me better.* But the mattress was feather-soft and held her in its grasp. And Alan's hand didn't leave her knee. Johanna knew that her limbs wouldn't obey her, and she would not be running anywhere.

"Ah, Radamès, ah, Pinkerton!" How many times had she met her death at the hand of her beloved! Why couldn't she let Alan kill her too? One tragic loss more or less. One unhappy little life more or less. She knew that her role in life was to be a tragic heroine. Both in life and in her work. Both on the stage and in bed. The gods on Olympus would not set her free. They only let her parry with her hands and strive vainly with her vocal cords.

"Mi struggo e mi tormento, O Dio, vorrei morir!" [*] She let her voice ring in Alan's ear in the bed. Alan was startled and turned toward her. He looked at Johanna lovingly. *Does he love me for my voice? Or for what I am?*

"*Si,*" said Alan, slowly moving onto her, shielding from her eyes both the heavens and the cruel gods of Olympus.

*

"Is there anyone from Otto Tief's government still alive that you keep in touch with? Confess, come on, confess!" demanded the new, dark-haired, red-eyed investigator.

But there was nothing to confess. All of the woman's freedom-fighter friends had died, left by boat, or hidden in the forest. She had no connections with anyone any more.

"Names. We're interested in names!"

"You have a list of the whole government, you know better," she said; "I only helped my husband."

"Your husband confessed everything."

She knew that he couldn't have done that. He had had nothing to say. He had sat for two years hidden in a back room, away from the world. He could talk about the soup she cooked for him. About the yellowed paper of old newspapers.

"What instructions has your sister received from English intelligence? Why is she in Moscow?"

She knew that this would never end.

They want me to sell my own husband and even my sister. Who else?

They've closed the borders and ended the war. They need to create new enemies. Manipulate, lie, repress.

She knew that her strength was ebbing away. She breathed heavily and pressed her lips together.

Then came the offers.

"Think carefully. If you start to co-operate with us, we can get you rehabilitated from your crimes."

What crimes? She didn't understand these words, but she understood the workings of logic.

"That wouldn't be a bad thing, in your circumstances," explained the investigator.

"My husband – what has become of him?" she asked.

"His situation doesn't concern you."

"And what is his situation?"

177

Silence.

"Is he alive, dead, in prison, out of it?"

The interrogator surveyed her through half-closed eyes.

"He's been sent to a camp," he replied drily.

"After he confessed everything?" Her voice had taken on an ironic note for which she didn't have the strength, for irony required a superiority she no longer had. She summoned her powers nevertheless.

"What confessions are you still expecting from me? The kind that would get me the death penalty?"

The investigator stopped and slammed his fist on the table. "Take her to the Dushegubka cell!"

*

Alan had instructed Johanna, advised her, on how to act to get an exit permit. But he could not fight his wife's battles for her. For both of them, so that they could meet again. He could only do battle on the airwaves. The result of that depended on whether the listener's receiver was switched on or his voice was echoing in the vast expanse of the ether. Through the airwaves he could transmit both destructive criticism and burning love, and its effect depended merely on a movement of the listener's hand. Click. To turn his voice on or off. Monitoring organizations were listening or recording it. Alan had to be careful in his actions on the airwaves. The BBC did not allow improvisation, the use of the airwaves for personal purposes.

Here they now stood in each other's embrace, not knowing whether they would ever meet again. Despite the fact that they were now husband and wife officially. Perhaps Johanna would be sent off to an even colder land. But if Alan submitted an application to move in with his wife, the KGB would exploit it immediately. It would be trumpeted for propaganda purposes and he would be forced to collaborate. But what would his colleagues in the opposite camp think; what would he think himself? He was an Englishman after all. Alan shook his head without moving his neck muscles. He merely gazed at Johanna with a prolonged stare, without saying anything, without making a move. They were locked in each other's arms. The movements were invisible, their words were soundless.

The time for farewell had arrived, when time stands still and the memories of the moment may roll forward or backward only in recalled images. Yet they still felt the warmth of each other's bodies, the touch of their breaths. If they listened carefully they could hear the excited beating of each other's hearts. Johanna was trained to control her emotions, but now pearls glistened in her eyes. Was this planned in the drama of her life, really? Alan would have liked to repeat the previous scene, rest on Johanna's warm moist skin, hide himself inside her once again.

"*Внимание, поезд на Псков отравляется с девятого пути.* Attention! The train for Pskov is departing from Platform 9," came the voice of the station-master from the megaphone.

The guard levered the bolt next to the door and gave them an impatient look. *One moment more,* thought Alan, hugging Johanna especially hard. *I will retain this moment in memory.* Then he let her hands loose, but Johanna did not release him from her arms, as if she wanted to take him with her.

"*Провожающим выйти из вагона!* Non-travellers leave the carriage!" announced the conductor reprovingly from behind their backs.

Johanna's arms relaxed. Now they could only see each other's eyes. Alan retreated down the steps back to the platform.

The iron door of the carriage closed between them with a loud crash.

Alan watched from the platform as the train slowly departed and thought how merciless the rails are. They carry lovers apart from each other, without looking back, not stopping once. Calmly but certainly the train wheels roll into oblivion. Now it was time for him, too, to sit in the familiar Pobeda provided by Intourist, where he was awaited by his escort and the chain-smoking driver, to start the journey to Sheremetyevo airport, where there was a tiny hole in the iron curtain.

*

Quandyk shrugged his shoulder, from which hung an empty string bag. The whole family and even the neighbour's boy, brought along for the occasion, stood behind him in the nocturnal sugar queue. It was good that the boy had agreed to come along. Sugar was distributed for every mouth, and the boy's mouth for sugar was the biggest. He was hoping that little Botakoz would be taken into account for the distribution. She, too, had a beating heart. She too was a Soviet citizen. This country was immense. Quandyk had left his homeland, because there too everything had changed with time. There were few of the old traditions and practices left. Russian expressions had invaded their language and blended with native words, some of them without a proper equivalent. For many of the words and concepts were so alien that they couldn't be translated. Now they had been sent, under the banner of the friendship of peoples, to another friendly republic, where nobody had expected or accepted them. Johanna the neighbour woman had tried to be kind to them, but she did not have their hearts. No one here knew the hospitality of the peoples of the steppes. They didn't take their shoes off before sitting on a carpet, they didn't appreciate the value of tea-leaves. Quandyk partially understood Johanna. This woman was used to living in a lumber-room of used furniture and singing ear-splitting songs. She needed space for furniture, not for people. She had a shortage of tolerance and of carpets. *She doesn't understand the importance of carpets to us, she only notices their size and colour. No one understands our culture here. People only look and nod, but they don't understand our speech. No one sits on the streets or makes friends with foreigners. Everyone seems to be rushing somewhere, but where? The Almighty is merciful to mankind and every moment granted by him should be appreciated and enjoyed. One shouldn't walk past his gifts. But here no one is allowed to talk about that. Nowhere any longer.*

Quandyk sighed at the thought, and turned around to take a look at his family. Most of all he was worried about little Botakoz. What sort of a person would she grow into? Here she won't learn either carpet-weaving or stone-baking of bread. At least she wasn't alone here. They had their own family cell here. It was sad to look at this boy, who looked like an orphan. The boy shifted from one foot to the other and had curled up. Quandyk patted the boy on the shoulder and said: *"Ну и холод!* Sure is cold!"* The boy smiled back and nodded.

"Скоро утро. It will soon be morning,"* Quandyk consoled the boy, took off his jacket and placed it on the boy's shoulders. The boy shook his head, but still wrapped himself in the folds of the jacket. *Good boy, so calm, independent,* thought Quandyk, resting his eyes warmly on the boy's face. *If he were from our people, he'd make a good son-in-law. And a suitable husband for Botakoz.* Joy-bringer turned his gaze to the brightening eastern sky. The sun was rising and bringing greetings from their distant home.

*

Johanna was almost happy. When she played the piano, did the washing-up, made the boy's bed, her gaze involuntarily turned to the ring on her fourth finger. Although it was bulky and made of reddish Soviet gold, it was the most precious treasure in the world. More valuable than Cleopatra's jewels, the gold of the Nibelungen or the Queen of Sheba's ring. She didn't yet know whether it was a magic ring which would help her to perform miracles. Some miracles had already happened, however. The boy was back at home with her. When she had opened the door of her home with her ringed finger, she found the lost boy in front of her. The boy looked like a shaven-headed visitor from another planet. Yet alive and well. A little thinner and grown-up. A self-satisfied Marco Polo, who had returned from his journey of conquest.

The new settlers had not taken off on their oriental flying carpet, but pushed out her furniture and taken up residence on the carpet. Well, what was to be done? Johanna knew how to appreciate antique handicraft, and genuine lambswool too.

Johanna's marital and family status had suddenly changed. She was now a married woman, though she didn't know if she would ever see her husband again. A shiver went through her shoulders at that thought. Johanna went to the window and pushed the ventilator shut. Alan had arranged a visa for England for her. And one for her potential foster-child, the 'lost' boy. It was another matter whether they would ever be let of out this wonderland, for every worthless Soviet citizen did at least have the price of a serf on him.

Anyway she now had an invisible bond with Alan. The adventures in Moscow had in turn brought them closer together; the trench friendship had made them companions in battle. The official document also made their secret affair of the heart legal now, for both the domestic and the enemy camp. Johanna still didn't know how to announce it to the world, whom she could tell about it. She didn't even know how her friends would react to this news. She felt that someone was following her as she came home. As an indirect foreigner she evidently now had someone on her tail. But she felt she was still in Alan's tender embrace, and she hoped that the power of the man's touch would protect her still.

Johanna took from the sideboard her English tea service and started laying the table with a sense of pleasure. Her writer friend was supposed to pop in and listen to the world news with her on the crackling radio. Now that radio had taken on a new significance here in the house. Her legal husband was hiding in the wireless case.

*

Alan was walking to the BBC again. He turned into Drury Lane; Bush House was not far away.

He felt relief at no longer having to look over his shoulder. He strode past a building that had been hit by a bomb, now surrounded by new scaffolding. Although London had suffered damage, there was still hope of recovery. The main thing was that the healing scars of this city did not acquire an alien overgrowth. That the old individuality and uniqueness of England be preserved. He was glad to be able to walk on the left side of the road and that the traffic was no longer on the right. The left-hand world had left a very right-handed impression. Every sort of polarity was missing in the totalitarian world. This was not simply in the human sphere. The one-party system, which could easily be misused.

Alan's senses had been sharpened in Moscow by the constant checking and self-censorship, which he applied in the knowledge that he was being monitored in turn by the state system. Thus he wrapped himself in the paranoia of multiple controls. *How had the state taken over the human role unnoticed? People were serving the state, the state didn't serve people.* All powers from top to bottom seemed to be concentrated on feeding the invisible present. Was this system really alive, or was it a matter of phantoms, molluscs without a face? *Perhaps the army of worker bees were feeding a queen bee who no longer existed? One who had perished in the flames of revolutionary terror?*

Alan did not know that. He could only paint an image before his eyes of an unseen Politburo, malevolently moving tin soldiers on a red broadcloth, planning the next famine or war. Or the next act of terror or sabotage, to pull the reins even tighter, increase surveillance and raise the productivity of its worker bees.

Could such a system be possible in the future in good old England? Would the citizens here give away their comforts and independence, their human rights? Would they let the system invisibly grow over their heads and ensnare them in its web? Even invade the privacy of the white Edwardian terraced houses, where everyone had their own door, their own little garden gate, their own patch of lawn?

Alan felt Johanna's hand still in his palm. He was carrying her with him. He knew that the system had not yet remodelled Johanna in its own image. That Johanna still had her thirst for freedom, inspiring playfulness, infectious imagination... He had to save Johanna from the jaws of the system before it swallowed her up, digested her and moulded her into its excrement. *Did all systems, more or less totalitarian, do that? Perhaps I too am the excreta of the British Empire, without noticing it?*

Absorbed in this meditation, Alan had arrived before the pillared doors of the BBC World Service.

Alan stepped inside the door of the building convinced that, in the end, all the rocks would be broken. The freezing of rain and thawing of ice, the pressure of winds and storms, create cracks even in stones. Water expands as it changes to ice and erodes a hole in a mountain. That is a natural process. If nature is subjected to such changes for millions of years, then the Soviet Union and the British Empire will be subject to them too.

*

The boy sat down in front of the wireless wedged between Johanna and the visiting writer. Auntie turned the sound down a little and pressed her ear closer to the wireless, so that the new neighbours behind the wall wouldn't hear what they were listening to. The boy was gripped by this conspiratorial activity, though he didn't understand English. It was exciting to listen to something you weren't supposed to hear. Even if you had to do it with enemies of the people. The Pobeda man had said that Auntie was associating with those. The writer didn't look much like an enemy of the people, for he was wearing an ordinary creased shirt and baggy old trousers. His glasses had thick, round ivory frames too. In the film that the boy had seen in Russia the enemy of the people wore a monocle at the end of a shiny chain on one eye and tight, crisply pressed black trousers. *Yes, going on his appearance this chap doesn't match up to a proper enemy of the people,* observed the boy, wrinkling his nose. The radio snapped and crackled, but Johanna expertly turned the round radio dial, manoeuvring it with the Englishman's voice. A new gold ring glittered on her fourth finger.

"Mr. Churchill said in his speech yesterday in Zurich," Auntie Johanna interpreted the Englishman's talk briskly, "that a structure must be given to Europe... in the framework of which it is possible to live in peace, security and freedom... We have to create something like a United States of Europe." At this the enemy of the people eagerly shook his head, and Auntie also smiled and pressed her ear even closer to the radio box. Then something much more interesting came out of the radio.

The Englishman said the word *automobile,* which even the boy understood.

"At the Paris auto salon," announced Auntie Johanna, "the new American automobiles, with long bodies and new colour schemes, attracted the eye."

Now the boy stuck his head between the other heads and listened attentively.

"It's about the new Cadillac model," Auntie Johanna explained in a whisper, "which has a specially streamlined effect. This new model is in a metallic… well, mother-of-pearl colour."

"I know," nodded the writer. "The Cadillac's back wheel is almost covered by the mudguard."

"What sort of car is a Kädilläkk?" the boy now eagerly asked the enemy of the people.

"A big oval American car, with rear mudguards just like wings," explained the writer. "It runs as smoothly as a ship."

"Is it bigger than a Pobeda?"

The man screwed up his nose and waved his hand. "Of course it's bigger and much prettier. And the engine is more powerful."

This fact made the boy sad. He would have liked the Pobeda to be the most beautiful of all. But there was no mention of the Pobeda in this report. *You can't really believe enemies of the people,* the boy consoled himself. In the film they had been lying all the time and in the end they set fire to the People's House.

When the broadcast ended, Auntie turned to him and said in a half-whisper: "Don't tell anyone what you hear on BBC radio. It would only make it hard for you."

So Auntie does have a secret, the man was right, thought the boy.

Auntie looked dubiously toward the wall of Quandyk's room and added: "Now for balance we'll tune the radio to the Moscow station."

"Vnimaniye! Govorit Moskva!" cried the boy proudly, imitating the voice of the man on the Russian station from memory. Auntie looked at him with horror in her eyes, and started twiddling the dial on her radio. She found some new station, where a woman was singing in Russian, and turned the sound up especially loud. Against the background of the Russian lady's singing they discussed in soft voices everything they had heard on the English radio. They sat quietly, following every movement and word.

"We let the system lie to us, push us into a corner, strip us bare, keep us in a cage," said Auntie Johanna excitedly.

"Churchill's right. As a counterweight to the Soviet Union they should create a proper federation of Europe," said the writer, the enemy of the people. "Then they wouldn't hand us over to Stalin every time he raps his fist on the table."

The boy was sure that Uncle Stalin never rapped his fist on the table. He was sitting in pictures everywhere with such a calm and friendly expression. Even his whiskers laughed.

*

The boy walked up the grey stone steps of the house on Narva Road. The corridor was dank and smelled of piss. He tried to take two steps at a time. It was quite hard, because the steps were higher than in the Russian colony. He was already on the second floor. He stretched out his hand, rose on tiptoe and pressed the doorbell of number 6. The bell buzzed like a mosquito on the other side of the door. The door had a big round glass eye. Someone's shadow appeared behind it.

Then the door opened with a slight creak. There behind it was the man.

"Come in, come in, come in," he said, and marched ahead of the boy through the hall and into a room.

This conspiratorial apartment was sparsely furnished and without distinguishing features that one could recall or dream about. *It's as if someone lives here, but doesn't,* thought the boy. Yet this was a nice place where he and the man could meet.

"How is my hero doing?" asked the Pobeda man, looking at the boy encouragingly.

"Doing well," declared the boy, stepping over by the window. The view of the yard wasn't exciting. Beyond the narrow backyard was a wall that one couldn't look or climb over.

"Yesterday I drove a new ZIS," said the man. "A real limou-

187

sine. It has a really long body."

"Great," enthused the boy. He recalled yesterday's news about the automobile show, where there was a mention of bright new mother-of-pearl-coloured cars. He added confidently: "You know, there are even bigger cars in America. Have you seen a Kädilläkk?"

The man's face showed interest. "I haven't – where did you hear that?"

The boy thought about how to say this better. *Auntie mentioned that I mustn't talk about listening to English radio.*

"Your Pobeda is the best of all, other cars don't count. And you're the best driver," he said, trying to change the subject.

The man followed him with a chuckle. "The Pobeda is the best, but tell me anyway where you heard about this other car."

"I suppose somebody was talking on the radio..." said the boy hesitantly.

"In Estonian?" the man asked suspiciously.

The boy looked for a new explanation. "Oh no, not the radio. A funny man was visiting Auntie," he said, choosing his new tack. "He said the new American limousines are very big. All colours in mother-of-pearl. Even two colours." The boy's face had turned lively. "What is mother-of-pearl?" he asked, looking fixedly at the man.

"Mother-of-pearl is a false sparkle. It has no pearls in it. It seems to reflect the paint metallically, but actually it breaks up the paint. So who is this funny man?"

The boy thought for a moment and described the writer. "He has grey hair, a big flat nose, bleary eyes and horn-rimmed glasses, and he writes a lot."

"Another one interested in cars. What's his name?"

The boy hesitated for a moment and thought about his aunt's admonition. "I don't know the writer man's name."

"Does the writer man talk to Auntie only about cars, or also about weapons?"

"Weapons?" exclaimed the boy. "No, mostly about cars. When the English and American navy gets to Tallinn harbour, they will bring us mother-of-pearl cars." The boy strained his memory. "Kädilläkk and Rolsroiss cars. Then they'll create a federation here in Europe."

"When will these ships arrive here?" asked the man, looking at the boy intently.

The boy shrugged. "Who knows... when Uncle Chochill says."

"Perhaps Auntie even has a radio transmitter? With headphones and a microphone?" he queried.

"No." The boy shook his head. "I would have seen that. Then she wouldn't be listening to the radio all the time, she'd be doing her own broadcasts." He looked at the man with interest. "Do you have a transmitter with headphones like that?"

"Not yet," he replied as if regretfully, "but I'd like to find one." He paused. "If you hear anything about a radio transmitter, tell me. Then we can play our radio game too. But let's continue for now with the detective game."

He put his hand in his pocket and took out a five-rouble note. He handed it to the boy.

"Here's some pocket money for you." The boy's eyes widened as he took the crisp note between his fingers. He had never had his own money. Until now he had mostly handled kopecks.

"We'll investigate other people's secrets," admonished the man, "but nobody must know about our secrets!" He put a warning finger to his mouth and stretched out his hand for a handshake.

The doorbell buzzed. The man went to open the door. A girl stepped inside. She seemed a little older than the boy, and had an absent look. The man led the girl into the next room and carefully closed the door.

"Till next time," he said to the boy and hurriedly showed him out of the door.

Interesting, thought the boy; *what is the man talking to the girl about? Are girls interested in cars too?*

＊

This boy has a musical talent and an absolute ear. I should start teaching him, thought Johanna.

The boy finished his song and drew a deep breath. His calf's eyes expected praise, but the feathers on his rooster's breast had gone fluffy.

"Good! You sing very well," said Johanna. "Although the words of the song are of questionable value. Perhaps we'll try some other song."

Johanna got up energetically and sat on a round revolving piano-stool. She opened the piano lid and played the opening chords.

"Why don't you like the words of my song?" asked the boy, a little offended.

Johanna raised her hand from the piano keys. "Not all songs have to be about Stalin. There are many famous men in history. Even here in Estonia. You don't have to sing only about politicians, but also about dreams, hopes, love. Politicians come and go."

"Will Stalin go too?" asked the boy. "Our trainer told us Stalin is eternal."

Johanna looked at the boy in astonishment.

"I hope not. Stalin's men are driving around in trucks picking up people who fight for the independence of the Estonian state. Those people are our heroes."

Now the boy was perplexed, as if recalling something. "But Uncle Stalin loves heroes."

"Stalin's heroes have taken over our country. There are heroes and heroes. One man's hero may be another's enemy. Real heroes like your father are fighting for our freedom, but we're not allowed to talk openly about that now." Johanna paused and asked in a friendly tone: "Have you thought about your father? Why he went away?"

The boy lowered his eyes and shuffled his feet.

"Maybe he didn't leave of his own free will. Maybe he was taken away," Johanna added cautiously.

The boy raised his eyes. "Who took him away?"

"Stalin's men in trucks. The Black Raven."

Am I saying too much, wondered Johanna, and changed the subject. "Do you want to learn another song, about Estonian heroes?"

The boy looked crushed by the burden of Johanna's words.

"I don't feel like singing any more," he said in a doleful voice. "I'd like to go home and look for my whistle and kaleidoscope."

"Good idea; we must bring you a change of clothes from there too." *Poor boy. I've confused him,* thought Johanna. *I've tangled up his mind.* She went over to him and hugged him. Then she combed his cropped head with her fingers, as if hoping that combing it would help to bring order to his confused mind and straighten out his thoughts. "The grown-up world is very complicated."

*

Johanna and the boy were strolling through the summer dusk of the town. At this time of year it never got completely dark. They were on their way to the boy's house. Johanna noticed how the boy's eyes glowed at the sight of the familiar stack of firewood. He let go of Johanna's hand, ran to the stack and stopped to study it. He prised at the pile as if looking for something.

"What's up?" asked Johanna, stopping on the pavement.

"My steering wheel is gone," said the boy sadly, "and the gear stick."

"Somebody needed firewood, despite the warm weather," guessed Johanna.

She stepped over to the boy and consoled him: "Soon you can get a new wheel in London." Then she steered him by the sleeve toward the house. The windows of her sister's apartment were dark.

"The house is still in place and she doesn't seem to have moved," said Johanna comfortingly.

He inspected the house intently.

"She has moved. More plaster has crumbled on the wall, and someone has picked the lock."

Maybe someone has been here? Perhaps my sister? She should have a door-key, though, mused Johanna. *Thieves perhaps?*

They went in quickly through the entrance door and stopped at the door of the apartment. There were signs of woodworking on the door lock.

The boy looked at Johanna. "Maybe Daddy couldn't get in… and put in a new lock?"

Johanna pressed the doorbell. They waited a long, pregnant moment.

The boy knocked hard on the door.

Still silence.

"I know which window will open," declared the boy to Johanna and ran out of the entrance.

"Wait," cried Johanna, but he had already vanished around the corner.

Johanna followed the boy around the house and saw him already climbing over the window-sill and prising the window open. It did indeed open. The boy jumped inside.

"Open the door from the inside," cried Johanna after him, and hurried back to the house door.

She rushed to the entrance again and stopped at the apartment door. The boy was not to be heard.

I hope he hasn't been hurt.

Johanna pressed the doorbell again. Now she heard the boy's steps. The boy tinkered with the latch and then opened the door. He looked at Johanna with a shocked face, as if he had seen a bogeyman behind the curtain.

"The apartment is full of somebody's things, but they aren't Mummy's or Daddy's."

Johanna entered the apartment and saw the signs of a stranger's life. Bundles again, old Soviet suitcases.

The same story, familiar props, commented Johanna mentally on the new state of the apartment.

The boy went back to look for his things. He opened the door of the hall cupboard and out of it fell a pair of new felt boots, fastened together.

Familiar geography, thought Johanna, without knowing what to tell him. The boy continued opening doors and pulling out shelves. Then he rummaged in cardboard boxes. Finally he found his clothes in a plywood box.

"New people have moved in here too, like at my house," said Johanna cautiously. "Empty apartments don't exist any more. There are none."

The boy's face was flushed.

Johanna knelt before him and explained: "I know, it isn't fair... but you have to understand the fact. New people are being brought into our country. Every day. And others are being taken away..." She stroked his head. "Do you want to take anything with you to my place?" Johanna paused. "Our place... our home?"

The boy didn't answer. He merely stared bewildered at the unrecognizably changed living-room. His own former bedroom. He had suddenly grown a year older, without growing taller.

*

What's happened, thought the boy. Although it had been nice to wander around, this was his home. Now he would have liked everything to be as before. Mummy busy at the stove and Daddy smoking in the back room. "Let's go," said Auntie Johanna. "There's no point in arguing with the newcomers. They didn't move here on their own initiative."

"I'm not going anywhere, this is my home," he said.

"Since they changed the lock and you climbed in the window, they could call the militia and say that we've broken in and stolen something… We don't need more problems."

"I'll tell them I've lived here six years," he replied.

"The militia won't listen to you. When they find out that your daddy's in jail and your mummy's a wanted person, it will all be over."

Wanted person, he thought – *what's she talking about?* "I'm not going anywhere," he repeated.

Aunt Johanna sighed. "You could have appreciated your home earlier. You don't know how I had to fight for you, to bring you back from Russia."

He looked at Aunt Johanna, not believing her.

"I had to personally beg the head of security to get you sent back," she explained.

She's twisting and lying again, he thought. "It was the nice man who brought me back," declared the boy sternly, "not you."

Aunt Johanna now looked at him a long time and asked: "What nice man? The one that visited Mummy here?"

He noticed Aunt Johanna's expression, which had suddenly become ominously serious.

The boy was silent.

Again I've said something I shouldn't. He kept his mouth resolutely shut and regretted that his tongue slipped so easily. Sometimes the talk came tumbling out faster than he could think.

"Is that the nice man who drives the Pobeda?"

He turned his back on Aunt Johanna and started again rummaging through his old clothes.

"Are you still meeting that nice man that you brought here to Mummy?" Johanna persisted. Aunt Johanna now seemed downright angry.

He thought that he shouldn't bring the man into this any more. He'd promised to be silent.

"No," he said, " – now where are my trousers with braces?"

He continued rooting in the clothes box.

Aunt Johanna didn't seem to hear him, and carried on criticizing.

"All your problems started with that man. Both Mummy and Daddy – and now Mummy's hiding from him."

The boy didn't want to hear his aunt going on any more, and pursued his search: "Where's my peaked cap? Where's my short-sleeved striped shirt? And where are my yellow socks?"

"That nice man destroyed your family. Somebody has to tell you that," he heard Aunt Johanna's raised voice say over his own words.

"… cap, yellow socks," repeated the boy, throwing aside the box. He went to the window and looked out. The man's Pobeda had stood there. He wanted him to come now and take him away.

"There are no informers or traitors in our family," his aunt's voice went on echoing.

The boy pressed his fingers deep into his ears and screamed: "I don't want to listen to you any more! Don't say any more! You're an enemy of the people!" He ran out of the door and slammed it behind him. He felt tears welling in his eyes. It was nice here on the street. The cool air blew against his face. He looked at the woodpile, his bus, and recalled how he had sat here with the man and held the Pobeda's steering-wheel in his hands. That had been a happy day. The man could not be bad. They had listened to the wireless and sung. They had driven past the house and then past a big car and the boy had turned the wheel to the left. There was a prison van in front of the house. Now he could clearly see men in leather jackets jumping out of it.

The boy didn't want to think or remember any more. *Auntie's talk isn't true. The man said I am a hero.* He started striding along the street, but he didn't know where to. Behind him he heard the clacking of Auntie's heels resounding on the evening pavement. He didn't look back.

*

Enemy of the people, thought Johanna. *Fairy tales of the new life…*

How much are we allowed to teach, whose eyes can we open, Johanna wondered. *For with opened eyes you see things you don't need to see. A sighted person doesn't tend to be happier than a blind one.* She watched the boy walking in front of her. Fighting invisible dragons. *Fairy tales are full of evil dragons and fire-breathers. Am I the stepmother, waiting with my poisoned apple?* Johanna sighed. *My apple isn't even poisoned, it's simply sour. Why should I sour the boy's happy naivety if his parents didn't? And now they've vanished without trace. In hiding, in exile, in a camp or dead?*

I should tell the boy that dragons in real life are more fatal than in fairy tales and he has unwittingly become one of them, and a target for others.

Johanna strode along the darkening street after him, not knowing where he was taking them. She was carrying the boy's clothes and his whistle, which he had found in the box. *Is the boy running away again? Is he forgetting everything?*

Who was the heroine in Dostoyevsky's Demons, *who understood nothing in her holy naivety? She stayed alive, for since she didn't understand evil, evil passed her by. Everyone else who saw it perished. But what if the one who doesn't notice evil starts unwittingly destroying others? What can be done? How can she be brought into line?* Johanna didn't know if the boy was beyond her control. The boy and the system that was supporting and destroying him.

She heard the clacking of her own heels, echoing in the emptiness of the darkening street. On the road to Golgotha, at the edge of the universe… *Will the footsteps still echo as hollowly as they do here now?*

*

The sounds in the corridor and the next cells had immobilized the last particle of the woman's will to live.

From time to time reason came from the dark corner of the cell and she calmed down a little.

She sprawled, curled up and addressed the wall: "The boy is pure. We have spared him from all ideological poisons, all state systems, so that nothing would overshadow his childhood. The boy is good, only inquisitive. That is what a child should be." She heard her own voice now and fell silent.

What am I doing? she asked herself. *I'm talking to the wall about the boy. So what if there's a microphone in the wall?*

But I'm not saying anything dangerous, I'm only talking about my pain.

The tin roof gave off an almost visible heat. Here under the roof there was little air and it was burning. She needed to drink. She hadn't had a drink for two days. Or how many? Who could count them?

The dushegubka, the interrogator had said. *Take her to the dushegubka.*

Right at the beginning of the war she had read about the *dushegubka*, the Soviet mobile gas-chamber, like the Nazi Gaswagen, in which lethal exhaust gas was forced inside the cabin while it was being driven. But she had not been taken to a vehicle, but into a covered cell blazing with heat. Was that the nickname of the cell, or was it just a warm-up for the journey? She only knew that it was worse here than in the cupboard. *What will be next?*

Before her mind's eye once again the faces of her interrogators rose like ghosts, merging together and forming a composite image which did not belong to this world.

She rolled on her back and stretched out her legs. The floor scorched her bare legs. She drew her knees up rapidly. She lay as if on desert sand. *Is this what Dante's Hell was like?* The floor

197

was too hot to lie on. But during the day the walls and ceiling were hotter than frying pans. She could have roasted potatoes on them. *My head is a potato,* she thought.

Enough: my life is over, it's past, finished, gone, she mused. *We loved, hoped, fought for independence and lost. Others will come in my place who will carry on fighting.*

The boy is the only reason left to live. But not as an informer. He can't be brought up without dignity. If I lose myself, I can't give anything to anyone else. That's why it's best to let go of life. Again she felt the hands of uniformed men on her body, forcing her back onto the stool. She saw the look of the interrogator, expressing nothing. Only the bloodshot eyes bored into her, with no mercy in them.

Again she heard endless questions, saw different questioning faces, repeating the same thing: Confess!

She could not escape from that repetitive image.

She had known it was bad in prison. But she hadn't known how bad. Who could have guessed? Worse than bad, crueller than cruel, more unjust than that injustice that is defined in the dictionary of correct usage. Or the code of civilization.

Did such a code exist? It was merely lodged in our consciousness, depending on the degree of depravity or the naivety of a good nursery.

On the point of fainting, the images and concepts of reality became fragile and crooked.

Suddenly she became worried that she no longer remembered the boy's face, its precise lines. They became amorphous before her eyes, without finding a final form.

She moved, tried to rise to a sitting position, but her muscles had no strength. Only her heart throbbed. She sprawled out again, turning on her side.

It's best to lose my memory, she thought; *then I can't answer a single question. Let them beat me if they want. Soon I won't feel anything.* She wanted again to be buried in sand dunes. The sun was at its zenith and golden beach sand might be good. The sand scorched her legs, but what of it? Somewhere the

Pobeda 1946

waves of the sea were lapping. Somewhere.

*

The boy was sitting on the leather seat of the Pobeda again. Sitting next to him was not the man, but his mother.

"Stretch out your leg, then you can reach to press the accelerator."

He looked at her, surprised.

"Press the pedal to the floor and drive straight into the sea," she told him.

Indeed the car now sped down the limestone coast, drifted through the sand and plopped into the water. Yet it didn't sink to the bottom or capsize, but remained floating on the surface. He rowed it onwards like a boat, jolting through the crests of waves, moving further and further out to sea.

"Don't look back, speed on towards foreign shores," said Mummy.

However, the boy felt uneasy amid the choppy big waves of the open sea. He pressed the brake and tried to turn around. As they turned, a frothy wave sprayed in through the car window suddenly and carried Mummy off with it.

"Now you'll have to go on alone," shouted Mummy from the foaming waters.

"Mummy, wait!" he shouted, turning the wheel with all his might. He tried to drive after her, but she had vanished without trace into the waves.

"Mummy, Mummy!" cried the boy, sitting up in bed.

The room was dark, and at first he didn't understand where he was. He was pleased that the bed felt warm and dry.

Now Mummy might come back, he thought, lying back down again. He snuggled better under the blanket and turned on his other side. As if hoping that on that side he would dream more peacefully.

*

The man knew that no one knew what he actually felt. Not even he himself knew. He wasn't allowed to feel, and it simply wasn't possible in his job. Mercy and bad conscience were not a part of his profession. Nor for the difficult professions of doctors, firefighters, butchers, dog-catchers and rat-poisoners. All doctors had in their secret compartments of memory a list of patients who died because of medication or wrong diagnosis. All judges had a list of the innocent condemned. Every achievement in history demanded its victims, and when the times changed, the faults could be corrected and the victims posthumously rehabilitated. The man didn't think about what would happen if another power took the place of his, and his head were suddenly on the chopping-block of history. It wasn't worth wasting your nerves on such a thought. You had to serve the power as best you could. Sometimes badly, when it failed.

He wasn't guilty. He had tried to be good. Been charming and attractive. Offered love. Given flowers and chocolates. But they didn't help. The woman had run away. What he couldn't get by being good he had to try by being bad. And he and his team didn't have to do that any more. There was another department for being bad, and they enjoyed being bad. The woman had made her choice. She herself was guilty. But mistakes had occurred even in the bad game. She hadn't withstood heat or pain, cold or sleeplessness.

The man hadn't believed his eyes when he got the report about the woman that morning. Died under interrogation. Corpse liquidated. This was not how he had planned it. But his colleagues had overstrained her or incorrectly assessed the state of health of the accused, her reserves of strength, hunger for life. The operation had been drawn out and the patient died.

The woman's decease had been unexpectedly quick. She

had been more fragile than the others. A true snowdrop.

He took a hasty look at the woman's file, as if hoping to find something in it. But there was nothing. The system had done its work. He felt a sudden desire for a smoke and fished a packet of cigarettes from his pocket, but it was empty. He crumpled it up and threw it in the waste-paper basket.

*

Here on Freedom Square there was no more freedom, though there was still space, thought Johanna. Freedom is a relative concept, isn't it? Freedom Square had become Victory Square. From the window of the Kultas café the other side of the square was graced by the façades of the Palace Hotel and the Gloria Palace cinema. Johanna would have liked to watch some Hollywood film, but those were no longer shown here. A handful of people had made revolution on this square too, with support from Soviet agitators and armoured cars. The square was empty now, idling in its mediocre midday quietness.

This outward peace was in contrast to Johanna's internal disquiet, just as before a performance. When the heart is beating fast, the face has changed to an expectant mask. Instead of the words of songs, Johanna was repeating Alan's thoughts. Unknown tactics, learned by heart. It was important to do it convincingly. The audience mustn't be allowed to notice the actress's fear. Nor should the major-general. Over and over again she repeated Alan's thoughts in her head.

The major-general arrived punctually, as soon as the hand of the clock had passed the full hour. There was dignity in the man's posture, heaviness in his step. His shirt collar was unbuttoned and his tie evidently in his pocket. *What else is he hiding in his pocket,* thought Johanna anxiously and summoned a smile to her face, emphasizing a friendly distance. The major-general greeted her graciously and took a seat on the other side of the coffee table.

"Are you glad about the boy?" he asked triumphantly by way of introduction.

"Very. I thank you from my heart." Johanna manifested her gratitude and thought: *Straight away we submit to favours and debts of gratitude.*

"So what's new in your life?" asked the general with the same friendliness.

As if he didn't know, thought Johanna, and replied: "And my little ship landed in the harbour of marriage too… and I have new neighbours. I might have to move to my husband's home and free up some living space." Johanna now looked at the general with an inquiring gaze.

"That would be a shame," replied the major-general with unfeigned surprise. "Who will sing Tatyana for us?"

"There are plenty of young Tatyanas," replied Johanna, feigning tiredness, trying to downplay her worth; "I should sing Tatyana's mother, Madam Larina, or retire."

Now the major-general raised his eyebrows, shook his head with a grin and raised an admonitory finger.

This man is at least chivalrous, thought Johanna, broadening the smile on her lips.

"You should carry on singing Tatyana, on whatever stage, and bring honour to our musical culture."

Yes, keep on dancing and singing to your tune, thought Johanna, extending her hand.

"Let me go and I'll be eternally grateful to you. I'll praise your –" she coughed – "*our* land and music."

The major-general's gaze grew sterner, but the smile did not vanish from his lips.

"It depends on your work – what obligations you take on."

Johanna made herself look even more candid, downright beseeching. "Let me go as a free person, without contracts, without obligations." She tried to anticipate the general's offer, so as not to create an embarrassing situation, to avoid a No. "I'm only a singer. I can't think strategically, or conspire. I won't become an employee. Only a friend." Johanna nailed her pleading look to the major-general's eyes. But the minister of security's look was not softened by this. He silently shook his head.

"It doesn't work that simply."

Now I'll have to use Alan's strategy, she decided. *There's nothing left but to go on the attack.*

She straightened her back and said: "My husband promised to ring you; he told me to ask you if you'd like to give an interview."

The major-general's expression grew imperceptibly more serious. "I don't give interviews. That's why we have intergovernmental press staff."

"Alan wanted just to talk to you. About us. The east-west alliance. Family reunification and problems associated with that. To make it an everyday news story."

Now Johanna had thrown the gloves off, and the general had noticed that. War had been declared.

Johanna didn't change her expression or betray emotion, but continued: "Your name will be famous in the international press. The BBC is listened to all over the world, maybe even by Comrade Stalin."

"I'd leave the fame to you, and I wouldn't invoke Comrade Stalin's name." An icy tone had come into the major-general's voice.

Johanna pretended not to notice it. "Why not," she replied. "The BBC has reflected us – their ally in the war – well."

"Recently that radio station has been very hostile towards us."

Now we're on a collision course, thought Johanna, letting her face express indignation.

"Then maybe Comrade Stalin wouldn't like it if the BBC repeats your name every day. Being conspicuous may also be dangerous." Johanna paused briefly and furrowed her brow thoughtfully. "If we think of Marshal Zhukov now…"

The major-general's face was now stiff. No smile relaxed his cheeks any more.

"You're drawing premature and dangerous conclusions. I will not be blackmailed. I'm not afraid of a hostile propaganda station." The head of security was calling Johanna to order. "Don't forget that I'm a decorated major-general."

But Johanna did not retreat from the front line.

"Your name might influence diplomatic relations and the reputation of the Soviet Union. To escape the annoying international news, it will be easier for the system to sacrifice you." Johanna paused theatrically. "Yes, you'll be given one more medal and then sent on your way, to join many of your predecessors. No one can know the reactions of Comrades Stalin and Beria."

A waitress with a preoccupied face and wispy hair had arrived at their table. "What can I get you?" she asked sternly, wiping the table with a wet cloth and unwittingly spoiling their battle.

Johanna turned her rather strained face to her. "One coffee with cream, please," she said charmingly, and turned her gaze back on the major-general.

The major-general took an ostentatious look at his wristwatch and took out his wallet. "I'll pay for the citizen's coffee, but I must go now." He placed a five-rouble note in the waitress's tray and got up.

"Honourable Comrade Minister," said Johanna, remaining seated sphinx-like in her chair. "Nobody wants war. There are no winners in war, only losers."

The major-general gave her an ironic look and turned around.

"Especially if something were to happen to me…" Johanna's words hung in the air behind him.

When the major-general had left the café, Johanna cast a glance at the big mirrors on its wall. She didn't know whether she had just signed her own death sentence. Here, in her favourite café.

Once before the war, when she had got caught in an

unexpected rainstorm, they brought her a famous Kultas morning-coat. Just while her jacket was being dried and ironed. At the same time she could browse in the international press. Here she could freshen up with coffee and freshen her foreign language skills with newspaper articles. She liked fresh poppy-seed buns and fresh political news. The approach of war was understandable in all languages, like a familiar opera libretto.

Now, however, it was constantly raining, there were no longer any foreign papers, the newspaper *Uus Eesti* (New Estonia) now bore the name *Rahva Hääl* (Voice of the People) and nobody ironed the customers' clothes here in the café any more.

*

The major-general's thoughts were a little unsettled. He knew that he must not let himself get confused. Not even when his honour had been wounded. Especially when he had not been shown the respect to which his rank entitled him from everyone else. He was not used to civilians threatening him. That a foreign radio station would ring his secret work number. Just as well that his secretary had answered. But they would certainly ring again. He should change the number. No-one could be trusted. Not even his own staff. Not even the operations section could protect him.

The major-general was not an emotional man. And yet, in his youth, his face had always gone red when he got angry. Not any more now, in golden middle age, when all colours were tinged with the yellow of early autumn. Or rather, the gold, like the medals on the chest of his parade uniform.

The major-general meditated on whether he should give the order to liquidate Johanna.

We needn't even arrest her. We could use chemicals from

Laboratory X in Moscow, to make it look like a natural death, leaving no traces. But what if the foreign radio blames me by name for the singer's death? There's only one head of security with a major-general's epaulettes in the Estonian SSR, and that's me. Reactions from the Kremlin, though, were always unpredictable.

No, thought the major-general, *especially if they're playing the missing Johanna's songs on air. That way the liquidation of one single enemy would take on musical proportions. I'm not going to offer that pleasure to the melodramatic minds of opera lovers. I have other local cultural figures to settle scores with, and foreign radio won't go on the attack against me for them.*

The major-general knew that even war heroes, the victors, had been arrested after returning home, generals had been demoted and removed from their positions. Nobody knew what could anger Stalin, upset his mood. In that sense the singer was right. The general knew that the *Хозяйн* skilfully played everyone against each other like chess pieces[*] ... and then Check! Checkmate! At a stroke he eliminated those who made a fuss, rocked the system or drew too much attention to themselves.

If the hostile BBC radio really were to start calling him by name, it might be fatal for him. The Soviet system didn't tolerate criticism.

In order to achieve an advantage in negotiations, you always had to make concessions. In order to get economic aid, new loans or territorial advantage, you had to constantly wash enemies and prisoners clean, nourish them, dress them up and send them back home... or exchange them for your own people beyond the border. For yesterday's enemy may become tomorrow's ally, and *vice versa*. Even the opium of the people, religion, had been exhumed at times during the war and taken out of its coffin, to please the Americans before the Teheran conference. Later the clerics were put back in their coffins and laid to rest... and yet! The major-general knew this better than others. He had been a cadre working abroad and had heard the Kremlin clocks striking at close range. Even Estonia was the 'near abroad' for Moscow. A border buffer zone, which had to be quickly appropriated.

Stalin was unpredictable. Even Beria could make nervous unexpected decisions. The Master had once said: "A KGB operative has two paths: promotion or prison." Since he was already the minister, there were few alternatives. A threat from a British spy and his singer accomplice had to be considered seriously.

Everything was changing all the time, so that no-one could feel at ease. Divide and rule, always. The acronym NKGB had been changed overnight into MGB, the ministry of state security, and he had unobtrusively become its minister. A few years ago he had started as a member of the NKVD. Not only the names of streets changed, but also the institutions where he worked, and their composition. Changes of bosses came with every new wave from Moscow. Fortunately those breakers had not crashed on these shores yet. The names changed, but the work stayed the same.

The major-general opened Johanna's file and leafed through the entries. It was time for rearguard action.

"Correspondence of a dubious nature..." he read. "Sister refused to collaborate, died under interrogation..." *Senseless story. That major didn't deserve a new Pobeda. Just drove around tooting.* The major-general had overestimated him. The head of the operations department had failed at the job of surveillance, letting the singer travel to Moscow unnoticed, to form a professional alliance with an enemy alien. *He could have neutralized the singer earlier. Instead he wasted time on her sister and her family. And on the little brat too. A cadre like that is fit only for the kindergarten.*

The major-general sank into thought. If he now acceded to the singer's ultimatum, Moscow might once again accuse him of losing a potential agent.

He took a fountain-pen and made a note in the file: "Following the performance by the singer A.L. in a BBC radio broadcast, and considering her close relations with an employee of the radio station, it seems risky to send her as our agent to London, where she might come under the scrutiny of the British secret service."

He read the note over again, half-opening his mouth at every word, and then made a correction in ink: "Under the watch of the MI6 secret service."

But if they ask why the opportunity was ruled out at the right time...? Who is to blame? Why was a possible new informer let out of our hands? The major-general furrowed his brow. In that case he could refer to serious flaws in the work of the operative.

The major-general looked for a decree form in the drawer of his desk and wrote on it: "Charge of violating the rules on conspiracy." He raised his eyes from the paper and thought for a moment.

The chief of the operations department may be charged with excessive personal ambitions, failure to pass on evidence to the appropriate instance, neglecting the opportunity to prepare an operation at the appropriate time – what else? He let the fountain pen scratch over the smooth paper: "Charge of spending money without appropriate sanction, wasting funds assigned to the department, misuse of operational technology."

A scapegoat had been found. One always had to be found, they always existed. The major-general decided that someone had to pay for his humiliation.

What times these are, he thought, *when the country's leading officials have to worry about their reputations. You can never know whose head will be on the chopping-block next. How hard it is to work when you have a bad cadre and you have to constantly fear losing the Master's favour.* "Radio," he grunted gruffly between his lips; "in the old days it was newspapers, now it's radio. What will they threaten us with tomorrow?"

*

Alan was rearranging the furniture. It was difficult to shift anything from its place, where it had stood for half a century. Used to its own place. Leaving ineradicable traces of itself on the floor or walls.

His new Soviet wedding ring had got stuck behind the bedside table, but that had not dimmed his love.

But it was strange to look at his own hand.

Alan wiped the sweat from his brow with his sleeve and looked around anxiously. A double bed didn't seem to fit in this room. *Or should I give up the chest of drawers? No, that is a Hepplewhite piece, a memento of my grandfather,* he decided. *Or the card-table? But Johanna loves playing bridge. She might even take up patience here alone if we don't find work for her.*

Alan had counted up the numbers that were easier to separate than join. It was always like this with finance. A plus sign broke down easily into two minuses. It might be difficult financially: a wife and perhaps a school-aged step-child. Alan struck out his bottom lip and blew air up into his nose. But it was too late for regrets, and he didn't want any regrets. The excitement of Johanna's possible imminent arrival stifled all his worries and fears.

It was so good to be rid of his bachelor life before his brain went soft and his strength deserted his muscles. Before his position and status would no longer be of any concern.

The antique wall-clock in the corner began to chime. Alan pricked up his ears and added up the hours. Rearranging the furniture had already taken up the whole afternoon. Now the home improvements required some purchases before the shops closed their doors. And his wallet had to be opened. Alan screwed up his nose at the thought, but eventually he would have to get used to the new reality. *For whom am I saving money?* Now the opportunity to spend a little money, to enjoy life was opening up. It was easier to do that with Johanna.

Alan knew that his lucky moment had arrived. Never mind what he thought or how much he grumbled. This was the woman he was waiting for, longing for, in love with. He had always loved her, without admitting his feelings to himself. And only a tiny impulse like the Second World War or the Iron Curtain was needed to make him realize that simple fact. That was how it was with him. A little slow to sort out his feelings and take action.

He could live with Johanna through opera libretti. Feel like Don Giovanni or Mephisto. Johanna had called him by all the names of legendary male heroes and looked at him fondly. *So that look will not fade, her smile will never be dimmed.* This was the only thing in the world that had a concrete value to Alan at the moment. He had left Johanna detailed instructions on how to talk to the general. But he didn't know if that would suffice.

That's enough meditating, Alan decided. *Still, I could buy the boy a school satchel. A stepchild's pleasure is reflected mainly in the stepmother's eyes.*

*

The boy was striding at a rapid pace towards town. Auntie had said that the writer man had been ar-res-ted. That meant: got into trouble. Was that because of what the boy told the man? Was it because of the mother-of-pearl cars? Or only because he was an enemy of the people? Was Auntie telling the truth? Was it true?

The boy's steps were longer today than usual, but Pikk Street still lived up to its name 'Long'.

He had been searching for the Pobeda man since visiting the apartment on Narva Road, but nobody had opened the door after he rang the bell. Yet the boy had glimpsed the flash of a shadow in the eye of the door and had given another long buzz of the bell. Finally a strange man had appeared at the door and said that today wasn't the right day. And it wasn't the right one, but the questions wouldn't leave the boy in peace. He didn't want to wait until tomorrow. The boy remembered the man's workplace, where he had been taken after he had run away from Auntie's place. It was a large house on the corner of Pikk Street. Not far from here.

He spelled out the name of a house on the corner of a narrow cross-street: PAGARI. *Hmm, 'Baker' – maybe they bake cakes here as well,* he thought. They had driven to the yard of this house in the Pobeda. There must be a gate somewhere. He walked around the house and found the gate on Lai Street. Now it was closed. He pressed his face against the iron lattice and peeped inside the gate between the bars. He saw the familiar Pobeda and behind it a big prison van. It seemed to him that he had seen that big van somewhere before too. *Wasn't it in front of my own house?* it occurred to him. *On that first ride with the man?* He felt a lump in his throat and swallowed it. "Bus driver, keep your eyes on the road, look straight ahead!" the man had said. Hazily he recalled the men in leather jackets who jumped out of that van. "The Black Raven", Aunt Johanna had explained; "they travel around in vans picking up people who are fighting for the independence of the Estonian state... Those are our heroes." But the boy was a hero too, and he was even riding in a Pobeda. *Why are those two vehicles standing side by side here in the yard?*

"All your problems started with that man. With both Daddy and Mummy," he recalled Aunt Johanna saying.

"Your aunt has a secret that you don't know about yet," the man had said.

The boy no longer understood who was good and who was bad. Even in fairy tales there were good and bad fairies. People like Clever Hans, who was cunning, and the People Under the Stove of Estonian folklore, who told lies. In real life, though, everything had got hopelessly confused. The boy tried to work out who was telling the truth. *Is the man being cunning, or is*

Auntie lying? Who is a hero and who is an enemy of the people? Can one man's hero be another one's traitor?

The boy surveyed the prison van again and strained his memory. The men jumping out of the prison van now came back clearly into his mind, running toward his house. Then his crying mother as he stepped inside the door. *Were those two images mixed up? Like a complicated fairy tale that you don't understand at all at first? Where good fairies turn into bad witches?*

His head was getting sweaty. There were too many conflicting thoughts, and he didn't know where the truth lay. *What was Auntie's secret, what was the man's important, top-secret job?* "Your mother is in hiding from that man," Auntie had said. Everyone was saying things to confuse him. No-one wanted him to be on the track of the truth.

He watched the prison van again through the metal bars. Something bad came into his mind. He wanted to talk to the driver of the prison van. But the van seemed empty. Nobody was sitting in it. *I have to find the Pobeda man*, he determined.

The boy made another circuit around the house and found an entrance, but sitting at the guard's desk was a grim-faced man the boy didn't know.

"What's your business," asked the man suspiciously – "and who with?"

"The Pobeda man," said the boy. Funny, but he didn't know the man's name. Then he thought of Anna, the lady who had taken him to the Muraste children's home and to the Moscow train.

"Anna," he corrected himself; "she works with the Pobeda man."

The guard grabbed a telephone and rang someone. He ordered the boy to wait.

Soon the boy heard familiar steps on the stairs. The Pobeda man was approaching him as if smiling, and yet with a furrowed brow.

"I'm in a big hurry. What's the problem, bus driver?"

"I wanted to ask," stammered the boy, "whether my father is a hero or an enemy of the people?"

The man froze for a moment. "Didn't your Daddy ever explain it to you?" he replied, raising his eyebrows.

The boy shook his head.

"Then there's one more puzzle to solve," said the man in a cheery voice, but a strange glint had come into his eyes.

"You said my Daddy went to Russia."

"I don't know your Daddy. Maybe he did," the man replied. "Many people went, even you went there…" The man stared at the boy for a moment and then raised his briefcase under his arm. "Now I have to go. Can I drop you somewhere in the Pobeda?"

The boy shook his head. *I don't want to ride in the Pobeda any more,* he decided.

"It's better if you don't come to this house alone. We can meet on Narva Road," said the man almost reproachfully as he rushed out of the back door.

The boy fell into thought. He watched the man going. The guard eyed him with a surly gaze. The boy turned around and went out of the street door. Outside it had started to rain. He started striding back along Pikk Street. Now his steps were not so long. The street, too, had become shorter and more slippery. He seemed to have lost something. *Even the man won't tell me the truth.* Something bad had happened. As if someone else had gone away. Suddenly he felt very much alone.

From behind him the man's Pobeda drove past, spraying water from its tyres. *What a horrible car,* thought the boy.

No one can be trusted any more. I'll have to find Daddy and Mummy. Ask them.

*

"Auntie Johanna," said the boy, fingering his ear lobe, "I can't come to London with you now."

"Why, may I ask?" asked Johanna in a surprised voice.

"I have to wait for my Mummy and Daddy."

What's this? thought Johanna. *The leaving blues? Of course it's hard to leave your parents' home.*

Johanna bent down to the boy and took him by the shoulder. "But you know, darling, that I can only take you with me. Your Daddy's in a camp somewhere in Russia, and your Mummy won't be let out of the country. I don't even know if they'll let me go to England."

The boy's face was still sulky.

I have to turn this song into a major key, thought Johanna. "Believe me, you'll get to like London. Big houses and plenty of splendid cars. You've never travelled in an aeroplane before."

For a moment a sparkle came into the boy's eyes. Then he sank back into a sulk.

"But when they come home, we'll both be gone. Without saying goodbye."

"They went without saying goodbye too." Johanna reminded the boy of the sad fact.

But the boy seemed oppressed by something heavy. *The burden of guilt?* thought Johanna.

"You're not to blame that they went away. You acted without wanting to, without knowing…" she said in an assured tone.

"Yes, I am to blame," said the boy, with downcast eyes.

I shouldn't have told him about all this, Johanna thought regretfully, taking him by the hand.

"Let's go and sit on the sofa and talk it over." *Now that I've wrestled with a thousand devils,* thought Johanna.

"If you don't like it in London," – Johanna was beginning a new libretto – "you can come back to Tallinn."

"I would like to ride in a Jaguar… once."

"Yes," agreed Johanna, adding grandly: "That's a much more valuable car than a Pobeda."

Boys and their cars, she thought. *What do they see in a means of transport? It will be good for me to be with him in London, play the choral conductor, when Alan's at work,* she pondered. *But I'm leaving my audience, my friends… even though most of them have vanished… At least I have the boy.*

*

Simon had grabbed the old-fashioned telephone receiver and conveyed an order: "Exchange! Connect me to the head of the Russian Service."*

His gaze looked toward the future, though his feet were crossed on the carpet of a floor from the colonial past.

Alan was seated in a deep Victorian armchair in Simon's office, where he couldn't move.

"Hello! When are you going to recruit more staff for your department?" breathed Simon into the receiver, now in a much gentler tone. "I have a good candidate for you. Clear diction, speaks several languages…"

As he watched Simon's nodding head and waving left arm, the images of Simon and Johanna merged before Alan's eyes, as they both loved to gesticulate while talking. Not just with one hand, but with both. She extended them slowly as if singing on a theatre stage.

She'd have to go through a training course in not waving her hands, not rustling her papers. In learning the specific BBC manner of speaking. But would she want to learn to do all that? As a singer she would hardly be able to find work here. Maybe only in an operatic choir. And being at home would soon bore her…

Simon listened patiently to the beeps coming from the

receiver and added cheerily: "I'll send the application. I'll make my own recommendation."

Alan sighed. *Poor Johanna. From one secretive world to another. Or maybe only half-secretive. They say that Soviet citizens can't live without Soviet power. It will crush their spirits if someone isn't eavesdropping on them or tailing them.* Here Alan could offer Johanna in return some invisibly vibrating wavelengths in the radio war, a different kind of ideological battle. So even the historically crushed Estonia was sending one of its own singers over to combat the ideology here.

Simon put the receiver in its cradle and threw his head back self-consciously.

"The timing is very good, old boy." He paused and winked suggestively. "And I can't call you 'old boy' any more… In any case they are planning to expand the department. Of course they'll want to see Johanna first. Do background checks. She'd have to do some tests."

Simon beamed his benevolent smile at Alan: "We can't let her be a burden on your salary."

"But if the KGB recruits her before she leaves?" asked Alan.

Simon spread his arms nonchalantly: "Then we recruit her back. You'll have a double agent for a wife. Double the salary!" Simon let out a gust of chesty laughter.

Alan wasn't in a laughing mood. He was imagining Johanna's amazed face. Her brow furrowed with worry. "You mean to say it's so simple…"

Simon got up from his armchair and rubbed his hands. "If she's no good for the big microphone, with her pretty voice she can be a radio operator, a contact for the Forest Brothers. In their dark bunker burrows they're sure to enjoy hearing a familiar timbre from the stage of the *Estonia.*"

Alan was feeling bad. He stared at the worn pattern of the Persian carpet before the toes of his shoes. A relic from the fading British empire.

"Johanna's an intelligent woman. She knows a few foreign languages, she might be good…" he said.

"Of course, of course," interjected Simon. "We'll find an opening for her. She will be a new star in the local émigré community… if she has the right mentality."

Mentality! Thought Alan, raising his eyes indignantly. "Simon, please don't forget that they have the same mentality as we do. For twenty years they've been a part of our friendly zone. Before the war the Tallinn passport checkpoint was one of our Baltic intelligence centres. Why should I, a civilian, have to explain that to you, with your military intelligence background?"

"I know, I know" – Simon silenced his arguments. "The Balts are reliable and decent. They just can't co-operate among themselves."

And what am I needed for? thought Alan anxiously. *If the Russians recruit Johanna and MI6 sets about converting her, then my life will be put in danger too. I'll be pushed in front of a Russian tank. If Soviet intelligence gets a whiff of all this, they might want to replace their disobedient informer. Maybe with her spouse… Unintended damage. A car accident in unclear circumstances, an unexplained fire…*

He had told Johanna: "Don't let them recruit you. Say that you're just a singer. That you know nothing about politics. That you have a poor memory." *Of course, Security would never believe that. Otherwise how would a singer learn her lines by heart for three-act operas?* He had rung the major-general's number himself, but only spoken to the secretary. He hoped Johanna had won the duel. Alan didn't know what compromises would be demanded of her. How great was her desire to get to the free world, or how great was her love for Alan? Was it great enough to leave the Soviet Union as an intelligence agent? Alan didn't believe so. Johanna had been open with him. As open as women can be. He had never fully understood a woman's inner world, it was true. Now the schoolroom of private life lay before him.

Alan turned his face thoughtfully to the window. Towards freshly watered summer greenery. A damp, fine rain had begun to fall. The sun had just been shining, and now... How quickly the weather changed. Climates and alliances, how quickly they changed.

*

There was a knock on Johanna's door. At the door stood a stiff-looking girl in a grey outfit whom she had never seen before.

"There is a wish to talk with you. Would it be possible for you to come outside for a few minutes?"

"Is there a wish to arrest me?"

"No. It's only a friendly conversation, which won't take more than half an hour. Get dressed and don't worry."

Johanna put her shoes on with trembling hands and put a jacket on her shoulders. She wanted to take her handbag with her.

The girl watched her every movement like a hawk.

"There's no need to take anything except keys."

Johanna silently followed the unknown girl.

A beige Pobeda was parked in front of the house. The rear door opened and the major-general stepped out of it.

"A pleasure to see you. I was missing you, and I thought I'd take a little walk in Kadriorg Park with a pretty lady for company."

He took Johanna by the hand and directed her toward the pond.

"I've been thinking about your request," continued the major-general in a hushed tone. "I'll let you go, but only if you behave like a Soviet citizen and don't blacken my good name or that of my country."

He squeezed Johanna's hand and looked her in the eye.

"Do you promise me that?"

Johanna smiled, feeling relieved, and summoned up her friendliest expression.

"Naturally I do. If you let me leave in peace, I will remain your admirer and friend."

The major-general led her closer to the pond, where a fountain was murmuring.

His gaze turned to a white swan in the middle of the pond.

"Look, what a beautiful bird. Such a shame that it's alone." The major-general's voice was now hard to hear; it was muffled by the sound of the fountain.

"Just yesterday there were two of them here. You see, it can happen even with birds."

He leaned in very close to Johanna and said in a soft voice: "But if you mention my name on the air, in émigré circles or to English intelligence, you too might disappear unnoticed. If you do that, it will reach me. Believe me, all the intelligence services are interlinked. They know what's happening here. We know what goes on there." He paused a little and let his eyes roam over the park. "We have our own people in London too. Everywhere. And something unexpected might happen to you. You'll be quite accidentally hit by a car. You'll be struck by an unexplained bout of illness. To say nothing of the troubles that will befall your relatives and friends here. You understand me, don't you?"

Johanna looked at him intently.

He continued: "You don't even have to answer me. This talk between us never happened. We were simply taking a walk in Kadriorg Park in summer. Do you promise me?"

Johanna nodded. "That means you'll simply let me go?"

"How can you deny love," said the major-general almost chivalrously, directing her to turn around. They started walking back toward home.

Is there really some hope, she thought.

"Not all operas have to end tragically. Come tomorrow to the Passport section, where you will get your exit pass. Bring with you two photographs and your Soviet passport."

"Thank you," said Johanna. "And you'll let my boy go too?"

The major-general stopped for a moment.

"I can't authorize that. You aren't his mother."

Are the problems starting again, Johanna reflected anxiously. "But he is now my foster-child."

The major-general looked at her almost regretfully. "Only a temporary foster-child. An exit permit for the child would require the parents' permission. It's a complicated procedure. If you ever get all the agreements and the necessary documents, you can make an application." The major-general added with feigned friendliness: "You can apply by letter later as well."

If only my sister would turn up now, thought Johanna, and asked: "Is there any news of my brother-in-law?"

The major-general shook his head. "I wouldn't worry or trouble my head right now about anybody else. I recommend you not to get involved with other people's destinies and offences. Worry about yourself. I can't do any more for you."

"But I'll need the agreement of the child's father," Johanna persisted.

"If the child's father is an enemy of the people and imprisoned, the mother's agreement is enough. But it's a time-consuming procedure." He lowered his voice. "Don't delay now. Your own situation isn't certain. I'm doing all this only because I'm an admirer of your talent."

Is he threatening or flattering? wondered Johanna, sizing up the general with her eyes. "Tomorrow I'll bring with me one of my records with a dedication to you."

The major-general tightened his grip on Johanna's hand.

"Don't write a dedication. It'll be etched in my memory. But don't forget that all this is based on our mutual promises alone. Everything can always change in life. As they say, the world is small."

Johanna swallowed. *What to do with the boy? How to find my sister?* One door had opened and another closed.

They walked arm in arm in the depths of the vernal park, and from afar one might get the impression that they were bosom friends or a loving couple.

*

For the man too, the time had come to bid farewell to the house. He let his eye wander slowly over the walls, ceiling and door-lock of his office. The door had again been opened and unexpectedly closed behind his back.

He wondered how he had been left out of the game, or rather, lost control of it. He had followed the British agent's correspondence with the singer, and yet he had been unable to decipher the codes in their letters or radio broadcasts. Maybe Johanna had a transmitter after all or they used an unknown messenger. There had been no use for informers either. The woman had not taken on the work, and the housing administration had made a mistake, placing the wrong people in the singer's house. The new settler Quandyk had nothing suspicious or relevant to say about the singer. The arrested writer didn't know, or didn't say, anything.

Sending the boy away had been a mistake. Through him the man might have discovered something earlier.

Everything had happened too fast. Cho-Cho-San had slipped out of his sight and married her Lieutenant Pinkerton in Moscow. The general had taken over the case and pushed him aside, and even taken the Pobeda away from him. Was his error so great that he had to be sacrificed? The system he had served so eagerly had now cast him out. The man understood that the system spares no one. He had received a decree dismissing him from the service. More exactly, he had been shunted on to inter-institutional work. As always, as the director of some hotel or school. He had not even been demoted to a sub-unit of the on-board KGB railway service. Once again life had led him to the wrong side of the tracks, and now the big trains were passing him by. He should have been passing on correspondence to the counter-intelligence department. He didn't have sufficiently trained staff. Only stupid operatives. And Anna. The baton had to be passed on.

Now that girl could become someone else's nuisance.

The man knew of the purges in the ranks of the party and security services. He had heard what happened to the first generation of revolutionaries, even members of the Politburo. False complaints were written about everyone; everyone could be slandered and betrayed. Everyone could obstruct everyone else's path. Somehow the man had thought that this wouldn't happen to him, that times had changed. *But does human nature change, does the system change?* He closed his eyes and let a film of the future run rapidly before them. He tried to see again what he had seen before. An ever-improving network, ever more reliable security measures, microphones, cameras, telephone lines… but the film started to crackle, the frames to jump, the images got distorted. The film in the camera caught fire, the fire made ever-growing yellow blotches on the black and white celluloid. The man knew that what had happened to many of his predecessors was now happening to him. Accusers had become the accused, prison guards were prisoners. Suddenly he knew that no-one would escape the fire unsinged. He turned off the camera in his eyes. He no longer wanted to see the future. There was something ominous now about that happy vision of the future.

He opened his eyes and pulled open his desk drawer. As if wishing to check whether anything of his was left in there. Evidence, dangerous references. But the drawer was empty. He closed it again, took his coat off the peg and left the office without looking back. He passed through the secretary's adjoining room. As always, Anna wasn't there.

He left the office, took a few steps along the corridor and stopped. A heretical thought occurred to him. To see that room of which no one here ever spoke. The place where many interrogation victims came to the end of the road. Previously he hadn't wanted to see it. He was an operative. He was just fulfilling his duty. He talked, persuaded, lured, forbade, provoked, imprisoned, dispatched, recruited… His work was restricted to words, to papers. His hands were clean. He tried to do everything for the best. And yet even he was being dispatched from here. At least on his own feet. He wanted to feel better than the rest just one more time.

He turned from the corridor onto a little staircase which led to the basement. He passed the execution room, the former military gas shelter, whose wall was pock-marked with bullets. He walked along the badly lit basement corridor and wanted to see the room where the woman, or what remained of her, had been taken.

He opened the door and looked into the secret chamber of the basement at a large pulverizing machine which had a powerful electric motor to grind up finely everything that was thrown into it. Up on the ceiling was a hatch from which material was cast down directly into the jaws of the pulverizer. The ground-up material descended into a concrete tub over two metres long, to which lime and water were added. *I wonder, was this machine actually invented?* he thought. He cast a glance up at the hatch, which was now closed. The operator of the machine was out on his lunch-break or having a smoke.

The woman's last journey would have been through here. *Was this better or worse than burning to ashes in a crematorium or decaying in a common grave?* He stared at the effluent channel on the floor. But there was not even a trace of lime in it. The meat-grinder had done its work. You couldn't keep hauling corpses out of the security building in the middle of town. This was practical, a necessity of life. If the living disappeared, then so did the dead. History would be silent about this. *I have to keep moving,* he thought; it wasn't his business to dissect his own feelings or the methods of the system. *It isn't my task to explain them either to myself or to the world outside.*

He had to forget this building now and start dreaming about something else. The smoking break had passed without a smoke, or the smell of it. Memories, too, dissolved in the air like the non-existent smoke. He felt a secret satisfaction in the fact that he was free to leave this building himself, and close the door behind him. He was still privileged. He belonged to

Ilmar Taska

the elect, he was serving a system, subject to orders, obeying commands. He was not embittered. He mustn't be. For otherwise the burden of the system's actions would have been his to carry.

It was time to bend his steps toward a new posting. *Director of the Pioneers' Palace – that job title doesn't sound too bad.* He faced new challenges, new tasks, boys and girls in Pioneer scarves. It was for him to organize the move to the new building on Veetorni Street. As part of the secret operations department he had had plenty to do with children. Now there was a use for his experience in his new job.

His imagination fled, against his will, back to the future, where children's faces were reflected back from bright screens, large and small, opposite which they would sit, or which they would carry with them. They would raise them before their eyes and put them to their ears. They would confide to those glowing screens their great and small secrets. He, however, would sit in the Centre in his clean, spacious air-conditioned room behind a huge bright screen and see and hear everything. Monitoring them all. He wouldn't need to get up, or sit in the Pobeda any more, or hunt anyone down in the street. He looked at the boot key of the Pobeda. Even that had to be handed over. No doubt he would be buying another decent car, bypassing the queue and by order of the Director of the Pioneers' Palace. Series production of the new Moskvich was expected as soon as next year.

*

I can't leave the boy alone here, thought Johanna, knowing at the same time that she couldn't take him without her sister's permission. She wet her upper lip with her tongue. How long must she wait? "I shouldn't delay leaving," the major-general had said. Johanna had left messages for her sister, but she

224

couldn't officially search for her.

I wonder if she got caught, was arrested? – the mad thought went through her head. *Hardly* – Johanna nipped that suspicion in the bud. *She was wearing my dark wig, my clothes. She wouldn't be recognized.*

Was the general telling the truth, pondered Johanna, *is the parents' consent really necessary? Or does he want to keep the boy as a pawn so that I won't dare to say anything about him in England?* She frowned. She understood that the general was only letting her out thanks to her threat, Alan's strategy. *Otherwise he would arrest me straight away.*

Johanna rubbed her temples, as if it helped to improve her mental activity. *How good it would be now to consult Alan. Perhaps the boy really could be sent for from London? At least one of us would be out.* Alan had said something about the Red Cross. It should be possible, through that organization, to apply for reunification of family members. *Does the Soviet Union respect the Red Cross? Or any cross at all? The Cross of Christ and the Star of David were buried long ago.*

Johanna wasn't sure of anything. But she had to act, move forward. She couldn't stay here any longer. The noose seemed to be tightening. First her brother-in-law, now Villem the writer. By marrying a foreigner had she automatically become a traitor, and a foreign agent as well? She knew that if she stayed here for the boy's sake, her connection with Alan would be broken and the general would certainly pay her back for the threat. As she came away from the passport desk, some man in a grey dust-coat had followed her. Even as she looked back at her front door she had spied him further down the street. He didn't even try to hide. *They'll give me a sign openly, terrorise me for a few days.* She felt like a weightless being, hovering between two worlds.

Will they trust me on the other side? Or will the London police tail me as well? Have I become an alien everywhere? Lost the care of all the gods? Anxious thoughts circulated in her head.

In London now I'll become an immigrant. A new settler.

She looked at the boy playing with his kaleidoscope in the corner of the room. *Who could look after him until his mother turns up?* All Johanna's friends were bohemians. They all gave birth only to works of art. They had all served only their muses, as she had. Of course there were some proper family people among them too. *For example…* Johanna pondered. Nobody came to mind. Individual people had individual friends, unmarried people kept company with unmarried people, parents with other parents. She belonged to the first group, even though her marital status had changed and she was now a temporary foster-parent. *Temporary, really?* Johanna knew she would be doing everything possible in London to make it permanent.

Such choices, thought Johanna, glancing into the next room. A heart-rending pentatonic song could be heard from there. The boy had taken up his tin whistle and was trying to imitate the oriental melody coming from behind the door.

"As soon as Mummy arrives, you'll tell her everything," said Johanna, turning to the boy, "and you'll start filling in papers so that you can come after me – do you promise?"

The boy nodded. "But before that I want to look for Daddy."

She didn't know how to answer. Nobody knew where to look for him. Was there even any use in looking? Men rarely came back from the camps.

"You'll have to start learning English, you understand?"

He nodded again and made calf-eyes at Johanna, while blowing cacophonously on his pipe.

Maybe it's good anyway if he comes a little later. I'll have time to settle into a new place and prepare school things for him – she tried to calm herself. She got up from the sofa and stepped over to the bureau. "Come here." She pulled open the lower drawer.

"I'm leaving a letter for your mummy and a little money for you." She followed the boy with an anxious look, as he surveyed the banknotes with interest. *He's otherwise independent and smart, but… There is no better option at present.*

She eyed the boy inquisitively. *This boy has my father's facial features. He's one of my family. My father abandoned me when I was a little older than he is. Now he's been abandoned too. Will I abandon him as well?*

"I'll come and visit you," the boy tried to convince her. "I want to ride in a Jaguar."

"Yes, but can you manage on your own until then?"

He nodded self-assuredly.

Now Johanna would have liked to cry, but she took him by the hand and walked decisively over to Quandyk's door. She knocked.

"Yes, yes," was heard behind the door.

Johanna opened the door to another dimension, which smelled of spices and baby's nappies. There was nothing left of what once had been her bedroom. It had been transported to another part of the world, Central Asia.

"I'm leaving," she said in Russian. "You'll have to look after my nephew. Until his mother turns up."

Quandyk let his eyes rove from Johanna to the boy and said: *"Конечно. Мы заботимся о нем.* Of course. We'll look after him." Quandyk's wife turned to the boy and smiled. *"Я изпекла пирог. Хочешь?* I've made some pie. Would you like one?" "I'd like one," nodded the boy.

"Он для нас как родной сын. To us he's like our own son," said the wife, turning to Johanna.

Little Botakoz made a jealous noise from her basket.

"Какая ты конфекта. You're such a sweetie," said Johanna enticingly, gazing at the baby.

The boy went over to the basket and cautiously took Botakoz in his arms. He started rocking Botakoz gently, and the little girl fell silent.

Johanna looked at the newcomers and the boy from the threshold. *What a holy family,* she thought.

She turned in the doorway with a sigh.

It was time to start packing her bags. *How will I fit my whole former life, the house, the antique furniture, the piano, the scores, the books, the memorabilia… into two suitcases?*

*

The boy no longer wanted to think about anything but his father.

I-want-to-see-Dad-dy-I-want-to-see-Dad-dy…

Playing that rhythm in his head, he felt omnipotent. In marching time the power seethed in his body. From his memory he picked out the names of all the camps. He knew that they were in Perm, Vyatka, Novosibirsk, Vorkuta, Urzhum, Slobotskoy and Verkhodursk. Those were the homes of the children who travelled back with him in the cattle wagon. They had told him so many details that the boy had the feeling he had already been there. Now he only had to sit on a train and travel through all those places until he found his father. The Black Raven had taken his father away and now the boy had to rescue him. He hadn't known then that the Black Raven and the Pobeda were friends. But now he knew. He wanted to talk to his father about the trenches and the grenades, and sing him the heroes' songs that he had learned in the colony.

First of all he had to get to Moscow and change trains there.

England was closed up, the key of the lock was broken in two, was the rhyme of a hide-and-seek game that went through his head. Now he didn't want to think about a gleaming Jaguar or the city of London. He didn't want to eat or sleep. He felt that he had to cut out the images of mother-of-pearl cars from his aching head, so that his father's features wouldn't be blurred. Nothing in his world now was more important.

There was no time to lose. Daddy was waiting for him somewhere. For several long months already. He decided that as soon as Auntie left, he would take a little money from the drawer and get on the train.

*

Are they really letting me go, thought Johanna as she saw the stewardess closing the door of the aircraft.

Johanna watched from the porthole the worn propeller under the wing, waiting for it to turn. The aircraft jerked and the propeller really did start to revolve. *And they really are letting me go,* Johanna now realized; it was coming true. Becoming a fact. *They're letting me go free. No strings attached!* Emotion overflowed into Johanna's thoughts.

What about the boy... my sister... my friends! Would she yet manage to rescue anyone, help them? Did her exit into the free world actually mean freedom, or would she have to carry everyone and everything with her, worry, wait, yearn? Would her dreams in London be haunted by the streets of Tallinn; would her walks in Hyde Park mean Kadriorg Park for her? Would she be driven mad in the alien sunspots by familiar shadows, the faces of the abandoned? People who were no longer in her life, maybe not in anyone's? Not alive at all?

"Citizen passengers, the Aeroflot crew welcomes you on board this Li-2 aircraft. Our aircraft is flying on the route Moscow – Budapest – Vienna – London..." resounded the cheery voice of the steward on the half-empty flight... *and will never come back into my life. Gone are Mäekalda Street, the sea breeze and the morning birdsong. Maybe some migratory bird will fly back to me,* she consoled her troubled mind. She produced a handkerchief from her sleeve and wiped the mascara from her eyes.

I never wanted to leave my homeland, thought Johanna, *and now I'm doing it anyway. I'm leaving my home, my language, my audience, my theatre. Or may I keep them all inside myself? Or will they be replaced? The domestic citadel has vanished, the language is distorted, my audience has changed. The stage on the scaffolding of the Estonia Theatre was built by Mefistos, commanded by sorcerers. Were they waiting for angels and the garden of paradise?* Johanna thought of Alan, of his shy smile in a cool gaze, the strength and warmth of his hands. He had not abandoned her to her fate.

He is full of an inner sunlight, thought Johanna; *perhaps he'll let it shine on me too.*

The aircraft engine blasted ever louder and the asphalt under its wheels rolled ever faster. The birch grove glistening ahead rolled past her like a bouncy stage-set painted on canvas. Was this a memory from another reality or of one of many stage-sets? Before Johanna's eyes, surrounded by birch trees, there rushed the writer, the artist, the baritone, the political instructor, the boy, her sister and crosses, crosses, crosses…

The Red Cross too? Should she turn to them now?

Then the shaking subsided. The wheels had risen from the dark asphalt into the air and the aircraft was pressing its heavy body through the evening clouds as if feeling relief, as if releasing itself of its metal burden.

It's easier to breathe now, she noted. The heaviness in her shoulders had diminished. The earth's gravitational force had decreased. Yet she was breathing compressed air and flying in a daring aircraft belonging to Aeroflot, whose growing network of flights extended across the lands and seas, spreading like a spider's web across the whole planet.

*

The boy liked the way the electric bus with horns whizzed away when it started, faster than other buses or cars. It didn't seem to need to change gear, it didn't tire of speeding. Yet on a bend it would jerk, and then you could hear a rattle from the roof. The lights went out inside the trolleybus. Accompanied by a long electric signal, its front door opened and the driver got out from his cab, cursing. The horns of the trolleybus had fallen from the wire. The boy was seized with anxiety, his nerves wracked. He saw the bus driver flashing past the lateral windows. *Did he get angry and is he now going away?* he wondered. He asked the lady sitting next to him to let him past, and pushed himself through the wall of standing passengers.

"Whatever next!" fumed a passenger in a straw hat. "Now we'll be late for work."

The boy climbed quickly out of the open front door and followed the driver to the bus queue. The trolleybus driver had put on mittens and was playing with ropes. He tugged first on one horn and then the other again. Like a fisherman reeling in a line in the water. Finally he managed to adjust both antennae back onto the electric wires. One antenna gave off a fine spark and then the neon lights in the trolleybus began to burn gaily again.

The driver took off his mittens and turned back to the front door of the trolleybus. The boy hurried behind him so as not to be left behind.

Great, thought the boy, and took an important professional decision. He wouldn't become a bus driver after all, but a trolleybus driver. He recalled the slogan on the wall of the Russian colony: *"Коммунизм – это есть советская власть плюс электрификация всей страны.* Communism is the Soviet state plus the electrification of the whole country" – the meaning of which he didn't fully understand. *In the future, are the electricity lines supposed to stretch out over the whole enormous country, so you can travel by trolleybus from Vorkuta or Moscow to Tallinn?* In the meantime he would just have to hunt for Daddy and Mummy. *Perhaps they'd like to ride on a red trolleybus too.*

He was now standing right behind the driver's cabin and pressing his nose against its window. The more people came on board, the more the lady towering behind him squashed him against the glass. He no longer felt alone, there were so many people, so much buzzing.

He mentally counted the roubles he had got from Auntie

Johanna; he had three left altogether. That should be enough to get to Daddy. And if he fell short, he would travel on the train roof like the bag boys.

"Citizen passengers, step forward, move closer together," cried the conductress. "You aren't the only ones wanting to get somewhere."

Can the victory of Communism come like this? thought the boy. Those were the words that the Pobeda man and the trainers kept repeating. Then he thought of Auntie Johanna, sitting in a long-bodied mother-of-pearl Jaguar talking yet another incomprehensible language with the radio man. For a moment the scent of Auntie Johanna's perfume invaded his nose and his shoulder was touched by her warm hand, but he shook it off with one rapid shrug. First he had to find Daddy. Without him he wasn't going anywhere. He wanted to be back on the woodpile, at home like in the old days.

More and more people came on board. The trolleybus was filled with warm fug and he was no longer cold without a jacket. He felt a hope that this was the trolleybus that would really take him to Daddy and the bright future. He looked out of the window and imagined himself soon standing on a square like that with his Daddy. *We'll look for Mummy too, we'll buy a new car… and we'll all drive together in it to London to visit Auntie Johanna.*

The conductor called through the trolleybus from behind him: "Next stop: Ploshchad Pobedy. Victory Square." The boy looked inquisitively through the driver's glass. In his eyes were both curiosity and exhaustion.

Joyful music boomed from the street loudspeaker. The horned bus kept on rolling, quietly whirring, on its scheduled route to the town's Lenin Prospect.

It kept on rolling.

NOTES

p. 21   The National Committee of the Republic of Estonia was formed in March 1944 by underground resistance movements, and planned to establish a democratic provisional government upon the withdrawal of occupying German troops.

p. 31   Forest Brothers, anti-Soviet resistance movement, called bandits by the KGB.

p. 104   Vobla is Caspian roach.

p. 108   One fine day we will see a plume of smoke rising. (Italian.)

p. 114   The Estonian Communist Party daily newspaper during the Soviet era, the 'Voice of the People'.

p. 124   General Laidoner: Estonian politician and military leader in the first Republic 1918-1940.

p. 125   Otto Tief: head of the temporary government of Estonia between the Nazi and Soviet occupations, 1944.

p. 126   Soviet scouts. All pupils had to become October children (named after the October revolution) before graduating to the Pioneers.

p. 144   A reference to a passage in the Estonian national epic poem *Kalevipoeg*.

p. 176   I am suffering and tormented. Oh God, I would rather die! (From Puccini's opera *Gianni Schicchi*.)

p. 206   'The Master'. Senior security officials referred to Stalin by this title among themselves.

p. 215   The BBC Russian service commenced on 26 March 1946.

Ilmar Taska

AUTHOR' S NOTE

Today, when the blood vessels on our planet's arms are bulging again – demarcating new boundaries, expanding passport checks, travel bans, increased security surveillance and growing migration, it is time to measure the distance or nearness of the past. Since fiction permits creative freedom, I could undertake a journey in time to Tallinn, London and Moscow in the mid-1940s.

In the late 1930s, all of Europe's larger and smaller nations held negotiations with Stalin and Hitler, while peaceful alliances gradually transformed and became military in nature. The parcelling out of Europe took place after the war ended. Overnight, allies became enemies and the Iron Curtain suddenly separated family and friends.

While doing research about this period and its people, I understood that my characters have to tackle ethical issues, deal with loss of trust in institutions and fellow countrymen, and the loss of personal freedom under intensifying surveillance in a growing totalitarian state. The regime was invisibly growing and expanding, reducing people to nameless numbers. As it is for the boy in my novel, it was hard to know how to orient oneself in a world where changing ideologies and regimes were suddenly colliding. The characters in this novel are a composite portrait of post-war people and systems, seen from both sides of the Iron Curtain.

Thinking about history will help create the future. Is it

possible for us to avoid the mistakes of the past while we carry the past in our own DNA as we move towards tomorrow? New paths stretch before us: our own path will reveal itself better if we do not forget that the world is round, and seen from space, the whole planet appears very small and friendly.

I thank all the people who have given me encouragement and a helping hand with the novel, and I'd also like to thank the unseen but ever present spirit of time.

Ilmar Taska

TRANSLATOR'S AFTERWORD

When this dramatic novel first appeared in the original Estonian, it was accompanied by an Afterword from the author, acknowledging all those who had helped him in researching the story. It is not a directly autobiographical tale, but it is based on events that shaped the lives not only of the author's family but of many thousands of Estonians who are living today. The era of Stalin cast a long shadow over the history of this small and often-occupied country, and still does.

In 2016 a new national museum opened in Estonia's second city of Tartu. Visitors can walk along a 'time-path' through various eras of Estonian history, and the generation that has grown up since the country regained independence in 1991 can relive the privations and suspicions of their parents' and grandparents' era, which are now starting to fade into the mists of history. Estonia is now a modern, progressive, wired-up, western-oriented democratic nation, but if there is such a thing as 'national character', a lot of it – a certain pragmatic reserve and cautiousness – can be explained in terms of the frightening events that unfold in the pages of this novel. This story may be fiction, but it is certainly not far-fetched fiction.

The tale of the nameless man, woman and boy, and the cast of other named characters is based on a short story for which Ilmar Taska won much praise and a prize in 2014. Encouraged by the critics' praise, and moved by his own family's experiences, Taska, who was born in 1953, the year of

Stalin's death, expanded the tale into the present novel. On one level, it is a story that any of the heirs of the Soviet dominion can relate to, and on another level it is peculiarly Estonian. As its translator, I have tried to make it a tale that English-speaking readers can also relate to. In one respect that was easy, for there is an important English element to the plot: the love-interest of the story. England is a country that the young protagonist in the novel can barely imagine; and likewise, I've borne in mind that most of the readers of this book can barely imagine life in distant Soviet Estonia in 1946. Part of the challenge, and much of the fun, of working on this novel has been the need to make these events accessible to a twenty-first-century English-speaking reader.

For a start, there is the title: *Pobeda 1946* as it originally appeared in Estonian. After much debate, the publishers, the author and I agreed to add 'A Car Called Victory' for our English audience. *Pobeda,* the name of a moderate-sized, almost luxurious saloon car produced between 1946 and 1958 by the Molotov works in Gorky, Russia, means 'victory' in Russian. My worn copy of *The Observer's Book of Automobiles* from 1955 does list it but it gives scant detail: "Pobeda saloon: B.H.P. 52. Weight 3,000 lb. (Other details not available.)" There was a lot of Iron in that Curtain, as well as in the car.

Ilmar Taska was born in Siberia; both of his parents' families had been sent into exile there after the Soviet invasion of 1940 and before the Nazi invasion. The Nazi occupation did not last long, of course – soon the Soviets were to come again and reconquer the Baltic countries, including Estonia. Taska came from a diplomatic family – his grandfather was serving at the Estonian Embassy in Paris at the time of his mother's birth. His diplomatic career ended when, under the terms of the secret protocols of the Molotov-Ribbentrop Pact of 1939, the Soviet Union annexed his country. Taska recalls: "In the last surviving photograph of him, he is posing as protocol chief together with the Estonian president and the Soviet ambassador as they warmly shake hands. Nevertheless, that handshake did not spare him from a trip towards the Ural Mountains in a cattle car even before the fighting began. His next post was as prisoner in a Gulag camp. My father (a student of architecture) and paternal grandfather (simply an innocent talented artist) rode the same train cars to Siberia. The first deportation trains that departed on 14 June 1941 were filled with intellectuals of Estonian nationality, as well as of Russian, Jewish and other nationalities living in Estonia. The Soviet KGB plotted its relocation policy well. Some were taken away, others were brought in to replace them and ensure the 'correct' mentality."

All this redistribution of power in Europe in the years leading up to the war, and on up to 1946, when our novel is set, was an issue in which Britain might have at first attempted not to involve itself, but ultimately it too was entangled. The new dispensation in which our British protagonist in this novel finds himself engaged, on both the professional and the personal, emotional level, is puzzling and frustrating to him, full of intrigue and deception. He is a BBC newsreader, so he is automatically kept abreast of events that are shaping his own emotional life as the lover of an Estonian opera singer, separated from him by the new Iron Curtain, and whom he has to trust to adroitly manipulate those in power to enable them to come together and plan a new life. Embroiled in this intrigue is the foreground figure of the nameless boy.

This central figure has echoes in Taska's own life: "Like the small boy in the novel I lived in two realities, one at home, another at school. I began to search for an answer to the question about what really happened to my parents and grandparents. I did not know how to orient myself in a world where one person's hero is another's traitor. I understood that I have to keep everybody's secrets."

The name of the car in the title is loaded with significance: Victory. The Soviet Union had just defeated Nazism in the previous year, and the centralized economy celebrated this victory with a little splash of colour and luxury. Never mind that the styling was modelled heavily on the 1942 American

Plymouth: it conveyed a promise of a better and more prosperous future. Compared with the drab military-style vehicles that populated the rutted roads of the Soviet Union, the Pobeda was a real head-turner, especially to a little boy. True, ownership of such vehicles was restricted to the *nomenklatura* and loyal servants of the State like the Man in our story, at least at first, but that fact, too, served to enhance the authority of the State. And this desirable object becomes the focus of our young protagonist's increasingly desperate conflict of loyalties.

Apart from writing fiction, Ilmar Taska has built a successful career in films and television. He founded the first national private television network in Estonia. Before that, even as a child he was a reporter for the National Radio. He worked in Hollywood as a film producer and director. Thus he has experienced the values of both totalitarian socialist propaganda and the capitalist West. Perhaps there is also something of the author in his British newsreader character Alan: caught between two ideologies.

This novel has been a best-seller in Estonia and has already been translated into several other European languages. There are many peculiarly Estonian and more generally Soviet references in the novel, which will be self-evident to adult Estonian readers, but won't be so clear to the English-speaking reader. The references to aspects of Estonian culture I have tried to put in context with a few additional explanatory words and an occasional note. The frequent passages of Russian were a bigger problem. Rather than pepper the novel with footnotes, the publishers and I decided to provide the translations in the text alongside the originals. Part of the mystery and terror of the little boy's world was his confrontation with this alien language. It too has potency. Words have weight, even when they are incomprehensible.

Christopher Moseley

DORRIT WILLUMSEN

Bang: A Novel about the Danish Writer

(translated by Marina Allemano)

29 January 1912. In a train compartment in Ogden, Utah, a Danish author was found unconscious. The 54-year-old Herman Bang was en route from New York to San Francisco as part of a round-the-world reading tour. It was a poignant end for a man whose life had been spent on the move. Having fled his birthplace on the island of Als ahead of the Prussian advance of 1864, he was later hounded out of Copenhagen, Berlin, Vienna and Prague by homophobic laws and hostility to his uncompromising social critique as journalist, novelist, actor and dramaturge. Dorrit Willumsen re-works Bang's life story in a series of compelling flashbacks that unfold during his last fateful train ride across the USA. Along the way, we are transported to an audience in St Petersburg with the Dowager Empress Maria Feodorovna, to a lovers' nest in a flea-ridden Prague boarding house, to the newsrooms and variety theatres of fin-de-siècle Copenhagen, and to a Norwegian mountainside, where Claude Monet has come to paint snow and lauds Bang's writing as literary impressionism.

Dorrit Willumsen's *Bang* was awarded the Nordic Council Literature Prize, 1997.

Bang: A Novel about the Danish Writer
ISBN 9781909408340
UK £13.95
(Paperback, 398 pages)

VIGDIS HJORTH

A House in Norway

(translated by Charlotte Barslund)

A House in Norway tells the story of Alma, a divorced textile artist who makes a living from weaving standards for trade unions and marching bands. She lives alone in an old villa, and rents out an apartment in her house to supplement her income. She is overjoyed to be given a more creative assignment, to design a tapestry for an exhibition to celebrate the centenary of women's suffrage in Norway, but soon finds that it is a much more daunting task than she had anticipated. Meanwhile, a Polish family moves into her apartment, and their activities become a challenge to her unconscious assumptions and her self-image as a good feminist and an open-minded liberal. Is it possible to reconcile the desire to be tolerant and altruistic with the imperative need for creative and personal space?

A House in Norway
ISBN 9781909408319
UK £11.95
(Paperback, 175 pages)